Be6.
D.Todd.
JR AA
M.Tabl.

KNITTING BONES

KNITTING BONES

MONICA FERRIS

THORNDIKE
CHIVERS

This Large Print edition is published by Thorndike Press, Waterville, Maine, USA and by BBC Audiobooks Ltd, Bath, England.

Thorndike Press, a part of Gale, Cengage Learning.

The text of this Large Print edition is unabridged.

Other aspects of the book may vary from the original edition.

Set in 16 pt. Plantin.

Printed on permanent paper.

LIBRARY OF CONGRESS CATALOGING-IN-PUBLICATION DATA

Ferris, Monica.
    Knitting bones / by Monica Ferris.
      p. cm. — (A needlecraft mystery) (Thorndike Press large print mystery)
    ISBN-13: 978-1-4104-0548-7 (alk. paper)
    ISBN-10: 1-4104-0548-6 (alk. paper)
    1. Devonshire, Betsy (Fictitious character) — Fiction.
    2. Women detectives — Minnesota — Fiction. 3 Needleworkers
    — Fiction. 4. Needlework — Fiction. 5. Minnesota — Fiction.
    6. Large type books. I. Title.
    PS3566.U47K58 2008
    813'.54—dc22   2007051035

BRITISH LIBRARY CATALOGUING-IN-PUBLICATION DATA AVAILABLE

Published in 2008 in the U.S. by arrangement with The Berkley Publishing Group, a member of Penguin Group (USA) Inc.

Published in 2008 in the U.K. by arrangement with the author.

U.K. Hardcover: 978 1 405 64496 9 (Chivers Large Print)
U.K. Softcover: 978 1 405 64497 6 (Camden Large Print)

Printed in the United States of America
1 2 3 4 5 6 7 12 11 10 09 08

ACKNOWLEDGMENTS

Every time I write a mystery, I learn something new. This time Mariah Flor, personal banker at Wells Fargo, told me how to detect a particular kind of bank fraud, who is in charge of detecting it, and what the process is for uncovering its extent. Rosemary Kossel showed Betsy how to do mitered knitting — and me, too. Professor Kevin McGowan at Cornell University, ornithologist, told me some things about crows I didn't know. And Ron Plaman of Excel Pawn and Jewelry told me how small an amount one might raise on a really expensive watch.

ONE

Fall's brilliant colors had faded; threadbare Halloween was standing tall, waving gnarled fingers from every tree in Excelsior. Betsy Devonshire loved autumn, but business had kept her from a leaf excursion this year. She couldn't even enjoy its brilliant colors in her shop much longer. The needlework patterns of bright-colored leaves, jack-o'-lanterns, and witches would make way for the Christmas displays the day after Halloween.

Such was the way of the commerce world. The fall stuff had been picked back around the Fourth of July, the Christmas offerings had been planned before school started. One of the sad parts of owning a retail business was that the owner was always thinking a season or two ahead.

Right now, Betsy was browsing through a catalog from Lantern Moon, which made beautiful baskets. Betsy liked to use their

7

baskets to display needlework products in her shop, and she also carried their baskets for sale, especially the sea-reed rice baskets with their fold-in tops, very handy for carrying projects. Baskets made great Christmas gifts. But Lantern Moon was now also carrying knitting needles made of ebony, rosewood, and coconut palm, and needle cases made of silk, and Betsy was happy to add these items to her order. They would look nice next to a basket full of wool and silk yarns in winter colors of deep green, wine, and gold.

She was totting up the cost with a little sigh when her door sounded its two notes. She looked up to see her good friend and steady customer Jill Cross Larson. Holding on to Jill's hand was Jill's daughter, Emma, just going on two. Mother and daughter were equally fair, but Jill's hair was straight and pulled severely back from her face into a fat braid; her toddler's hair was fine and curly. Emma was walking sideways, reaching for a hat that Jill held in her other hand. "Mine, mine!" Emma was saying.

"Yes, baby, this is your hat," said Jill, handing it over. To Betsy, she added, "She was experimenting to see if she could throw it between parked cars into the street."

"Throw hat!" agreed Emma, suiting

action to her words. The hat, a warm knit helmet in bright blue, flew up and forward a couple of yards, landing on a low table covered with framed models of solemn pilgrims and comic turkeys. Emma giggled and tried to pull free of her mother's grasp.

"Hold on, Mighty Mite," said Jill, not letting go. She walked her over to the table and picked the hat off a frame. Holding it out of her daughter's reach, she said, "If I give this to you, do not throw it. Do you understand? Hold it, or wear it, but do *not* throw it."

" 'Kay," agreed Emma. Of course, on being handed the hat, she immediately threw it. This time it hooked onto a spinner rack of overdyed floss.

Jill looked around at Betsy. "Sorry," she said.

Betsy was laughing too hard to reply. Jill was a solemn sort of person. To see her coping with a daughter who had a wild sense of humor was amusing.

Jill again retrieved the hat and this time stuffed it in a pocket, placidly ignoring the outraged toddler's demand for it back.

"What can I do for you?" asked Betsy, using more effort to ignore Emma's screams.

"Two things: First, I want to sign up for

that knitting class that Rosemary is teaching."

That took a few minutes, while a check was written and a name entered.

Then, "Second, I want to invite you to go horseback riding with me."

Betsy smiled, in case this was the beginning of one of Jill's subtle jokes. "Ride a horse where?"

"Oh, out in the fields on my friend's farm. She has five horses. They're not being ridden as often as they should be, so she says I can come and ride any time I want, and I can bring a friend, too." Seeing that Betsy still did not understand, she continued, "You know how every so often we talk about going on a cattle roundup?"

It had long been Betsy's dream — her maternal great-grandfather had been among the last of the real cowboys — to go on a cattle drive. It was a dream Jill shared, though they had not managed to fulfill it even after years of talking about it.

Cattle rides, or roundups, still happened in the twenty-first century, but mostly as tourist attractions. There was a ranch in eastern South Dakota that had one, Betsy knew. But the tourists didn't just stand by the fences, applauding as the cattle streamed by; they got to join in, ride the horses, herd strays back into line, eat beans and wood-grilled steak around a campfire, and sleep on the ground. And they paid good money for such privileges.

"Yes, I remember. Are you saying she's going to have a cattle drive?"

"No, no. I mean, she does have cattle, a few of the Scottish Highland breed, very exotic — and delicious. But this isn't a roundup or drive, just a chance to re-acquaint our bottoms with a saddle."

"Hmmm," said Betsy, for it had been a long time since she sat on a horse. "When do you want to go?"

Jill went to the spinner rack of overdyed floss and turned it casually with one finger. "Lars has tomorrow off."

"Oh, Jill, not this week! I've got that EGA convention coming up!" Betsy, an officer of the local Embroiderers Guild of America, was helping to organize the national gathering of needlepointers. But she was also the sole vendor of needlework materials and was going to have to move almost the entire stock of her shop to the downtown Minneapolis hotel for a three-day weekend. That took considerable organization, and all of it in addition to the usual lengthy day of a small-shop owner: sales, restocking, book-keeping, cleaning, mending, filling special

11

orders, and keeping teachers and students in her many classes organized and happy. Not to mention the usual tasks of an unmarried person in today's America: laundry, cleaning, cooking, grocery shopping, even the occasional full night's sleep.

"Can't Goddy —" began Jill. Godwin DuLac was Betsy's store manager and essential right arm in the business.

"I am *not* going to let Goddy do my laundry!"

Jill laughed. "Laundry?" she asked. "I meant he can find someone to work an extra afternoon, can't he?"

Emma imitated her mother's laugh, and Jill scooped her up, then began walking very slowly toward the checkout desk. "Think about it," she said. "The sun on top of a horse's mane, rippling as he walks. The pungent equine scent, the rocking saddle, the breeze in your hair. The bawl of a distant calf, and a crow's fading call. The smell of drying grass and fallen leaves. The unwinding of stress." By now she was leaning in to Betsy's face, her voice low and thrilling.

Betsy's eyes closed. She was there, in the sunlight, with the crows and the creaking saddle. "Oh, gosh," she murmured.

"Business has been good lately, hasn't it?"

Betsy nodded.

"So you can send your laundry out for once. And you can afford that part-timer for one extra afternoon, too — not even the whole afternoon, just three hours. Lindsay's place is half an hour from here, so an hour there and back, and two hours to mess around with horses. Fat, quiet horses, nothing exciting, you won't even be sore the next day. She'll have them saddled and waiting."

Betsy meant to argue some more, but when she opened her mouth, all that came out was, "Let's do it."

The horses were indeed fat and lazy, perfect for two women who needed to relearn old riding skills. The day was bright and barely cool — global warming had come to Minnesota, and sometimes it didn't snow until mid-November.

Jill's friend Lindsay led the way out into a pasture where green grass was growing up through hay stubble. Insects buzzed half-heartedly, resurrected by the warmth. The sky was a cloudless blue, a deeper shade than in summer, and the air had a rough edge to it, carrying scents of ripe apples and dying leaves. The horses' feet crushed the dry stems of cut hay with a sound like bursts of elfin applause. As Jill had predicted, the distant lowing of a cow and cawing of a crow could be heard, while overhead a skein of Canada geese flew in an uneven formation.

Betsy, after ten minutes of discomfort, finally remembered how to relax her spine and settle into the saddle. She was riding a mare named Brown Eyes. Lindsay, leading the way, rode a beautiful light gray gelding named Fancy Pants, who had a dark muzzle and legs and a mostly white mane and tail. Fancy Pants snorted and danced his way across the field and Betsy was grateful not to be riding him. Jill brought up the rear on another gelding, a tall, quiet palomino named Goldie.

At the other side of the pasture, Lindsay showed off Fancy Pants's training by making him sidle back and forth while she opened and closed a gate without dismounting. The gate led to a dirt lane into a small wood. Fallen leaves crunched in a deeper note as they ambled among some big old trees. A jay flitted from tree to tree ahead of them, screaming, "Thief! Thief! Thief!" which alarmed an antlered buck into crashing off, his tail a white flag.

"Darn that old jay," grumbled Lindsay. "Usually when you're on horseback, the deer can't pick up the human smell and you can ride right up on them."

The trees ended abruptly at a steep bank, leading down to a stream. They started up alongside it. Betsy said over her shoulder to Jill, "I'm starting to feel competent, how about you?"

"Sure. What do you have in mind, a race?"

"No, but I'd like to see if we can get down to the water without falling off."

Lindsay, who was Jill's age, with light brown hair and eyes, said, "Yes, a race! Race you to the bottom!" and turned her horse, clapped heels to his flanks, and gave him his head. The horse took the slope, which was gravelly and thinly strewn with clumps of low-growing grass, in a series of dust-raising plunges, which she rode with ease.

Betsy, grinning, turned her horse to follow. But Brown Eyes snorted at such foolishness. She refused to go headlong, instead turning sideways to ease her way down.

Jill's tall palomino took one leap headfirst, almost throwing Jill over his shoulder. Then he turned sideways and imitated Betsy's mount, stepping carefully downward. Jill grinned at Betsy, relieved.

At the bottom, Lindsay was letting her horse drink from the stream while she looked up and laughed. "Cowards!" she shouted, making him snort and splash.

"Hey, this is my horse's idea, not mine!"

replied Betsy, perfectly happy with his caution.

At the bottom, they all let their horses drink from the stream. Fancy Pants pawed impatiently at the water, and Lindsay said, "Shall we see if they can climb up the other side? It's still my land over there." At the top on the other side was open pasture.

"Sure," said Jill, and she urged her horse up and out of the water.

The opposite bank was, if anything, steeper than the first, but with a kind of small plateau halfway up. Jill grabbed the saddle horn and hung on while her horse, sinking fetlock-deep into the gravelly earth, lunged upward. Betsy hollered, "Wait for me!" and kicked her horse to make it hurry.

But halfway up, Brown Eyes began to slide. Betsy started to get off, but had only one leg free when the horse collapsed, legs flailing. Betsy, with her other foot caught in the stirrup, felt a sickening pain as the horse twisted and rolled, trying to regain its feet. Then her foot came loose and the horse slid away, still struggling, down to the stream at the bottom.

Betsy tried to get her own legs under her, and screamed as the pain in her right ankle overwhelmed her. It was like a huge monster that darkened the sunlit sky over her head.

"Oh, my God, oh, my God!" yelled Lindsay, who had dismounted at the bottom. She began climbing up toward Betsy on all fours. "Don't move, don't move!"

"O-okay," Betsy stammered. She was lying on her back, and she dug her left heel into the soft ground to stay in place. Her voice was thin and shaky.

Suddenly there was a tumble of stones from above, then Jill was beside her. Betsy put a hand out, afraid Jill would try to lift her. But Jill said, "Lie still."

"I'm trying to." Betsy could hear Lindsay talking on a cell phone, calling for an ambulance. "Is the horse all right?" Betsy asked.

Jill smiled at her. "Yes, she's stepping on her reins down in the water, trying to decide how much trouble she's in."

"Our fault, not hers. Oh, God, my leg hurts so bad!"

"I know. No, don't look, it's twisted in a funny way. But there's no blood. You're going to be fine." She looked down the slope and called, "Lindsay, can you bring me your jacket?" Jill, very typically, had worn only a light flannel shirt for the ride. Betsy had a denim jacket on, but she was going into shock and had started to shiver.

"Anything else hurt?" asked Jill, looking

her over.

"No, I don't think so. But I think my ankle's broken."

"Yes, I think it is, too."

"Oh, Jill, what am I going to do about the convention?"

Jill smiled. "I don't think that's the big problem right now. The big problem is going to be getting you out of here. Should be interesting to see how they do it."

It was. And painful, too.

Two

The door to Betsy's hospital room opened, and Jill appeared in the doorway. "Hi, are you ready to go?" she asked.

"I guess," said Betsy. It had been five days since the horse had rolled over and broken not just both her fibula and tibia — the two long bones between her knee and ankle — but also torn the ligaments that held her ankle bone in place. The tendons were not torn completely loose, and they had a decent chance to heal if supported by a cast or brace. A surgeon had removed the marrow from the shattered larger leg bone and strung the pieces on a metal rod as if they were beads. The tibia was held in place by a plate with screws. The pieces of bone would grow back together, but the hardware was permanent. For the rest of her life Betsy would carry a card, signed by her doctor, explaining why she set off metal detectors in airports.

And meanwhile, she was unable to get around at all. This was not the kind of broken leg that allows for a walking cast, at least not for several weeks. She was instructed to go home and stay there, mostly sitting down or lying in bed, hobbling around on flat surfaces with crutches. No stairs, no prolonged moving around, and certainly no driving.

"Does it hurt much?" asked Jill.

"Not too much. So long as I lie still, there's only a kind of ache," she said. "Of course, they keep insisting I get up and move around — and now that you're here, there's going to be some serious movement, isn't there?" Jill had come to bring her home. Betsy's surgery had been four days ago. Her medical insurance mandated, and her doctor agreed, that she could finish healing at home. "And by the way, have you given any thought to how I'll get up to my apartment?" she asked Jill. Betsy lived on the second floor of a two-story building, which normally was great, because her needlework shop was on the ground floor. But there was no elevator.

"Lars will carry you," said Jill.

Betsy chuckled uncertainly. Lars was Jill's husband, a very large cop who could probably climb the stairs with her thrown over his shoulder, without even lightening his load by first taking off his gunbelt.

"Isn't he on patrol today?"

"Certainly. But our motto is 'To Protect and Serve,' and carrying you up to your apartment is service." Jill used to be a cop, too, but she had quit to raise her daughter, the adorable Emma Elizabeth.

"Jill, are you seriously proposing that Lars carry me up the stairs to my apartment?"

Jill's light blue eyes widened with sincerity. "Sure. Otherwise we'll have to get two or three men trying to carry you in a wheelchair, and maybe stumbling and letting go with you hanging on for dear life, and the wheelchair going over and over and you winding up at the foot of the stairs with your other leg broken, if not your skull."

Betsy wasn't sure if Jill was joking. She looked serious, but then, she was at her most serious when pulling Betsy's leg the hardest.

Jill was of Norwegian stock, and not the least inclined to let her feelings show — whether she was joking, angry, or penitent. She had apologized in her direct way — once — for instigating the horseback ride that led to the mishap, but she had not mentioned it again. Betsy was fine with that; it was nice to have a friend who didn't find it necessary to make endless demonstrations of sorrow or repentance. On the other hand, doubtless Jill felt responsible for getting Betsy home safely.

Betsy decided just to trust Jill. She would wind up safe in her apartment one way or another, because another thing Jill was, was reliable.

Betsy said, "Thank you for helping me."

Jill smiled, pulled her cell phone from her purse, punched in a fast-dial digit, and said, when the call was answered, "It's go for the transfer. We'll be leaving here within half an hour. Right." Her tone grew tender. "Bye, sweetums."

Betsy rang for the nurse, who helped her pack up her belongings: two bed jackets (knit by loyal customers of Crewel World), five pairs of bed socks (ditto), a potted plant, a half-eaten box of chocolates, a toothbrush and other bathroom items, a pair of crutches, a carrier bag of medicines, and several printouts of instructions for home care. These were put in a cardboard box, which was balanced on the arms of the wheelchair after Betsy was helped into it. She managed not to groan.

Then Jill wheeled her down the broad corridor to the bank of elevators, stepping back when a car arrived with a nurse, two attendants, and a patient on a gurney. "So, you want to go horseback riding again this weekend?" Jill asked Betsy while they waited for the patient to be wheeled out. An attendant was maneuvering a wheeled stand holding up two plastic bags each half full of a clear liquid, which was dribbling down a hose into a needle taped to the back of the patient's hand. He was an unconscious man with dark hair showing under the edge of his bandages and a lot of facial cuts and bruises.

Betsy made a tsk sound of pity, as Jill pushed her into the car and punched the button for the ground floor. Then, "No," said Betsy, chuckling, as Jill's question suddenly registered, "not this weekend. Maybe next if the weather is nice."

Tony Milan was vaguely aware that he was moving. And not walking but riding. In a car? A very distant alarm went off at that thought. But no, he was lying down. Maybe . . . maybe he was on a horse. No, of course not. Silly idea. He was doped up, and by the familiar muffled feeling it was on some kind of downer, something stronger than pot. Prescription pills, maybe, the good kind.

Rolling, rolling, rolling — wasn't there a

song with those words? A cowboy song. Something about a horse? Whoops, the rolling had stopped. And there were voices, a woman and a couple of men. Maybe a couple of women. His clothing was being messed with, he seemed to be dressed in sheets. Toga party? And now they were moving him, rolling or pushing him, he was sliding. Was he being mugged? He opened his mouth to protest and suddenly what they were doing hurt and he let out a kind of soft yell. One of the women said, "Hush, take it easy, you're all right," and covered him with something, like another sheet. But damn, his whole left side hurt, and his head, and the back of his hand, and his knee, and his right ankle . . . before he could finish his inventory, he was drifting back into the comfortable haze that only OxyContin can bring.

And then someone was calling his name. "Tony? Tony Milan? Wake up, Tony!" He opened his eyes and a dark-haired lady with brown eyes and an Aztec face was bending over him. He had no idea who she was.

He tried to ask, but his throat hurt and all he managed was a croaked, "Ur? Oo-oo."

"My name is Margaret, and I'm your nurse," she replied, just as if she understood his question. "You are in Hennepin County

Medical Center. You had an accident with your car. Do you understand that?" She was talking as if to an idiot. Of course he understood. "Wah," he said, which was nearly a word. "Hah, how —" Better. Lick lips and try again. "Howah lon I behn heah?" He seemed to have developed a foreign accent.

"Three days," she said.

That seriously surprised him. He'd never gone on a toot that lasted that long before. "Th-thu-reeeee?" The drawn-out vowel was because something started stabbing him in the chest. Only one arm seemed to work, he reached to touch the sore spot. Was she poking him?

"Lie still, don't try to move," she said. "You have some broken bones."

"Ah?"

"Don't you remember the accident?"

"Uh-uh." He'd been in an accident — was that because he'd been on a toot? Tony didn't want the police involved in this. He was scared, and began a struggle to remember. Somehow this started to involve his whole body, and a gentle hand came down on his chest.

"I said, lie still. You can't remember because you fractured your skull in a car accident."

"Amma gonna die?"

"No, though we were a little worried about you when you arrived."

"Wha' happen?" He sure hoped someone hit him, that he hadn't hit someone.

"A drunk driver ran a light. He's more badly injured than you, which is unusual."

"Yeah." Tony tried to nod — he had often joked about drunk drivers who walked away from accidents that killed other people — but the movement hurt his head.

"Amma hurt bad?"

"You have a broken leg, a broken arm, broken ribs, and a skull fracture."

"Wow. Car totaled, huh?" He liked that car, and it was paid for.

"What was left of it had to be cut open with the Jaws of Life to get you out."

"Wow. Wait, skull fracture?" His head was actually broken? No wonder it hurt!

"Yes, that's why you can't remember the accident."

"What day is today?"

"Monday. You had the accident on Friday."

"Wow."

She took his pulse, then tucked his good hand, his right one, under the sheet. "Are you in pain?" she asked.

Well, bless her, there was a question he

loved to hear! He nodded and began trying to look pathetic. Actually, he was in pain, he could feel it moving around under the drugs they'd already given him. Oh, wonderful to be in a hospital, where the pain meds were legal, where the chance he'd get some was amazingly, happily high. Which he hoped to be, real soon.

And there it was, a syringe just dripping with eagerness to sink into a vein — only she didn't put it in the vein, she stuck it in a thin, clear plastic hose — oh. That's why the back of his hand hurt. Gosh, not even the pain of a needle stick and here was the sweet, warm fog coming back again. He sank happily into it, even though someone at the back of his head was yelling, "*Three days?* Three days?"

THREE

It was Wednesday morning, around noon —
Betsy had come home on Monday — when
she looked up from her knitting. She was
lying on the couch in her living room, her
right leg supported on three needlepoint
pillows. From the knee down it was encased
in a hard, gray plastic foot-shaped case held
shut with Velcro straps. The toes poking
out the end of the case looked small and
forlorn.

She was knitting an afghan made of
squares of scrap yarn. She was bored with
it, but being fuddled with pain meds meant
she could knit only very simple patterns.

Her large and fluffy cat, Sophie, was
asleep on her stomach. At twenty-two
pounds, Sophie was a serious burden; but
the animal had taken it upon herself to be a
comfort to Betsy, a behavior so outside her
normal selfishness that Betsy hadn't the
heart to discourage her.

It was so quiet up on the second floor that both sets of ears picked up even faint sounds. Sophie's head came up only an instant before Betsy heard the footfalls of someone coming up the stairs. They were followed by a soft *tap-a-tap* on her door. "Come in!" Betsy called, because she knew who it was.

"Hello, hello, it's me!" caroled Godwin. He was her store manager, though he preferred Vice President in Charge of Operations of Crewel World, Incorporated. He stopped just inside the door, which let into a short hallway, to ask anxiously, "Are you decent?"

"Yes, yes," grumbled Betsy, who thought that an irrelevant question, considering her age, weight, injury, and the sexual orientation of the man asking. Nevertheless she pushed Sophie onto the floor so she could rearrange her old bathrobe, the thick one with the broad vertical stripes of gray and maroon, so it covered her down to her ankles. She lowered her needles and peered over her magnifying glasses.

He'd sounded all excited about something, but as he entered the living room he halted short. "What?" he said, surprised.

"What, what?" she asked.

"I don't know, you were giving me a look,

29

like you already know I did something wrong."

"I was? I didn't mean to." She took off the magnifying glasses. "Did you do something wrong? Is there trouble down in the shop?"

He relaxed and came forward. "No, no, nothing like that. But have you seen the news today?" He was starting to get excited again.

"No," she confessed. Though she was not taking so many of the most strenuous meds, she still found she lacked any desire to see what was happening in the real world, possibly because she lay helpless here at home so there was nothing she could do about anything. "Did I miss something?"

"Girl!" said Godwin. "Did you *miss* something? Only the biggest scandal ever to hit EGA!"

Betsy stared at him. She hadn't been able to go to the convention, of course, being either doped into semiconsciousness or actually in surgery while it was going on. But Godwin had brought her all the details once she was awake and able to take notice. Others reported that he had done a superb job of running the Crewel World booth at the event. Neither he nor any other visitor had even hinted at a scandal. And, anyway, the Embroiderers Guild of America was hardly a place one would find a scandal of any size, large or small. She tried a smile, thinking he was jesting, or at least exaggerating, but he didn't smile back. "You're serious!" she said.

"You bet I am!"

"So tell me!"

"Well, you know how they were selling that heart canvas to raise money for women's heart disease research," he began.

She nodded. The local EGA group had begun selling a painted outline of a Valentine heart on canvas right after the last annual convention. The inside was divided into seven sections, each to be filled with a different stitch. There was a competition to find the best composed and executed set of stitches, entries to be displayed at the convention for members to vote for. Betsy and Godwin had both been consulted by several people putting together their designs — and been glad to sell them the materials needed to work them.

"Did you know they raised over twenty-four thousand dollars?" asked Godwin.

"I knew it was going to be at least twenty thousand," said Betsy. "They said as much at the last meeting I went to."

"Well, the Heart Coalition was so impressed that they sent a man to the banquet to pick up the check — and he's gone. So's the check."

"Gone?"

"Yes, gone. Gone, as in run off, vanished. *With the check.* The police are looking for him, but so far no luck. That's what the news is saying. Mrs. Germaine is downstairs, and she's really upset."

Mrs. Germaine was president of the local EGA chapter. Betsy said, "She should be — everyone in the guild should be. Twenty-four thousand dollars was a lot of money to raise, and it's a lot of money to lose!"

"No, no, sweetie, you don't understand! The man who disappeared with the money is her *husband!*"

Betsy had to try twice before she could exclaim, "No!"

"Yes! Mr. Bob Germaine came to the banquet, made a nice speech, gave me the eye, and walked out with the check."

Betsy shook her head as if to clear it. "I don't think I'm following you."

"I went to the EGA banquet, remember? You told me to use your ticket, since you couldn't go. That's why I was actually there, an eyewitness who watched him take the check from Ms. Pickens, the EGA Treasurer, and make a small thank-you speech. Don't you remember me telling you about that?"

"You told me about the banquet and the check presentation. But that's not what I mean. Why did EGA give the check to Allie's husband?"

"Because he was the honcho from the National Heart Coalition they sent to pick it up."

"Bob works for the Heart Coalition?" Betsy held up a hand. "Wait a minute, I knew that. How could I forget that?"

"Possibly because Allie came up with the idea of the Women's Heart Disease fund-raiser?" suggested Godwin.

"Yes, she did. So what? Oh, I see what you mean: She didn't want to underline the fact that her husband's employer would benefit from a heart disease fund-raiser."

"That's right. She talks a lot — a *lot* — about Bob, but ever since EGA started that Women's Heart Disease fund-raiser, she never let the fact that her husband is an executive with the National Heart Coalition escape her pretty lips."

"Do you suppose the idea was really his? That he used EGA as a fund-raiser?" asked Betsy. "That *would* be a scandal."

"You know I love you," said Godwin. "And that you are my very favorite boss in all the wide world."

Betsy frowned at him. "Do I hear a *but* in there somewhere?"

"But," said Godwin, nodding. "The question is not whether or not he asked his wife to use EGA to raise money for the company he worked for. I mean it might be a scandal if it's true, but not nearly as big a scandal as his taking the check and leaving town."

"Oh," said Betsy. She definitely had to cut back on the meds. "I suppose people are saying that if he really did run off with the check, then this whole thing might be a plot between the two of them to steal the money. That *would* be a scandal!"

Godwin raised a slim forefinger, indicating he had a thought about that. "Twelve thousand dollars apiece seems kind of small potatoes for people in their income range."

Betsy nodded. "Well, yes, you're right. Besides, if it was both of them, why is she still here?"

"She wants to talk to you."

"No, I mean, why didn't she leave town with him?"

"I don't know. But right now this minute she is downstairs all agog to speak with you." He frowned. "Is *agog* the word I want?"

"I don't know. What does she want to talk to me about?"

34

"About helping her find out what really happened to him, of course!"

"Goddy, look at me! I can't go sleuthing! I'm stuck inside this apartment for another ten days — and I can't drive my car for six weeks after that! How on earth can I possibly investigate when I can't go anywhere?"

The note of distress in her voice brought Sophie back up onto her stomach. "Uff! Easy, cat!" But when Godwin came to lift the animal down, she said, "No, leave her, she thinks she's helping."

Godwin stopped and looked at Sophie, who was "kneading dough" on Betsy's abdomen. "Are you sure?"

"Yes. And actually, it's kind of nice having her within reach all the time."

"Okay, if you say so. Where were we? Oh, Allie wants you to help her — and yes, I told her all about how you can't go anywhere. But she says she just wants to talk to someone who might believe her when she says someone kidnapped her darling Bob. Someone who can give her some ideas about what to do, where to look."

"Oh, for heaven's sake! Don't the police — ?"

Godwin interrupted, "The police have put out an all points bulletin asking for help capturing one Robert Henry Germaine, wanted for grand theft, theft by fraud, and — something else, I can't remember what. They have a photograph of him." Godwin frowned. "It's not a very good photograph, which is pretty clever of Mrs. Germaine."

"What do you mean?"

"Remember when Mary Kuhfeld lost a lot of weight and had a Glamour Shot taken of herself all made-up to look like a model?"

"Yes."

"Well, her husband said that if she ever ran away from home and he didn't want her back, that's the photo he'd give the police."

Betsy laughed, and the jiggle made Sophie jump down and stalk off. Betsy said, "I see what you mean. Allie's helping her husband hide by giving the police a photo that doesn't look much like him."

"That's right."

She nodded. "Well, that's understandable. And clever, certainly." She thought briefly, then suddenly flashed on something he'd said earlier. "What did you mean, he gave you the eye?"

"I mean, during his speech, my good old reliable gaydar went *ping!* So I smiled at him as he went out and he smiled back. I actually think he would have stopped, but he was surrounded by about half a dozen women who were escorting him out, talking sixteen to the dozen to him."

Betsy laughed. "His wife might not have liked that, Goddy," she said.

"His wife wasn't at the banquet. She was at a meeting of chapter presidents."

"During the *banquet?*"

"I know. It was supposed to end before the banquet started, but they got caught up in something — no one knows what — and had their meal sent up."

"Still, I can't believe he'd actually give you the eye with people who know Allie watching."

"Unless he knew he would never be seeing any of them again," Godwin pointed out. "One of the women told me they walked him out to his light blue Lexus in the parking garage, and he drove off, never to be seen again."

"You really think he's gay?"

"Well, my gaydar is generally reliable, but I'd never met him, and never even seen him, until the banquet last Friday evening. Have you?"

Betsy thought. "Now I think about it, no."

Goddy shrugged. "Maybe his gate swings both ways. You can feel her out about it, if you like. May I send her up?"

"Oh, I don't know —" Betsy didn't mind so much that Godwin saw her in dishabille, but Allie Germaine was a different story. Betsy looked around at the mess in the room, at her ratty bathrobe, and recalled that she hadn't had a tub bath since the accident. "My hair, this place —" she said.

"I'll get you a comb. And this place isn't so awful, really. Here, let me put some things out of sight." He picked up the cat and a trashy novel and headed for the bedroom with them.

Betsy called after him, "But what if she expects more than I can do?"

The door closed and Godwin came back. "Oh, please don't say no! She's sitting right in the shop, ruining the ambience." He rummaged in her purse, coming up with a comb, mirror, and lipstick. "Please, please?" He handed her the comb and said, "She's so upset and sad, and she says you're her last hope."

Betsy looked despairingly at her face in the little mirror, then over it at Godwin's pleading expression. "Oh, all right. Send her up."

Godwin waited until Betsy finished with the comb and began applying lipstick, then hurried out. Betsy put away her knitting and tried to smooth some of the wrinkles out of the robe with her fingers. It was too big on her so it covered the even more wrinkled nightgown under it, and the ugly plastic casing under that. She had barely gotten past the wince of pain any movement of her leg brought when there was a light tap on her door, which Godwin had left ajar.

"Come in, Mrs. Germaine!" she called, and braced herself. She was sadly certain she would not be able to help this woman.

FOUR

Tony Milan had read the story in the *Star Tribune* — the first time in a long time that Tony had read a newspaper for more than the sports and comics — and watched two follow-up stories on the morning and evening news. He learned that Robert Germaine, Account Executive of the National Heart Coalition, had run off with a check for over twenty-four thousand dollars. The check had been presented to him by the Treasurer of the National Committee of the Embroiderers Guild of America. It had been collected by EGA for women's heart research. Germaine had last been seen getting into his car in the parking ramp at the Hotel Internationale in downtown Minneapolis, to which he'd been escorted by five members of the local chapter. The police were looking for him. There was a photo on page six of the newspaper that Tony recognized as a copy of the one that was on the wall of the third floor of the Heart Coalition's headquarters in a long row of executive portraits.

So maybe Tony had been put off by the presence of all those women walking Bob Germaine to his car — because Tony was supposed to have that check, not Bob. His plan had been to go to the hotel, waylay Germaine as he was leaving, and take the check. Then around three on Saturday afternoon he was to drive to the airport. Tony had had a plane ticket to Madagascar, best of the few countries left that had no extradition treaty with the USA, and an almost-authentic passport. Instead, here he was, four days later, in a hospital bed.

But now Germaine and the check were both missing. How had that come about?

He had no idea.

Tony had spent at least an hour last night trying various methods to recall what happened four days ago. He had some experience in recall, having been through a dozen or more drug- and alcohol-induced blackouts. He could usually get a glimpse of events, but not this time. This made him wonder at first if maybe he'd had the car accident on his way to the hotel, but the nurse said he arrived at the hospital around eleven that night. Where had he been? His plan called for him to be at the hotel around half past five, and he remembered leaving work in time to do that.

Last night he'd fallen asleep while trying to shake loose the memory and so triggered a dream about it, a dream in which he'd ridden a horse out to the airport and hit Germaine on the head with a black Nike sports bag after which some woman had presented him with the embroiderers' check as a reward.

Which he was sure was not what had actually happened.

Maybe in some kind of weird coincidence, Bob Germaine really had stolen the check himself. Funny how Tony hadn't spotted Bob as a fellow crook; he was generally pretty good at that. Still, Tony's acquaintance with him was slight; about all he did was glimpse him in his office as he handed his secretary a fistful of mail twice a day. Though now he remembered that he had sat through a speech Germaine gave to the staff a few months ago, about increasing efficiency. Tony had thought to ask about getting a motorized mail cart, but something about the look of the man changed his mind.

Wait a minute. Tony thought hard. Somewhere, sometime, Tony had heard Germaine practicing a speech. In a big empty hall, maybe. Someplace where his voice echoed. Tony could actually remember some phrases from it; it was a speech about gratitude. There wasn't a big hall at the Heart Coalition headquarters, so where had that been? Tony had been standing near enough to touch Germaine — maybe. The more he tried to tease the memory from his head, the more it turned to smoke. It was probably another dream, because what would a mail-room clerk be doing listening to an account executive practice a speech?

Tony had had ambitions to rise through the ranks when he came to work for the Heart Coalition. He got the entry-level job through the assistance of Post-Prison Friends, an organization that helped people on parole get honest work. He actually meant to go straight this time, after his second trip to the joint.

However, and understandably, most companies weren't interested in hiring a two-time loser, particularly someone with a record of theft on top of drug use and drug sales. But one — a charity that was feeling charitable — consented to give him a chance. He had to start at the bottom, of course, so he was given a place in the mail room. He'd thought janitorial was the bottom, but Janitorial Services was unionized, with good pay and full benefits. Such a high-tone department was not willing to consider hiring an ex-con on parole. Mail-room clerking was the real entry level, at least at the Heart Coalition. The work was easy enough, sorting mail by name and department, taking a cart twice a day to pick up and deliver letters and packages on three floors. Then weighing outgoing mail and putting postage on it from a meter. A woman who worked in the mail room showed him the ropes — it turned out he was her replacement, and after four days of letting her carry most of the weight, she was gone. After that it was just him and Mitch. Mitch was grim, a pissant about everything. The woman had bored him enormously, of course, being a know-it-all female, but she had nothing on Mitch for bossiness.

So, naturally, Tony quickly came to hate the job. He stuck at it, having been serious about going straight, but after four months he was thoroughly fed up. The work was boring and the mail room full of petty rules, like starting the morning mail run at nine-thirty, not nine-twenty or nine-forty, and keeping the mail room picked up — what was the unionized janitorial staff for, any-how? And Mitch was an everlasting pain in the ass, always finding something to ride Tony about. So Tony decided to fall off the honesty wagon. He began by lifting an item here and there, but it wasn't enough to make staying with the job worthwhile. Then he remembered a con a fellow inmate had told him about, and here he was in the perfect place to try it.

To his delight, it worked, and soon he had an extra, if irregular, income that enabled him to have a life outside of work. It might have gone on for years — so long as he didn't get greedy enough to make anyone notice — but Tony couldn't resist continuing picking up items here and there that the owners left right out in the open. Cell phones, wallets, watches, and rings (people took them off when washing their hands), gold pens, iPods, once even a take-out mu shu pork lunch that smelled too good to resist.

Mitch eventually began remarking about things going missing — and Mitch didn't know the half of it — so Tony decided this was a clue he'd better quit. If Mitch found proof Tony was a thief, it might lead to an investigation that would reveal the great scheme Tony was running. Tony began to look for a good reason to quit — then found out about this big check coming in. Twenty grand, maybe more. What a swell good-bye to the place if he could intercept it.

Usually talk about a big check didn't reach as far down as the mail room — no need to tempt the peons, after all — but this time it did, because it was unexpected. It wasn't the result of a fund drive, this was something extra, run by a bunch of females who did embroidery-type sewing. Tony once had a shirt covered all over with hand-done embroidery, an expensive gift from a friend. Tony had seen a photograph of a pink heart they'd embroidered — the boss made a poster of it and put it up in the lobby of the Heart Coalition. These females were embroidering these hearts and selling them, and instead of a couple hundred bucks, they had raised twenty grand.

Tony had taken a good look at the poster, because it had the embroidery club's logo on it: *EGA* in fancy lettering. He'd recognize it when the check came into the mail room. Getting his hands on this check — and not having to take the deep discount he'd get if he merely sold it to a fence — was going to make a sweet good-bye to this stupid nothing job and pissant Mitch, and the suit-and-tie jerks up on the third floor. He was going to sting these people good.

Then came the bad news: The check

wasn't going to be mailed in, the Heart Coalition was going to send someone to pick it up and thank the embroidery ladies in person.

What a gyp! That check was *his*, good as in his hand, until some big shot took it from him. What was wrong with sending it through the mail? Bigger checks had come into the mail room, Tony had seen them. And wasn't a written letter better than a verbal thanks? Jerks, all of them, from the embroidery ladies to the big shots upstairs. They were the thieves, taking the check away from Tony, after it was almost right there, in his hand!

So all right, all right, a little thought brought a new idea, a different way to get hold of the money. They were going to send some hotshot executive to pick it up? Fine, Tony knew where the event was being held, he'd go over there himself. It was a downtown hotel and it had an attached parking garage. Someplace, in some lonesome corridor or down in the dimly lit garage, he'd mug the executive and take his watch and wallet. By the time they figured out the check was gone, too, Tony would have run it through his system, pulled the cash, and be long gone. He made a point of refreshing his memory of what this Germaine fellow looked like so he'd know him outside the hotel.

Then . . . something. Tony was pretty sure he hadn't done the mugging, or it would be Bob in the hospital, not him. But instead, there was a police hunt for Bob Germaine.

So what the hell had happened?

Damned if he knew.

"Tony?" asked a voice from the door. He looked over and there was the pissant himself, in person.

"Hey, Mitch!" said Tony, pretending to be glad to see a familiar face.

"How're ya doin'?"

"Aw, I'll be all right once they let me up," growled Tony, posturing just a little. In fact, they'd had him out of bed this morning, and he'd been surprised at how far away from his eyes the floor was.

"When do you think they'll cut you loose?"

Tony grinned. "What's the matter, you miss me?"

"Would you believe I do? We got a temp in there now, and I'm not sure he knows how to read. So have they said anything about letting you go?"

"As a matter of fact, they have. The doc came in this morning and said maybe tomorrow. Problem is, he said I should stay home for a week, to finish healing. And then there's going to be a problem walking — I'll need crutches for three weeks, and a cane for a while after that. I messed my knee and my ankle up good."

Mitch grimaced. "That's too bad." Then he smiled. "And it didn't do your handsome face any good, either."

Tony smiled back. He was a good-looking man, much better looking than Mitch. "Well, my face will heal." He didn't add "But yours won't," but Mitch got the jab anyhow, and his smile went away.

Mitch said gruffly, "Well, we'll hold your job for you. You've got some sick leave coming and there's even some vacation time — four days, I think. So you'll get a paycheck for a while. I want you to call in every couple of days to let me know how you're doing. What the hell happened, anyway?"

Tony shook his head. Funny how the truth was all right this time. "I haven't got the slightest idea. I have a skull fracture and the doc says it gave me a severe concussion. I remember leaving work, and I think I remember driving out of the parking lot — and then it's just blank. I left work around five, and the accident happened around ten or ten-thirty. I was in the hospital when I woke up. My car is wrecked, the ambulance people had to use the Jaws of Life to get me out, but I don't know how it happened."

"I'll be damned," said Mitch. "You're sure you don't remember a thing?"

"Not a thing. It's been bugging me, I can tell you. The doc says parts of my memory may come back, or I may never remember any of it."

"Well, I'm glad you remember clocking out of work. We coulda been hit with a workers' comp suit."

"That's my boss," cracked Tony. "Always looking on the bright side."

FIVE

Allie Germaine was about thirty-five, maybe a little older, of medium height, very slim, with bright brown eyes and short-cropped, dark, curly hair. She wore a copper pantsuit ornamented with a red scarf, and low-heeled copper shoes. Normally so vital she virtually thrummed, today her energy seemed barely adequate to get her up the stairs and into the room.

"Hello, Mrs. Germaine," said Betsy, speaking gently because she was so shocked by Allie's obvious fatigue.

"Hello, Betsy," replied Allie in a low voice. "I want to say how sorry I am about your accident," she added, a tiny bit more forcibly. Allie's good manners would prevail on her deathbed, even were she to be crushed by a steamroller. "Sorry to be taking so long about this, and please excuse the mess," she'd murmur before expiring.

Betsy replied, "Thank you — oh, and

51

thank you for the cookies, they were delicious."

"You're welcome, of course. We all love you and miss you in your darling little shop. But I'm not up here just to exchange pleasantries, of course. Betsy, the most dreadful thing has happened."

"Yes, Godwin was just telling me. I'm afraid I haven't been watching the news lately, or I would have known. Here, sit down and tell me more."

"Thank you." Allie sank into the upholstered chair set at ninety degrees to the foot of the couch. She relaxed for just a moment, then looked up at a high-pitched sound. "What's that?"

"Oh, it's just the cat. I had Godwin put her in the bedroom so she wouldn't bother us. She loves visitors; she hopes they'll feed her."

Allie smiled a tight little smile, then sobered. "It's all been like a nightmare; I simply cannot believe the things the police think Bob did."

"What do they say he did?"

"Well, that he's a thief! That he took the EGA check and made off with it."

"Was it presented to him personally?"

"Yes, of course. He made a thank-you speech on behalf of the Heart Coalition when it was handed over. That was at the banquet Friday night. Then he was walked to his car by five EGA officials, who watched him drive away." Allie swallowed a sob. "The EGA officers say he drove off in the car alone, no one was in it with him. And — and he hasn't been seen since. The police are out to arrest him."

"But you think —" prompted Betsy.

"I don't know what to think! He wasn't there when I got home from the event, but that didn't bother me, he often goes for a drive after making a speech — he gets so wired that he needs time alone to get his heart rate back to normal. Driving relaxes him. I was so exhausted myself, I took a sleeping pill and went straight to bed. I slept right through till nine the next morning — good thing it was Saturday. When I realized he hadn't come to bed, I thought he might have slept on the couch — sleeping pills sometimes make me, er, breathe a bit heavily — and then gotten up early Saturday morning and gone to the office to turn in the check. It wasn't until around noon that I got worried. I called his office and got no answer. And I couldn't think what to do."

"You didn't call the police?"

"No, not right then. I should have; I mean, it was ridiculous to think he'd go off somewhere with no warning. I knew he wasn't in an accident, he always has plenty of identification in his wallet, so someone would have called. And if he was kidnapped, I'd have gotten a call about ransom. It was when I started that conversation with myself, about a ransom, that I realized how worried I was. I just couldn't think why he wasn't at home." She offered a painful smile. "There isn't a family history of amnesia, either."

"Had you quarreled about something?" asked Betsy.

"No. We haven't had a serious quarrel about anything in quite a long time. We were on the best of terms that day; after all, it was at least partly my doing that the Heart Coalition was getting that rather nice check. And his getting the Heart Coalition to lend its name made the fund-raiser important, so more people joined in. Denise Williams designed the heart — she did a great job — and we had some really lovely entries; I'm sorry you couldn't be there to see them. I kept telling myself he was all right, that any minute he'd call with some silly reason for not coming home. I was thinking about calling the police when they came knocking at my door."

Betsy, remembering what Godwin had

said, asked, "Did Bob sometimes do that? Stay out late or all night with some silly excuse for it?"

Allie raised her eyebrows in surprise. "Never all night. Once in a while he gets into an intense planning session or caught up reading a complicated survey and will come home late. Or he'll get to playing a new computer game and just forget about the time. I've been married to him for sixteen years, and his excuses for staying out late have never gotten less lame or sounded more like him."

Betsy nodded. "So either he's been leading a double life since before you married him —"

"Or he's the creative, driven, exasperating, charming darling I've always known him to be," said Allie, nodding back.

"If he's that absentminded, he must keep some kind of calendar," said Betsy.

"Oh, yes. He says his iPAQ is the greatest invention since the calendar, that he'd be lost without it — once he learned to put all his appointments on it."

"Does he let you see it?"

"Of course. He downloads a copy of it onto my pocket PC at least once a week, and I send mine to his — I've got a busy life, too — so we don't book one another for engagements that conflict." She smiled. "And sometimes one of us will sneak in a luncheon booking on the other's schedule, just for fun, and we meet at a downtown restaurant."

"Was he supposed to be somewhere on Monday?"

"Yes. In fact he's missed two appointments and a meeting already this week. But he has a big one this afternoon, one he wouldn't miss for anything. He has to make a very important presentation to some members of the national board about an idea he has for a campaign."

"Was he nervous or upset about it?"

"He's always anxious about presentations. He's wonderful at it, but he gets almost sick with stage fright ahead of time. He walks up and down in the living room at home, practicing — it drives me out of the house when he's preparing for a big one like this. He gets so tense, he sometimes doesn't eat dinner the night before. But he never, ever tries to get out of them. That's why I'm certain now something . . . something dreadful has happened to him. Because he just wouldn't miss a presentation as important as this."

"Did you tell the police that?"

"Yes, of course. I showed a detective my

little pocket computer with his calendar on it, and he wrote some of it down."

"Bob didn't say anything to anyone at work about someone taking his place this time, just for this presentation?"

"No. When they called me today, I told them I still hadn't heard from him. I pointed out that his speech is on his computer at work, PowerPoint slides and all. I think they're covered; after all, it isn't as if no one else knows what it's about or how he planned to do it. It was like a Broadway production; there were a lot of people involved in planning and writing it. But they're very disturbed that he won't be there to make it."

"Do they think he ran off with the money?"

"I . . . I can't believe they do, not really. The police do, but the people at the Heart Coalition know him, they know how pleased he was that so much money was raised — it was his idea to ask EGA to do the project."

"Not yours?"

Allie smiled. "All right, we thought of it together. EGA loves to raise money for charity and we were looking for something for the national convention, and this just seemed a natural. But Bob did all the work on his end and some of it on mine, so of

57

course I let him take all the credit. But you see, that just strengthens my argument that he would not possibly have stolen that money. The credit he got for the project was far, far more important than twenty-four thousand four hundred and seventy dollars."

"Suppose, just for a minute, he did take it," said Betsy. "What would he do with it? How would he cash it?"

"It was never cashed."

"What?"

"As soon as we were notified on Tuesday morning that the check hadn't been turned in at the Heart Coalition, we called our bank. The balance indicated it hasn't been cashed, and we put a stop payment on it."

"Have you told this to the police?"

Allie nodded. "Yes, but it doesn't seem to have changed their minds that he meant to steal it, and that now he's staying away because he knows he'll be arrested if he comes home. That's why I'm here to talk to you. Betsy, you've got to help me!"

"Allie, I'd love to. But look at me, I can't even get down to the shop. What do you think I can do for you?"

"I don't *know!*" Her voice was a wail. "But there has to be something, someone you can talk to, to make them stop treating Bob like

58

a, a *felon!* He's a missing person!"

Betsy thought about that. It occurred to her that if the police thought Bob had arranged this whole fund-raiser in order to steal the money, they might also think his wife was a co-conspirator. So of course they wouldn't share all their conclusions with her. She said, "The police aren't fools, I'm sure they're looking at all the possibilities. They just don't talk about everything they're doing with the public."

"I suppose that's true. But you know some police officials. Can't you call one of them and find out what they're doing, what they're thinking?"

"Well, I suppose I could ask. Meanwhile, have you called around, asked some of Bob's friends if he's gotten in touch with them?"

"Yes, of course. Nothing." Allie gave an exaggerated, exasperated shrug.

Betsy wished she knew Allie better. It was not enough to know she was an ardent needlepointer and skilled knitter. She needed to know more about Allie and Bob's marriage, for example. And have a deeper understanding of Allie's character.

She asked, "If he's in hiding, what's he living on?"

"Betsy, we have ten thousand dollars in a

bank account he can access with a cash card, fifteen thousand in a money market account, and two credit cards, one with no limit on it. That's why it's stupid to think he would run away with a check for twenty-four thousand dollars!"

"Has he accessed any of these accounts?"

"Not the cash accounts, no." Allie looked close to tears again. "I checked the balances this morning, and when I saw they hadn't gone down, that's when I decided I needed to talk to you. I didn't know where else to turn. You've done investigations before; you're so very clever."

"Yes, well, before I could always get around to talk to people."

"Maybe I could talk to them, if I knew who to talk to. Maybe he's using his credit cards — that can be checked, can't it?"

"Yes, they can trace credit card use, including location, so if he had, they'd have gone there looking for him."

"Do you think he's . . . dead?" Allie asked in a very small voice.

"What do you think?"

"I think something's happened to him, that he's stuck somewhere and can't get home or call for help. Perhaps someone hijacked his car to get the check. Or just to get the car, and left him injured somewhere.

Or maybe he was on that drive and went off the road and he's in a ravine somewhere, hurt. The banquet was last Friday, five days ago. I have nightmares about him lying injured in his wrecked car, too hurt to use his cell phone, unconscious, maybe . . ." The pain in her eyes and voice was enormous, but she took a breath and continued bravely, "Yes, maybe dead by now. I've driven the route he would have taken coming home, but didn't see a car in a ditch. But if he went for a drive, there's no telling what route he took. Who knows where he is right now?" Tears overflowed and rolled down Allie's cheeks.

Wishing she could reach her, to put an arm around her, all Betsy could do was gesture at the box of tissues on the coffee table. Allie pulled two out and covered her eyes. Betsy waited, and in a few minutes Allie pulled herself together and blew her nose. "I'm sorry."

"Allie, I'm so sorry, too. Let me make some calls, maybe the police are taking everything into consideration." She took a breath and dared to ask, "What if we found him in a hotel somewhere with . . . someone else?"

Allie laughed softly. "That won't happen. But if it did, that would be worlds better than what I'm terrified has happened."

Allie wasn't gone ten minutes before God-win was at the door again. "Well? Well?" he demanded.

"I said I'd make some calls to find out what the police are thinking," said Betsy.

"You're not going to try to find him?"

"How on earth can I do that?" she retorted, gesturing at her leg.

"By asking *me* to *help,*" said Godwin, with an air of stating the obvious.

"Oh, I don't think —"

"Then you should, my dear, you should. For who has sat admiringly at your tender toes, absorbing your methods? *Moi!* All you have to do is tell me where you would have gone, if you could go, and *I* will go there, ask any questions you would want asked, and bring the answers back to you." He assumed a "thanks for your applause" pose, arms wide.

"Oh, Goddy, I don't know," she said. Godwin was intelligent, clever, and imaginative — it was this last that made her doubtful.

"Why not?" he asked. "I've already told you something nobody else knows, that Bob Germaine is gay."

"Now, hold on," said Betsy. "We don't

know that."

"I'm sure Allie Germaine denied it —"

"I didn't ask her," said Betsy. "She is in far too much distress to be asked a question like that right now."

"Oh, but that's the *big question,* the question that needs *answering,* the question that could lead to the *solution* to this thing!"

"I did ask her how she would feel if he were found in a hotel room with someone else, and she said that would be worlds better than finding him dead."

"Well . . . yes, I suppose, if that's the alternative," said Godwin. "But surely he'd've been found by now if he was killed in a car crash or something."

"I don't know. Every so often there's a news story about someone who ran off the road and no one saw the wreck for days, even weeks. That's what she's thinking happened, and she's upset that the police are searching for a thief when they should be looking for an accident victim. She says he sometimes goes for a long drive after giving a speech, to cool off, settle his nerves."

"Or," said Godwin, "maybe he went out partying to celebrate."

"With the check in his pocket? That sounds kind of irresponsible."

"Maybe he left the check in his car, in a

good hiding place. Maybe the car got stolen — it was a new Lexus, after all — and he's too ashamed to admit where he was. And it didn't get cashed because the thief didn't find it." He beamed at her. "See? I'm thinking like a detective already!"

Betsy nodded thoughtfully. "Yes, you are. Well, let me make my phone calls first, then we'll talk about you going out to sleuth."

SIX

Betsy was in her small kitchen, moving awkwardly on her crutches — the old-fashioned kind that offer support under the arms — while she got out the crackers, then stirred the pan of soup heating on her stove. She couldn't think how she would transfer the soup to a bowl and the bowl to the table, and so proposed to eat it out of the pan.

Sophie had already learned that for the time being (though she didn't know there was to be a limit on it) she was allowed on the counter, because Betsy couldn't put the animal's bowl on the floor and so fed her up there.

Then the doorbell rang. With an aggravated growl, she swung around clumsily to head for the intercom near her front door. The bell had rung again before she got there.

Holding down the intercom button, "Yes?"

she said in her crispest voice, a warning to someone with something to sell.

"It's me, I've got news!" Godwin, sounding cheerful.

Her physical therapist had been here earlier and had her doing more leg lifts than she ever thought she could. Her leg still ached, and she was in no mood for chirpy conversation. But Godwin said he had news, and if he could tell her something useful she could put up with chirpy, right?

"Come on up." She pushed another button, one that released the lock on the door downstairs, and went back to stir her soup, which was starting to bubble around the edges.

In less than a minute he was opening the door to her apartment. "Hi, good to see you up on your feet!" he said, coming into her kitchen. "And cooking, too, better and better."

"Well, I hate to say it, but all those lovely hot dishes people keep bringing are too high in calories for someone who does nothing but lie around all day. Which reminds me, my freezer up here is full of them, and three more came this afternoon. Can you take most of them down to the basement, to the big chest freezer down there? I'll write my name on them so my tenants will leave them alone."

"Sure, after I've told you what I found out."

She went to stir her soup. "Supper first. I'd've made a salad, but my lettuce has died. I figure chicken noodle soup can't do my figure much harm, even with crackers. Would you like some?"

"No, thanks, I've wined and dined and dined some more." He smirked just a little; he was dating that handsome fellow known as Dex who worked at Needlework Unlimited, so life in that respect was good. "And I'll hint in the shop tomorrow that what you need is not another hot dish, but someone to do some grocery shopping for you."

"That would be lovely. Thanks."

"But now to the big news: Bob Germaine has been very active in the gay community."

Betsy turned toward him so fast she staggered and nearly fell. *"What?"* she said. "You *saw* him? What did he say?"

He reached out to steady her, taking her by the shoulders. "No, no, I didn't see him," he said, mildly aggravated. "And no one I talked to has seen him for at least a week." He let go and stepped back. "Okay now?

"I'm fine, just fine," she said impatiently. "Well, then what did you mean that you found him active in the gay community?"

"I mean people I talked to know him. When I described the man I saw at the banquet, a lot of people said they've seen him around. He's kind of a party animal, they say. Only he uses a different name: Stoney Durand."

She snorted faintly. "Sounds like the main character in an old television show: Stoney Durand and his sidekick Giggles, fighting for justice in the Old West."

"Can I help what a man picks for a pseudonym? Maybe he watches old westerns a lot. Maybe he smoked a lot of weed in college."

"How did you describe him?" Betsy was thinking Godwin had only seen Bob Germaine once, and then from a distance.

"He's a little taller than me, with a better-than-average build, and dark brown hair kind of wavy on top and short on the sides. He has brown eyes and thick eyebrows. No earring. His hands are not the kind you get when you've done hard labor like construction or landscaping." Godwin held out his own slender hands. "Not as nice as mine, of course. His nose is just the least little bit retroussé. He wears a silver ID bracelet on his left wrist, the kind with flat links — I noticed it when he reached for the check and at the same time was shaking hands with the President of EGA. And people who know Stoney Durand say he always wears an ID bracelet like that."

Betsy, duly impressed with this detailed description, said, "Sounds as if you were really paying attention. Good for you. Still, that description could fit more than one person."

"Not the whole thing taken together," argued Godwin. "The hair, the nose, the eyebrows, the bracelet —"

"The name," said Betsy, by her tone only appearing to agree with his list. "I understand most people pick a fake name close to their own so they'll turn to look when they hear it. So I'd've thought he'd pick something like Hob LaLane rather than Stoney Durand. And also, if he's bi, has this Stoney ever been seen with a woman?"

"Not in the places I looked," said Godwin with a smile. "And anyway, he's got a woman at home."

Betsy turned off the burner on her stove. "So you are relatively sure this Stoney Durand is actually Bob Germaine?"

"Not relatively: positively!"

Betsy grimaced and shook her head. "What a shock this is going to be for poor Allie!"

Godwin's cheer dimmed considerably.

"Yes. And while there's no need to tell her this, some of the people who say they know him aren't as sweet as I am." He waggled his eyebrows to underline this.

Betsy's heart sank and she sighed. Then hunger prodded, and she turned back to the pan. She couldn't eat right from the stove with Godwin looking and so was at a loss.

Then he was beside her, putting a bowl on a plate, pouring the soup into it. "Crackers?" he asked.

She nodded toward them on the counter, and he took a few from the package and set them on the plate. The second drawer he opened held her silverware — he found it before she realized what he was looking for and told him where to look.

"This way," she said and went to the little dining nook at the other end of her kitchen.

She bumped her foot against the table leg and sat down with a grimace of pain she hoped he didn't see. He put the soup in front of her. "But he's still missing," she said. "You said no one's seen him for at least a week."

"That's right." Godwin went back for a napkin, then sat across from Betsy, watching as she crumbled a cracker into the bowl. "But I did find out the important thing, right?"

"Yes, unfortunately." Her ankle was throbbing.

"Do you think he stole the money to spend on his secret life?" He filched a cracker off her plate and nibbled at a corner of it.

"Do you think he thought he could just ride off with the check and no one would come after him for it?" retorted Betsy.

"Maybe he thought no one would go looking for him. You know, not guess he's gay."

"If he didn't want people to guess, he shouldn't go making eyes at handsome young men until he's away from the hotel." Betsy knew she was sounding grumpy, but now her whole leg ached. "Did anyone see the look you two exchanged?"

Godwin preened a little and touched his blond hair at the back. "I don't know, I wasn't looking anywhere but at him. But I see what you mean."

"So you see how something's very wrong about this."

"I don't see anything wrong. I'm thinking he met the love of his life a month or two ago and now they're starting all over again somewhere far from here."

"What are they living on then? Allie Germaine says he hasn't emptied their bank accounts. If he was willing to steal a check, you'd think he'd take at least some money from their joint accounts."

"Maybe the love of his life is rich."

"So why steal the check?" Betsy asked.

Godwin considered that a few moments. Then he said, "Maybe it was like a good-bye thing, taking that check. Good-bye to his job, good-bye to his wife, good-bye to everything and everyone who thinks they know him. Taking the check meant he was burning his bridges. He can't come home again now."

Betsy considered that. There was an ugly logic to it. A man living a lie decides to come out of the closet — and makes sure he can't go back in again. "It's hard to believe Allie could be so wrong about her husband. They have children — two or three, I think — and the oldest is in high school, right?"

"Two, and I think both are in high school," said Godwin.

"She said they'd been married sixteen years. That's a long time to carry off a lie, don't you think?"

Godwin shrugged. "It happens." He leaned forward and repeated more strongly, "I know for a fact that it happens."

"All right. But is it even *remotely* possible Stoney Durand is not Bob Germaine? *That we're not talking about the same man here?"*

The intensity of her look and voice made him squirm just a little. He said, "Look, I described him as best I could, and only two people named someone else — and one of them took it back when his friend said no, it was more likely Stoney Durand I was talking about."

"And the other person, the one who didn't take it back?"

"He said I was describing Al Gore." Godwin snickered. "I said, 'In your dreams,' and he said —" Godwin sighed romantically, and drawled, " 'Yeah.' "

Betsy sighed, but not romantically. She shifted slightly on the chair. Her leg was like a bad toothache.

"But you see," Godwin continued, "the consensus is, it's Stoney Durand. We both know the man I saw at the banquet is Bob Germaine. So I'm positive the man I asked everyone about is really Bob Germaine." Her doubting face made him uncomfortable. "I would have taken that photo from the newspaper with me, but it was such a bad picture. Could you ask Mrs. Germaine if she has a better picture? I'd ask her, but if she wanted to know more about why I want one, I might forget and tell her where I've been looking."

"Didn't they take pictures at the banquet?" asked Betsy.

"Some people at the tables did. You can just imagine how awful they are, with those little flashes, and too far away to do any good. But I didn't see them do that posed thing, where they hold on to a check big as a coffee table and smile pretty."

Betsy said, "I think the decision to send an exec from the National Heart Coalition came too late to have that humungous check made."

"How do you cash a check like that?" asked Godwin, diverted. "Can you imagine trying to put it in the car? Wouldn't it be funny to watch someone trying to get it through the door of the bank? Could you still cash it if it was in two or more pieces?" He grinned and popped the remainder of his cracker into his mouth.

"They aren't real checks," said Betsy, dipping her spoon into the bowl. "It's just for show. I remember reading somewhere that the real check is the normal size." She took a mouthful of broth and noodles, then put the spoon down. Pain had taken her appetite away.

Godwin asked, "Did you talk to the police about what they're doing?"

"Oh, yes. I called Jill, and she called the

investigator on the Minneapolis police force in charge of the case. His name is . . . O-something. Orrick? He told Jill his investigation is going nowhere. Germaine, he said, seems a very unlikely thief, but he is their only suspect. Jill told me he said it's because of the eyewitnesses."

"What about them?" Godwin asked.

"There are too many to doubt, and they're all telling the same story. They heard him make the speech, watched him put the envelope with the check into his pocket, and some of them walked him out to his car. So that part is clear. Orrick thinks it possible Bob Germaine got carjacked, but if so, where is he?"

"Do you think that's what happened?" asked Godwin.

Betsy repeated Allie Germaine's story about her husband going for a drive after the speech. "Jill said Allie told that to Orrick when they first talked to her, and that Orrick put out a call to law enforcement in the five-county area to look for signs of a car going off the road, and to check ravines and rivers for a light blue Lexus. But nothing so far."

"So maybe the car is on its way to New Mexico, driven by Bob Germaine. And in the passenger seat is this good-looking older

75

guy with big bucks."

"Why older and good looking?" asked Betsy, thinking Godwin had someone in mind.

"Why not?" said Godwin with a shrug, reaching for another cracker. "It's just that when I think of someone breaking loose at last, running off with a new lover, he's rich, handsome, and has these beautiful silver streaks in his dark, wavy hair."

Tony Milan sat on his dilapidated couch, his left leg in its dark canvas-and-metal brace resting on the stained old coffee table the landlord had probably rescued from the sidewalk. *What a dump,* he thought.

Beside him was a black plastic bag containing the stuff he'd brought home from the hospital. He'd already dug out the pain meds they'd given him, but he was still resting from getting from the curb into his garden apartment. He was afraid that if he didn't gather his strength before he stood to go into his bedroom, he might fall. And he was afraid that if he fell, he wouldn't be able to get up — his broken arm and leg were on the same side, plus his overall bruises and scrapes made even ordinary movement painful. He wished he'd accepted pissant Mitch's offer to help him into his apartment, even at the risk of seeing the packed suitcase inside the door. And the passport and airline ticket to Madagascar sitting on top of it.

Maybe it was just as well. Mitch thought he'd be coming back to work — and maybe he was. The airline ticket was no good anymore.

Anyway, he had no reason to run now, did he? He frowned over that for a while. Because he had been stealing checks from the mail room and depositing them in a special account he'd set up. There was absolutely no sign from Mitch that he, Tony, was suspected in that way. Of petty theft, maybe — but Tony hoped with all his heart that there were other petty thieves at the Heart Coalition, because a sudden stop to all theft during his hospitalization would be all the proof they needed of his guilt.

Thinking about his check-stealing scam brought up the question again: What happened last Friday? Tony had a good-enough plan to get hold of that check written by EGA. Okay, both Mr. Germaine and the check were gone — but why assume Germaine and the check had gone together? Maybe Tony had the check. His car accident may have been just that, an accident, with no link to the theft of the check. After all, no one said they'd found this big check written to the Heart Coalition in a pocket — they did search his pockets, didn't they?

Whoa!

Tony stopped thinking while he ripped open the black plastic bag that contained his personal effects. A big brown envelope contained his cell phone, his good ID bracelet with the flat links, a nice gold watch with a leather band — which he'd never seen before — and his wallet, which itself contained his driver's license, Social Security card, two credit cards. And $147, which was a lot more than he remembered, but nowhere near $24,000. In the big envelope was also a little brown envelope containing about two dollars in loose change, a small brass key with the number *36* written in ink on a strip of white tape on it, and a pair of what looked like real-gold cuff links. The change he remembered, but not the key or the cuff links. He put them aside and continued pulling things out of the bag. Up came a white dress shirt, covered with dried blood. His blood. It was odd to look at that and think that huge amount of blood had come out of him. He touched the big bandage on his head tenderly.

Hold on, he owned a white dress shirt, but he hadn't worn it to work last Friday.

And this one had French cuffs, which his didn't. That explained the cuff links, in a way. But why had he been wearing someone else's dress shirt and cuff links? Had he gone to a drunken hot tub party and put on the wrong shirt after? He smiled at himself — that would have been a typical accidental-on-purpose "mistake" for him. And it would explain the watch, too. But he had no memory of a hot tub party, and, in fact, didn't currently know anyone with a hot tub. He picked up the cuff links. They were plain, a small square sitting on a bigger square, and not new; but the weight and shine suggested high-carat gold. He put them down again, more respectfully. The watch was only a Bulova, but the strap looked like real crocodile. Taken from the same person who owned the shirt and cuff links?

In the bottom of the bag, in a big wad, was a black suit. He pulled it out. It was torn, cut, stiff with what was probably more dried blood, and here and there, caught in the folds, were a very few little cubes of glass. Oh, windshield glass, sure.

But the suit was once a very nice one. And it wasn't his. Tony didn't own a black suit.

He went through the pockets anyhow and didn't find the check. Had he left it at the party? In the car? Did the people who towed wrecked cars away go through them looking for valuables?

Wait a second, maybe he'd deposited it. He opened his cell phone and was pleased to find he had turned it off, so when he turned it on, it had a charge. He thought a few moments, then dialed a number that connected him to First Express Bank's automated service. He had a checking account there that would give the Heart Coalition a fit if they knew about it, and he loved not having to talk to a person who might later remember his call. Some more numbers and he got the balance on the National Heart Fund account he'd set up: "Four thousand four hundred thirty-two dollars," the female robot voice told him.

He disconnected. Okay, he hadn't deposited the check.

Maybe Mr. Germaine had it after all. Tony felt a stab of anger. He hoped Germaine was found and sent to jail. That would teach him to steal from Tony Milan!

Tony cast about for something to do. He wasn't able to go out of his little apartment and had always been careful not to let anyone know where he lived unless absolutely necessary. His home was a den, a place of safety, and the wise predator didn't leave hints to its location. So he couldn't invite anyone over.

His bank had his address, as did the bank unwittingly taking part in the Heart Fund scam. Some Heart Coalition employees also knew where he lived; for instance, the two women in Personnel and the pissant.

But no one else. Well, except the Domino's Pizza that he sometimes ordered a delivery from. He drew a lonesome sigh. But hold on, no need for a pity party. Tony could still talk to people, couldn't he? Some of his friends must be wondering why they hadn't seen him in a while.

Tony picked up the cordless phone on the coffee table, thought a few moments, then dialed. A male voice answered, and Tony said, "Hey, Billy, it's me, Stoney Durand!"

SEVEN

Jill was preparing Emma Elizabeth for bed.

"*I* do it!" shouted Emma from inside the nightgown, her little fists grabbing at the fabric. Jill immediately let go and Emma began a struggle to find the neck hole and get her head through it. She pulled at random, and when she couldn't find the opening she began bouncing with impatience, which didn't help.

Jill, amused, continued to refrain from helping, but she could not entirely smother a giggle. Emma stopped, listening to the sound. Her tiny nose could be seen in outline through the fabric, pointed at the ceiling. Jill laughed.

Emma laughed uncertainly. "I silly?" she asked.

"No, darling, you're not silly, but you look silly with your teeny nose." Jill reached out and touched it lightly with a forefinger.

Emma collapsed as if the touch had been

a blow. "Nose silly!" she shrieked. "*Toe* silly!" She kicked upward inside the nightgown, pressing her toes into the fabric, laughing heartily.

At other times Jill would have begun a hilarious search for the toddler's silly toes and nose, but it was already a little past Emma's bedtime and no time to get her daughter even more excited. Instead she began to sing a song about a farmer named MacDonald, and while at first Emma shouted with every verse that what old MacDonald had on his farm was a nose, pretty soon she was agreeing that here and there the chicken was going cluck-cluck and the pig oink-oink. Soon she allowed her mother to help her get the nightgown on. In ten minutes, she was asleep.

Jill went out into the living room and sat on the couch beside her husband with a little sigh.

"It only gets worse," said Lars, affably. "Pretty soon it's drinks of water and 'God bless Mommy' and just one more story."

"And how do you know all this?" she asked in a chilly voice, and then was alarmed at how real it sounded. But she saw him catch the slight twinkle in her eyes, and her alarm faded.

"I remember from when I was a baby," he

said, and stuck his tongue into his cheek.

She made a skeptical face at him.

"Okay, my mother said my baby brother was just like me, and I remember him being like that."

They sat in smiling silence for a few moments. Then Lars said, his massive brow corrugating in an effort to be diplomatic, "Hon, have you been thinking about going back to work?"

"Not really, why? Do we need the money?" She wondered if he had another costly purchase in mind — he was prone to costly, work-heavy enthusiasms.

"No, no, we're doing all right." Which at least meant his current hobby, a 1912 Stanley Steamer automobile, hadn't done anything expensive to itself lately.

"Well, why do you ask, then?"

"You'll think this is dumb, prob'ly, but yesterday I opened the suitcase on the top shelf of our closet because I forgot what it was doing up there, and I found it was full of Em's baby clothes. And a smell came out of them, just like she smelled when she was new, and all of a sudden I thought how nice it would be to have another baby."

He wasn't looking at her when he said this. Afraid she might laugh at him, she thought. "And you think perhaps the choice for me is either going back to work or having another baby?" This time the chill in her voice was not faux.

"No, no!" he hastened to say. "No, what I was thinking was that maybe you were thinking about going back on the cops. Because I know you miss it. But if you're not thinking about it, maybe you could think about a baby brother or sister for Em."

He still was looking away. So he missed the look of compassion she gave him. Back before they married, they'd agreed they wanted a big family, at least four children. But Emma was more expensive and a whole lot more work than either had anticipated. Most of the labor fell on Jill — which was okay, because it was her choice. And she loved it. Mostly. And just lately she had been thinking that one wasn't enough. It was kind of nice that dear Lars was thinking so, too.

Her silence drew his attention, and he turned to look at her, his pale gray eyes looking into her light blue ones. They both started smiling at the same time.

Godwin was watching an old movie on cable. It was Bette Davis month, and she was starring in *The Petrified Forest*. Bette Davis, he reflected, had been a terrific actress, sweet and vulnerable in some roles, defiant and angry in others, ironic and sarcastic in still others. Whatever the role called for, there she was, living it, graceful or clumsy, defensive and vulnerable, snotty, witty, beautiful — sometimes even homely, but always true to the role.

He was knitting another in his endless series of white cotton socks — not that he needed another pair. What he needed was an excuse for staying up late. Some customers who knew him would be sure to notice he was tired tomorrow and ask if he'd been out on a date. He didn't want to lie and say yes — but he also didn't want to say he stayed up late to watch a Bette Davis marathon. So he knit, because saying he got involved in knitting was almost the truth, and something Crewel World customers would definitely understand.

But he was really staying up late because he wanted to think. Like his parents before him, he had grown up doing homework while watching TV, sometimes with music also playing. He believed all those distractions somehow helped him focus.

But it didn't seem to work this time. Maybe because he'd seen *The Petrified Forest* before, several times, and he didn't think it one of her better efforts — Ms. Davis was very young in this movie, not the gallant ruin she would be many years down the road. It made him aware that one day he, too, might be a ruin — and not a gallant one, at that.

Which was not what he wanted to think about. He wanted to think about sleuthing. He'd thought he'd be a natural. Wasn't he nosy? Even nosier than Betsy, if it came to that. Wasn't he able to charm almost anyone into talking to him? Hadn't he gone to places where he knew he could get people to talk to him, where he knew many of the people he would talk to? And hadn't he found that Bob Germaine was living a secret second life? And yet the way she'd looked at him and his deductions . . .

He'd watched Betsy's techniques as she investigated crimes over the past few years. He'd hung on her every word at the end of her cases and absorbed her explanations. It wasn't hard, she always said. She'd just talk to people and gather their meanings, hidden and obvious, until a pattern emerged. And that's what he'd done, talked and listened. And he brought home lots and lots of good information.

So why did it seem to him that she wasn't fully satisfied with his results?

The deep thinking this was calling for was

getting a bit hard, so he reached for the remote and turned off the television. He continued working on the sock, which was one begun at the toe and ending at the cuff. He was at the cuff, knit one, purl one, very easy, and he liked a nice, long cuff. Betsy often said that knitting something simple freed her mind to think, to *ponder,* which she defined as a deeper kind of thinking. He sat back in his big, comfy chair, allowing his mind to ponder.

He hadn't done *everything* wrong. For example, Betsy had been very impressed with his idea that Bob Germaine had decided to come out of the closet with a big, bad, dishonest act, make a *statement,* so that was probably true — Betsy had a nose for the truth that was at least as good as his own.

But she had seemed particularly nose-wrinkly at his vision of Bob sailing down a highway with his silver-haired lover, which Godwin thought was a particularly fine piece of deduction. Why didn't she like that one?

He pondered that for a while before deciding it was too many for him — he'd read that expression in a Mark Twain story once upon a time and really liked it — "too many for him," meaning he just couldn't figure it out — that was sharp. But knowing it was too many didn't solve the problem. He knew his next assignment was going to be to talk to the women who had been at the EGA convention banquet, which was going to be a lot harder than talking to friends around the city. Maybe he'd better ask Betsy about her expectations, or at least get some solid instructions about his methods. That decision settled his mind enough that he could tuck his knitting away and go off to his lonely little bed for the night.

Betsy, struggling gingerly into a fresh nightgown, reflected on Godwin's efforts. Godwin had many talents, and his admiration for Betsy's sleuthing ability was as charming as it was sincere. But his ambition to emulate her, to be a sleuth himself, was, she feared, not something he could do reliably.

Godwin had gone investigating to prove his already-drawn conclusion that Bob Germaine was a closeted gay man. Which was almost all right. He had told Betsy that Germaine was gay before they talked about his sleuthing. The problem was, he found a number of people who helped support his theory, and felt his mission was accomplished. Perhaps if he'd talked to more people, he might have found some who disagreed with his theory, perhaps with facts to back them up.

But what put the cap on the thing, she thought, was his imaginative description of Bob Germaine driving his Lexus down a long highway with a handsome, wealthy, mature lover in the passenger seat — there was not a shred of evidence to indicate this scenario was more than a happy dream — and one close to Godwin's own heart. Who knew what Bob Germaine's dreams were?

She sank carefully into bed, laying sheet and blanket tenderly over her mending leg. She had a huge stretchy stocking pulled over the hard plastic "boot" on her left foot and lower leg to protect her sheets from its buckles and rough edges, but pulling it on had reignited the pain.

She had barely emitted a sigh of relief at successfully becoming horizontal when Sophie jumped up on the bed, on the other side from her usual landing spot, away from Betsy's wounded leg. Funny how Sophie had immediately understood that her mistress was injured and in pain, that the pain was located in her right leg, and that she, Sophie, while seeking to comfort Betsy, must not step on or bump the injury.

The cat, a beautiful, fluffy white creature with tan and gray patches on her head, down her back, and up her tail, was also very solid, and she joggled the mattress — and Betsy's leg — while making her way to Betsy's left side, where she collapsed with a purring sigh. Very gently she put one paw on Betsy's forearm. Betsy could not help smiling, and she stroked Sophie's dense fur, eliciting a deeper, more rhythmic purr. Giving and receiving comfort, Sophie was good to have around, Betsy thought.

Betsy was also, for once, grateful that Sophie was probably the laziest cat in the state. Long ago, a friend who owned a more energetic cat was sick in bed, and the cat wore itself out bringing her freshly killed mice, gophers, and once even a squirrel, in an attempt to nourish her mistress back to health.

Sophie, the queen of nourishment, did not hunt even to nourish herself. Possibly it was not her fault, possibly she was taken from her mother before her mother could teach her to hunt; it was even possible her mother did not know how to hunt, either. In any case, Sophie did not seem to know food could come from elsewhere than a human hand.

Betsy's thoughts had wandered off the topic, which was . . . what? The pain pill she'd taken after brushing her teeth was kicking in. Oh, yes, sleuthing. And Godwin's willing, enthusiastic, but not very good attempts at it.

So what was she to do? She didn't want to hurt Godwin's feelings by telling him he wasn't to do any more investigating. And, it wasn't as if she could go out herself. Perhaps, hinted her weary mind, she should just call the matter off. She'd done what Allie had asked, found that the police were, in fact, looking into other possibilities than that her husband was a thief. Still, it was an interesting case, and she was intrigued by its contradictions. Could she use Godwin's inept investigating somehow? Or was there someone else she could send out? Who did she know who might be more skilled at sleuthing than Goddy?

The pill began easing her gently into sleep. Her last conscious thought was: *Jill.*

EIGHT

It was late the next morning. Godwin was just starting to think about lunch: Should he go first, or send Marti, the part-timer? It had been a slow morning, and he was sitting at the library table in the middle of the shop, stitching a model Christmas stocking. It was cut out of a piece of canvas and he was covering it in shades of red, white, yellow, and green yarns in a bargello pattern. Bargello is beautiful with its sharply curved lines, and not difficult — if the first line is done correctly. Also, once under way, the stitcher can put it down and pick it up again very easily, a nice quality if one is (hopefully) constantly interrupted by customers. One trick Janet Perry suggests is to begin that first row in the center of the line. Leave half the yarn hanging, parking its end at one end of the canvas, and work the line to the end. Then come back and pick up the loose end and finish the line in the other direction. Godwin was doing an illusion pattern, where the center section had steeper and narrower lines, making it look as if it were partly folded.

He'd done the first row and then quite a few more rows when the door sounded its two musical notes. He put his work down and stood to smile a greeting. And then smiled more warmly. A tall woman with a serene Gibson-girl face and very pale hair pulled back in a braid was standing there in pale green wool slacks and matching soft flannel shirt.

"Hello, Jill!" he said. His voice went very high as he added, stooping, "And heh-woe to you, wittle darlin'!" to Emma Beth, who stuck a forefinger in her mouth and looked up doubtfully at her mother. Emma, even fairer than her mother, was delectable in wine corduroy overalls and a pink-and-wine sweater.

"It's all right, baby, you may say hello to Godwin."

"Woe," said Emma obediently, looking at him.

"Not into baby talk, is she?" Godwin remarked, straightening.

"Not too much."

So he made a silly face at the toddler, who suddenly warmed to him, grinning back.

Jill said, "Betsy told me she was going to send you to find out if Bob Germaine was leading a secret life."

"Yes, she did. And I did. And he is."

"Really?" Jill looked just a trifle taken aback. Since she rarely showed surprise, this gratified Godwin very much.

"Oh, yes," he said, preening, "I have a lot of contacts in the gay community, so I talked to a lot of people. And I described the man I saw getting the check at the EGA convention banquet. That was Bob Germaine, and they said that from my description, it sounded like Stoney Durand, who is quite well known in the community." Godwin raised and lowered his eyebrows in a complex way and Jill nodded comprehension.

"Well done," she said. "Betsy asked me to come over today and talk to her. Is she free?"

"Sure. Go through the back door of the shop, so she doesn't have to get up and answer the downstairs buzzer. Her apartment door's unlocked."

Jill didn't ask if she could leave Emma with Godwin, for which he was grateful.

Emma Elizabeth knew what a visit to Betsy's apartment meant. She turned left into the kitchen with a one-word cry of happiness: "Cookie!"

"Hi, Betsy!" called Jill. "It seems I brought the Cookie Monster with me by mistake. I thought I had my lovely, well-mannered daughter along."

"Cookie!" insisted the lovely daughter.

"The cookie jar is on the counter near the refrigerator!" called Betsy from her place on the couch.

"Cookie!" reiterated Emma, who could hear that magic word in any sentence, be it ever so long; and the next sound heard was the pottery lid being lifted off the pig-shaped jar.

A few moments later they came into the living room, Emma contentedly gnawing on a sugar cookie, Jill smiling a greeting.

Jill said, "Did you know Goddy can do the wave with his eyebrows?"

"What? Oh, that thing he's started doing when he thinks I may be missing a point he's trying to make. I bet he practices an hour in the mirror twice a week."

"Kitty?" asked Emma, looking around.

But Sophie had vanished in that magical way some cats have, the instant they hear a child's voice. Though Emma had a habit of spilling lickable cookie crumbs, she also loved to pull the cat's tail and whiskers.

Sophie knew she could gather up the crumbs after the child was gone.

Jill said, "The kitty is taking a nap. Would you like to take a nap?"

"No!"

"Her favorite word," said Jill with a sigh. "I was just downstairs, talking to Goddy. Were you surprised to find out Bob Germaine is a closeted gay?"

"I'm not sure he is. I have only Godwin's opinion."

Jill raised her left eyebrow and said, "I take it Goddy is not a detective."

"Well . . . he does his best. But in this case, he had an idea, and I think he only looked for information that would confirm it."

Jill cocked the other of her pale eyebrows. "Where did he get that idea to start with?"

"He is sure Bob Germaine returned a flirting smile Goddy gave him as he went out of the banquet hall last Saturday night. Therefore, according to Goddy, he is a deeply closeted gay man."

Jill's lovely features went still for several seconds. Then she said, "I don't believe it."

Betsy felt a sharp stir of interest. "Have you met Bob Germaine?"

"Certainly. I've been to the Germaine house half a dozen times — maybe more. I've spent evenings with them. And I have never had the remotest idea that Bob was gay. He's an artist, but more the serious kind than the flighty kind, you know?"

Betsy smiled. "More Russian than French, right?"

"I'd say he's definitely more suffering than romantic, if that's what you mean. He gets really intense when he's on a project."

"Allie said that about him. I wish I had met him, then I might have a better feel for this. What do you think, could he have been joking with Godwin? Does Bob know Goddy?"

"No, although he knows about him. Allie loves to talk about Godwin with me — she likes him at least as much as I do, and she's always telling Bob the funny things he says. But I don't think Godwin's ever been to their house, and I'm quite sure Bob wouldn't know him on sight. On the other hand, Goddy isn't the kind to receive a message when one isn't being sent, is he?"

"No, not normally. He broadcasts a lot, however. Maybe he saw something he liked in Bob, let it show, and Bob saw it. And, just kidding, smiled back at him." She looked inquiringly at Jill.

Who nodded slowly. "I suppose so. Though that wasn't exactly the right time and place for that sort of thing, was it?"

"I wouldn't think so — but I don't know Bob. You do."

"And I don't think he'd do something like that to someone he didn't know, especially when he was acting on behalf of his employer. But downstairs just now Godwin said that when he described Bob Germaine to people in gay hangouts, they said they knew him — but by another name."

Betsy nodded. "Stoney Durand. An unlikely pseudonym, don't you think? But Goddy told me Stoney Durand is a well-known figure among a certain set of gay people. A wilder bunch, if I read Goddy's euphemisms correctly."

"That's . . . different," said Jill, using the Minnesota understatement for *very strange.* "If Bob were gay — which I don't believe — I don't think he'd be the wild and crazy type. He'd be the quiet kind, the one you never knew was gay until he introduced you to his partner."

Betsy shrugged. "Well . . . maybe. I mean, if you're living a double life, and you have to keep all your gay feelings locked away most of the time, it seems to me that you'd want to let them roar at least a little bit when they're out for a walk. Take you, for instance."

Both of Jill's eyebrows went up. "Me?"

Betsy smiled. "Yes, you. You are this cool and calm person, and when you were a cop on patrol, you were so correct you could have given lessons to Sergeant Joe Friday. I was scared to death of you when I first met you."

"You were?" Her ice-blue eyes twinkled with amusement.

"Sure. Then I started hearing stories about you. My favorite was about the time you put just a drop or two of tear gas on the heater of Lars's patrol car on the coldest night of the year. He had to choose between freezing and crying his whole watch."

Jill thawed into a smile. "And you realized that I roar sometimes, too."

"Exactly. So I suppose it's possible Bob Germaine lets loose when he's out of the closet."

Jill nodded. "In the sense that anything is possible, it's possible. But I still don't believe it."

"That's interesting. Because now Goddy's all hot to go talking to people who came to the EGA convention."

After a short silence, Jill said, "Did you ask me over here to see if I would go with him?"

"Yes," Betsy admitted, and burst out, "I

don't know who else to ask!"

"Maybe you don't need to ask anyone. Maybe this is a job you can't do. Maybe you should tell Allie — wait a second." Jill held up a hand, palm forward, a cop stopping traffic, while she thought. "Remember when Goddy was arrested for murder?"

"Yes, of course I do. Why?"

"Well, you involved a woman lawyer in the case. She ended up working as a PI, right?"

"Oh, you mean Susan Lavery. She calls herself a 'recovering lawyer' nowadays. She's doing private-eye work." Susan was a regular customer in Betsy's shop — she claimed that she could sit anywhere doing needlework and no one, even the target of her stakeout, would realize it was a stakeout. A tall, thin, white-skinned woman with bright red hair, she was otherwise pretty conspicuous.

"You helped her change careers, maybe even saved her life," said Jill. "Don't you think she owes you a favor?"

"Well, she told me she does, said to ask her for help if I ever needed it." Betsy nodded twice. "Oh, wow, I wonder why I didn't think of her." She looked up at Jill. "I'm confused a lot lately. Could it be the pain meds?"

"I don't know. What are you taking?"

"Vicodin, mostly."

Jill smiled. "Oh, yes, a couple of Vicodin will mess up anyone's thinking. Nice stuff, otherwise."

"Actually, I prefer Darvon. I was given Darvon years and years ago after a dentist took out my wisdom teeth. I've never forgotten how marvelous Darvon made me feel." Betsy sighed. "I actually had my doctor write in my medical file that I was not to be given Darvon again, because I really, *really* like it." Betsy sighed again, remembering how Darvon smoothed all the bumps out of her life the three days she was on it. Then she looked up and saw Jill smiling at her.

"Vicodin does a good job, too, I see."

"Oh. Yes, I guess it does. All right, I'll call Susan Lavery. But I wish you'd work for me. Godwin trusts you, and you used to be a cop."

"But I never was a detective in the department."

"No, but you did very well on patrol — and that calls for a lot of decisions based on your interpretation of what people say and how they behave."

Jill nodded. "True. Emma Beth, come away from there!"

The child had fallen silent, a development

that should have drawn Jill's attention sooner. Now she was seen with one arm inserted nearly to her shoulder into Betsy's knitting bag. Beside her on the carpet were several balls of yarn and a piece of knitting with needles sticking out of it. She glanced over at her mother, absorbing the look of censure with her mother's own cool composure. "No," she said calmly.

"One," said her mother, just as calmly. "Two. Three."

The arm reluctantly came out. Jill went to praise and pet her daughter and allow her to help pick up the yarn. Jill asked Betsy, "Do you want me to hand you this piece you're working on?"

"No, it's nothing important. I thought you couldn't use that counting business on children until they were at least four."

"I thought so, too, then I came home from an overnight trip and found Lars had taught it to her. Thank you, Emma," she said, taking the last ball of wool from her and putting it into the bag.

Emma followed her mother back to the chair, then leaned on her lap to smile very sweetly up at her. "Cookie?" she asked.

"No. Lunch soon."

Emma's lower lip poked forward, then turned downward until it nearly touched her chin. Her beautiful blue eyes shone with incipient tears, but Jill only continued regarding her daughter with no show of sympathy — or anger — and Emma's lip slowly righted itself. The child sighed and looked around for some new source of entertainment.

Betsy said, "There's a pretty ball somewhere in this room."

Emma brightened. "Ball?"

"It's soft and it's red and green and gray and blue and gold. And there's a jingle bell inside it." Betsy had made the ball of scraps of washable velveteen as a toy for Sophie, back when she still thought it possible to tempt the cat to exercise. It was stuffed with old panty hose, nice and squeezable, and in its middle was a tiny golden bell inside a little plastic box. Sophie had spent several weeks contentedly watching it roll by. A couple of weeks ago Betsy had come across it while cleaning out the linen closet and decided that she'd give it to Emma.

"Where's the ball?" Jill asked Emma.

Emma looked around, then back at her mother and shrugged her baby shoulders.

"It's behind a pillow," hinted Betsy.

Emma studied Betsy as if waiting for further enlightenment, but Betsy merely winked and nodded. Emma looked around the room again and saw the brightly colored needlepoint pillow on the upholstered chair. With a glad cry, she ran to it and pulled the pillow away. But no ball was behind it.

She looked accusingly at Betsy, her lower lip threatening to do its trick again — then saw how Betsy was moving her head against the big pillow on the couch. Emma laughed and ran to thrust a chubby hand behind the pillow, and pulled out the ball with a loud shriek of delight. She spent the next several minutes clumsily throwing and kicking the ball around the room while Jill and Betsy talked.

"How's the healing coming along?" Jill asked.

"Oh, not too bad. There's still some pain, of course. And the exercises are aggravating. I think it's too soon to do all they're asking me to do. Leg lifts really hurt."

"Do you think you're reinjuring the bones?"

"They say I'm not, that the plate they put in there will protect it against the movements I'm doing. But it *hurts!*" Betsy saw Emma look at her with alarm and closed her lips firmly over further whining. She said instead, "I just wish I didn't feel so useless."

Jill said, "I think you need to give yourself

some time. As the healing really takes hold, you'll find plenty to do." She stood. "And now I think it's time we went away and left you to it. Emma Beth, what would you like for lunch?"

"Mackincheeeeese!" crowed Emma immediately, dropping the ball and trotting to reach for her mother's hand.

"Bless you for coming," said Betsy. "You really gave me a good idea. I wonder what other obvious thing I'm missing?"

"Me, too," said Jill, and she let the merest hint of a twinkle show in her eye. "Come on, baby, let's go home."

NINE

Betsy's curious failure to think of something so obvious as calling Susan Lavery left her shaken. What was the matter with her? Was it the pain meds? Or was it simply that she had eaten only a dry piece of toast for breakfast this morning, and nothing since?

. She got to her good foot, grabbed her crutches and did the "dot and go one" — her father's expression for anyone walking on crutches — into her galley kitchen to open a can of soup. She had very little appetite, which she would ordinarily consider a good thing, as she was generally in the middle of a fight between her waistline and her love of good food. On the other hand, the visiting nurse had warned her she needed to nourish her injured body so it could grow the new bone it needed to mend itself. She decided cream of chicken soup would be the easiest wise choice and balanced on one foot while pulling the tab that opened the can's top. She used the last of her milk to make the soup and actually ate most of it. And did feel better.

After lunch, she went to phone Susan Lavery at her home. She got Susan's voice mail and left a brief message. Susan's cell phone went directly to voice mail, too. Since she worked for a criminal defense attorney named Marvin Lebowski, Betsy called Marvin's law firm and talked to Mr. Lebowski's secretary.

"Hi, Phyllis, is Susan there?" asked Betsy.

"Oh, I'm sorry, she isn't. She's out all this week."

"Vacation or on a case?" Betsy had hired Mr. Lebowski to defend Godwin last year — which he did, very capably, with her help — and as a side effect of the case, Susan Lavery gave up her own position in a law firm to work for Lebowski as a PI.

"A case. She'll be gone at least all this week and possibly most of next week, too."

"Would it be possible to contact her somehow?"

"No, I'm sorry, she's out of touch unless it's a real emergency. Is this something that serious?"

"No, no. I wanted her to do some investigating for me."

"Maybe she'll finish up this week. I'll have her call you when she gets back in town."

"Okay. Thanks, Phyllis." Betsy sighed deeply and hung up.

She was back to deciding whether to let Godwin continue sleuthing or pressing harder on Jill to help.

"No," said Jill, on the phone. "I told you, I have a full-time job taking care of Emma Beth. Maybe when she's older, in first grade, say; then I'll think about it." Betsy could hear a smile in her voice as she continued, "Of course, by then I may have a little brother for Emma Beth."

"Say, you aren't —"

"No, I'm not — yet."

Betsy groaned inwardly. Jill in a nesting mood was not at all what she wanted. She teased cruelly, "I hope it's twins."

"Then I'll give one to you."

"Triplets?"

"The other one to Goddy."

Betsy laughed. "Can you imagine Godwin with a baby?"

"Now, don't cast aspersions, he might make a very nice parent."

"At the very least, his baby would be the best-dressed of the three." Godwin's sense of color and style were legendary.

"Seriously, Betsy, I'd like to help, but not by going out on a case. Maybe I can consult with Godwin, give him some hints about talking to people and how to judge whether they are holding back or lying."

"That actually might be a great help. Thank you."

Godwin was having a very interesting conversation with a young woman making her first quilt. "It's not just my first, it's my last," Sharon was saying. "I had no idea how complicated it was when I started it, or how long it was going to take. I could have finished a Marilyn Leavitt Imblum pattern in the time it's taken me just to accumulate the fabric and cut it." She was a short, stocky woman in her middle thirties, with thick, light brown hair tied back loosely at the nape of her neck. She wore a pink cotton sweater of a complex pattern she had probably knit herself. "It's not like I'm doing a fancy pattern, I'm just doing four-inch squares."

Godwin nodded sympathetically. "I've avoided quilt shops," he said. "The fabric is so gorgeous I'm sure I'd be tempted into quilting. *Just* the thing I need, another needlework project!" He looked around Crewel World, which didn't sell beautifully patterned fabrics. "So how can we help you?"

"Well, my theme for this quilt is chickens."

". . . Chickens?"

"I know, it's silly. But I must not be alone — there are dozens and dozens of fabrics with a chicken theme, especially if you include things like fried eggs and grilled chicken legs." She laughed softly, a little embarrassed.

Godwin made a pained face, and Sharon said, "Pathetic, I know. But eggs and fried parts are the reason we have chickens, right? Anyway, I've got two counted patterns already finished — one's a hen and the other's a rooster — and I didn't know what to do with them until I thought how cute they'd be in my quilt. But two's either too many or not enough."

Godwin smiled. "And you've decided they're not enough."

"Right."

In a few minutes they had rounded up Jeanette Crews's counted cross-stitch pattern Rooster Serenade, featuring two Mexican-style roosters — they'd finish at eight by eight inches, but that was fine; a booklet from Cross My Heart called Little Critters, which had a simple pattern of a rooster's head in it that could be done on low-count fabric to make it four by four; a small square painted canvas of a baby chick labeled Share One's Ideas; a punch needle called, simply, Rooster, designed by Rachel T. Pellman; a Cedar Hill sampler of a hen and chicks ("I'll leave out the alphabet and some of the chicks," said Sharon); a set of machine appliqué patterns from Debora Konchinsky featuring sixteen chicken patterns, if you counted the guinea hen as one; and another painted canvas of a Picasso-style hen — Sharon had the counted cross-stitch pattern of Picasso's rooster at home.

"There, that should keep me for a while!" she enthused at the checkout desk.

Godwin happily added up the charges and was happy all over again when Sharon did not gasp at the total cost or groan or decide to change her mind about some of the patterns. But as he was bagging up her purchases, she said in a much more sober voice, "Goddy, you were at the EGA convention banquet, weren't you?"

He paused to look at her. "Yes, I was. I got Betsy's ticket because she was in the hospital. Why, were you there, too?"

"Yes. I sat at a table with my mother and four other relatives — it was a combination stitch-in and family reunion at my house all that week. But we heard about the Heart

112

Coalition man running off with the check for the money we raised, and I wondered if Betsy is involved in the investigation."

"She wants to be, but her broken leg is keeping her at home for now." Godwin leaned over the big, old desk that Crewel World used as a checkout counter and murmured, "But I'm helping. I'm talking to people who know something about it and bringing the information to her."

"Really?" Sharon breathed, eyes widening. "I'm glad to hear that, because I think my mother has something important to tell you."

Ten

Tony was going desultorily through his mail. It had piled up a bit — he wasn't ever very interested in mail, unless it had a check in it, his or someone else's that he could glom onto, or unless there was a big sale on at Macy's, which used to be Marshall Fields, which used to be Dayton's. Odd how even the big companies merged and split nowadays. He could remember his grandmother's intense loyalty to Dayton's. Today you couldn't be loyal for long to any department store.

He quickly put aside a notice from the management company that ran his apartment building. He'd stopped paying rent a couple of months ago in anticipation of fleeing the country, but now he'd have to do something about getting caught up. That wouldn't happen until he closed that phony Heart Fund account, and getting out and around was too painful right now. His eye was caught by an envelope with a return address of the Minneapolis Impound Lot.

Oh, hell, his *car.* Which he'd been driving when he'd had the accident. Now he remembered how, once he'd been sitting up and paying attention in the hospital, he wondered what had happened to his car. And where it had gotten to. "Call the police," his nurse had advised him. "They'll know."

But Tony, for several good reasons, didn't like talking to the police. Besides, if the accident was so serious they'd had to cut him out of his car, then probably his car was not just toast, it was burnt toast, and he was no longer interested in it.

But maybe not.

He opened the envelope hopefully — and gave a sincere groan of despair. His car had been towed, the form letter inside informed him, and they were charging him eighteen dollars a day to keep it until he came to claim it. *And* it wasn't just the storage fee he owed them, there was also their "heavy-duty tow" charge of a hundred seventy-five, *and* their ninety-dollar "winch time" money.

"Huh!" Tony muttered, tossing the form letter on the coffee table. They could go whistle for their money.

But the notion of rent and now these car

115

charges made him uneasily aware of the thin state of his finances. He'd called the airline where he'd bought his ticket and spun the sad story of his car accident, but had they forgiven him the price of his ticket? Of course not; hadn't he been informed that the special bargain price he'd bought it for was absolutely not refundable?

And the twenty-four grand? That turned out to be a hatful of smoke. He wished he could remember what went wrong! He clenched his good fist as he sighed after the lost party time, the hot sun on the friendly beaches.

But so what? Right? So what? It wasn't as if he were on the street. He had some money in his wallet, and some credit left. Not a lot, but some. And there was the four thousand dollars in that Heart Fund account. That money was going to be a great comfort very soon.

Still, it would be good to run a con on someone, just to keep his hand in. Too bad his good looks were — temporarily, but still — marred by a huge black eye, a scabby cut on one cheek, and a swollen, purple ear. He could pull the "just need fifty more dollars for a plane ticket" scam, but that meant he'd have to stand for hours at the airport, which he wasn't up to — plus, he couldn't hustle away if a cop turned up. But he sure wasn't ready for the dance floor or even a bit of sleight of hand. It made him uncomfortable to realize that; he'd always relied on his charm, handsome face, and smooth moves to get him into the right circles and out again — swiftly, if necessary. It would be a few weeks, maybe a couple of months, before he regained that edge.

He pushed the rest of the mail aside. He'd gotten an uneasy glimpse of some bill-like envelopes from his doctor and the hospital, which he was sure represented the deductibles they mentioned when he'd checked out. What was the good of health insurance, anyway, if you still ended up paying out big hunks of money? It was a gyp! Well, he'd show them, he wasn't even going to open the envelopes.

So long as he could continue living in this apartment, and eating, and have lights to turn on at night, and warm water to bathe in, he was okay.

But that meant he'd better go empty that Heart Fund account — that con was over as far as he was concerned.

He'd show them his wounds and they'd feel sorry for him and probably not check his papers too closely. Like the fact that his ID card said Mail Room on it, not Chief

Financial Officer like he'd written on the application to open the account.

Better go while the going was good. He took a deep, energy-giving breath and rose to his feet. But he hadn't taken care to plant his crutch solidly. It slid across the low-nap carpet, and he fell. His head thumped painfully on the floor and spasms of pain shot through his injured arm and leg. He lay there for a minute, waiting for things to settle down. But his head only went from sharp pain to thick ache, and his arm and leg throbbed almost like they did when he first left the hospital. He lay there for several more minutes before beginning the long, slow struggle to regain his feet. Was this bad enough to warrant a call to his doctor?

No, he might ask him for a payment, so never mind.

But no going out to the bank today.

He lurched slowly into his bathroom, took a double dose of pain pills, and in five minutes was draped across his bed, letting the Vicodin ease the hurt.

He wasn't quite asleep when his phone began to ring. He tried to work the noise into the dream he was starting but it was too loud and insistent.

He waited for his answering machine to pick it up, then remembered that he hadn't listened to his messages, and the phone wouldn't transfer calls to a full box. Damn.

He rolled over and reached for the cordless phone on the bedside table. "H'lo?" he grumbled, thick-tongued.

"Tony? That you?"

Well, damn it to hell if it wasn't the pissant! "Yeah, Mitch, it's me. Whassup?"

"Can you come in to work tomorrow?"

"Whaaaat? I can't work yet! I won't be able to work for another week, maybe two." Or three. Maybe four.

"I know, I know. This is just some kind of paperwork deal. Take you half an hour, maybe."

Tony breathed heavily while he thought about it. He was going out tomorrow anyhow, to First Express Bank to close that account. The bank was maybe two blocks from the Heart Coalition Building. "All right. What time?"

"One o'clock all right?"

"Sure, fine. See you then."

They were in Betsy's apartment, which despite the dust and clutter retained its cozy elegance. The living room was carpeted in a deep red, with triple windows draped in chintz, some of whose flowers reflected the color of the carpet. There were standard lamps and a glass-fronted cabinet full of porcelain collectibles. There was a lamp with an angled lampshade standing behind an upholstered chair, beside which stood Betsy's carpetbag of needlework.

Godwin sat in the chair, Jill stood beside the lamp, and Betsy half-reclined on the couch in her rumpled flannel robe. Rain tapped lightly on the windows.

They'd been talking for a while about sleuthing techniques. Betsy was saying, "Goddy, it's important to have some purpose in mind, and to think up some of the questions you need answered to accomplish that purpose, before you to talk to Sharon's mother — or anyone, for that matter."

He nodded. "Okay — and I do, right? I want to find out if anyone else saw Bob Germaine smile at me, or if maybe he even winked at some other man."

Betsy and Jill both sighed. "No, Goddy," Jill said patiently. "You want to find out if they saw Bob Germaine at the banquet. You want to find out who, if anyone, walked with him all the way to his car. You want to find out what Bob said or did that they themselves saw or heard. You do not hint that you think Bob is gay, you let them tell you they think he was behaving gaily —" She stopped short and said, "Is that the right word, *gaily?*"

"No," said Godwin, "but never mind, I know what you mean."

"Okay. No trick questions, and don't let them know the answer you want."

"That's right," said Betsy. "Let the people you're talking to answer in their own way. And if they say something that doesn't confirm what you think happened — in fact, *especially* if it contradicts what you think happened, it's important to listen very closely. Don't even hint that you think they're mistaken or lying, but do ask questions that will allow them to give you lots of details and reasons why they think it happened the way they're describing."

Godwin nodded again. "Okay, I got that part."

"Good. Wherever the conversation leads, you just follow along and see where you end up. It may give you a whole new perspective on your theory because they are going where you thought they would go, only they have to get there a different way. Or you may end up some place you never dreamed of, some place where all your assumptions are proved wrong." Betsy reflected a moment. "All this sounds complicated. But do you understand?"

Godwin shifted a bit in the comfortable

chair. "I think so. The thing is, sleuthing is not what I thought it would be. You told me you just ask questions and sort through what people answer and the solution pops up out of that. But I've seen TV shows and movies where some detective starts out knowing who the bad guy is and is out to prove it.

Jill snorted softly. "You want to know something? There's been exactly one television show that is close to accurate about a cop's life: *Barney Miller.* And if you want to laugh, tell a person who works in forensics that you've learned a lot from *CSI.*"

Godwin grimaced, then nodded. "Okay, it's not like on TV."

"It's not all wrong," said Betsy. "Now that I've been sleuthing for a while, I can read what you might call the subtext of all that fiction. All this is there — it's just not spelled out. Because it's the boring part. If they did a TV show about a famous needlework designer, they'd leave out all the hours of pushing the needle in and pulling it out, I'm sure."

Godwin chuckled. "They'll never do a show like that, because if they left out the stitching, there'd only be fifteen minutes of show. What else?"

"Would anyone like a cup of tea or hot

cocoa?" asked Jill.

"Me," said Godwin promptly. "Earl Grey tea."

"Me, too, thank you," said Betsy. "Cocoa."

Jill went into the kitchen.

Betsy said, "When you're figuring out your questions, try to put them in chronological order. When did they get to the convention, did they stay at the hotel, did they have tickets to the banquet, where did they sit, like that. Take them through step-by-step."

"Okay, but what if I want to talk about who they saw at the banquet and they want to talk about something totally different? Like the new stitch they learned in a class?"

"If it's obvious they aren't answering your question, politely pull them back on task, and ask it again. If they still won't answer it, write that down. It may be important."

"But maybe — oh, wait, I get it! If they're evasive, there might be something they don't want to tell me, and a serious reason for that! Well, sure, that makes sense. You even told me once you draw conclusions not just from what they say, but what they *don't* say. You *are* brilliant!"

Betsy tried not to preen, and Jill poked her head out of the kitchen to say, "Now, let me tell you how you'll know if someone is lying to you."

"Oh, honey, you don't get to be my age and gay without having about ten thousand lessons in that." Godwin looked sad about that, but briefly. Then he smiled. "The good part is, my lie-dar works at least as well as my gaydar."

"That's true," said Betsy, who had seen him shame a patron trying to return a book or needlework gadget as unused with a mere knowing glance.

Jill came back with a tray holding three steaming cups — she'd made cocoa for herself. She put the tray on the coffee table, handed the cups around, and said to Godwin, "Just to comfort my heart, how about you tell me some of the ways you know someone is lying to you."

"Well, for example, someone's been looking at me but now he looks away before he answers the question. Or, he leans forward and looks deep into my eyes, which he wasn't doing before. If we're talking and he lifts one hand and says, 'I swear to *God*' or 'on my *life*' or 'my mother's *grave*,' the rest of that sentence is a lie." Godwin's eyes rolled upward as he thought, then he took a sip of tea and said, "If he says, 'Would I lie to you?' he probably will. If he says, 'Trust me,' especially if he touches me on the arm while looking into my eyes as he says it, I don't. If he gets furious when I doubt his story, it's a lie. If he suddenly gets up and walks around while telling me this part of his story, that's because he can't maintain eye contact while he lies. Which brings us back to the first way, doesn't it?" He smiled at Jill. "Did I miss anything?"

"Not so far," said Jill, hiding a smile behind her cup of cocoa.

Betsy asked, "Did you notice any of those signs in the people you were asking if they'd seen Bob Germaine flitting through under a false name?"

"No," said Godwin promptly. Then he frowned. "But I wasn't thinking any of them might be lying. Anyway, this is not the same thing, Betsy. I *know* Bob Germaine is gay."

Betsy and Jill did not reply and after a few moments Godwin said humbly, "But that's what we're talking about, isn't it? My not jumping to conclusions?"

"I'm afraid so," said Betsy.

"Maybe I should go talk to them again?"

"Yes, but not right now," said Betsy. "You need to talk to Sharon's mother, first. What's her name, anyhow?"

"Ramona," said Godwin. "Ramona Tinsmith."

Betsy said, "Tinsmith, that's a nice name.

After you talk with Mrs. Tinsmith, I'd like you to see if you can contact any of Bob Germaine's coworkers."

"He'll need an excuse for that," said Jill.

"The truth will do, I think," said Betsy. "We've been asked to investigate his disappearance by his wife."

"Something else," said Godwin. "I want to get a better photograph of Bob from Allie before I go back to my friends at the Eagle. Is there anything you want me to tell her?"

"Oh, I wish there were!" exclaimed Betsy unhappily. "I can't figure this out without listening to people!" She clenched her fists. "I *wish* I could get out and talk to people myself. I *wish* I could get down to my shop! I feel so *useless* up here!"

Godwin hastened to say, "You're *not* useless! You're giving me good advice right now. And, I come up here all the time with questions and the latest gossip from the shop. Which reminds me: A couple members of the Monday Bunch want to know if they can meet up here." He leaned forward and added in a confidential tone, "Bershada says when she broke her ankle, all her friends came around and cleaned her house for her, and she wants to know if the Bunch can do it for you on Monday."

Betsy, who had looked around her dusty, disordered apartment in a kind of panic at the prospect of the Monday Bunch visiting, turned now to Godwin and burst into grateful tears.

Ramona Tinsmith was shorter and stockier than her daughter, but otherwise she looked very much like her. She had even dyed her hair the same light brown color. She was wearing a silky green housedress and old-fashioned white Keds.

Her voice was deeper and warmer than Sharon's, and her blue eyes were surrounded by attractive laugh lines. She invited Godwin into her immaculate little kitchen, done all in black and cream, and without asking poured him a mug of coffee, then poured a second for herself. She sat down at a tiny round glass table in a corner and gestured at him to sit, too.

"Thank you," Godwin said. He got out a little notebook — it had a flowered fabric cover and sewn-in pages — then, seeing she seemed to be waiting for something, politely took a sip of the coffee.

"Milk? Sugar?" Ramona asked, rising. All of a sudden she was avoiding his eyes, which was making him uncomfortable.

"No, this is fine. Good coffee." Godwin

took another sip. Since he rarely drank plain coffee anymore — he liked Starbucks's half-caff triple grande nonfat caramel macchiato with whipped cream and nutmeg powder, with one Sweet'n Low and one NutraSweet — he didn't know if he was lying or not. "Please, sit down. This won't take long, and it won't hurt a bit." He chuckled. "I sound like my dentist."

Ramona smiled and relaxed into her chair. "I'm sorry, I'm a bit nervous. Yesterday I was completely sure, but today not so much."

Godwin let his mouth drop open in amazement. "I know *exactly* what you mean! I'm liable to say just about anything — until I see someone with a tape recorder or a notebook. Then I start dropping 'almost,' 'maybe,' and 'some people think' all over the place!"

Ramona's laugh lines deepened as she lifted her chin and laughed. "You are so right! I've been getting more and more nervous about you coming over and asking questions, until by the time you got here I was almost ready to pretend no one was at home." She took a deep breath. "But I'm over that now."

"Good," said Godwin. He found the pen in a shirt pocket and clicked out the point.

"Sharon said you had something to tell me about the EGA banquet."

"Yes." Ramona nodded, then leaned forward. "I don't think that was Bob Germaine up there accepting the check."

Godwin had begun writing this down, but stopped halfway. "Oh, now —" he began, and stopped. Betsy and Jill had leaned on him about this, hadn't they? And he'd resented it just a little bit. After *all* — now, now. After all, maybe they were right.

He cleared his throat and began again. "What makes you think that?" he asked.

ELEVEN

At noon the next day, Godwin went to the Sol's Deli next door and ordered a thick beef-on-rye sandwich with lettuce and tomato, a side of potato chips, two milks, and an extra pickle. He took the paper bag with him upstairs and tapped on Betsy's door. "Come in," she called in a slightly odd voice.

"Hello, hello, hello!" he said brightly, putting on a smile for her. But when he came in and saw her sitting in her overstuffed chair, wearing a silver peignoir that tumbled in lace over her knees, her hair washed and combed, her lips colored, the smile turned real.

Her head was turned slightly away as she tucked her knitting needles into a small ball of orange yarn. When she turned to look at him, he saw she was ashen, her eyes bright with unshed tears. He went at once to kneel at her feet. "What's the matter?" he asked.

"Nothing, nothing. Don't I look better?"

"You. Look. Mahhhh-velous! Except around the eyes. There you look like you're hurting."

"Well, I am, a little. I'm cutting back on the pain meds. And see how it helped? I'm no longer lying like a beached walrus on the couch, I'm sitting up and taking notice. And noticing what I've been missing. For example, the fact that the 'squares' I've been knitting for the African blanket are not exactly squares." She lifted the needles, which held a shape probably best described as a parallelogram.

Godwin was surprised into a snort of laughter. He reached and took the piece from her. "Well . . ." he said, thinking rapidly. "Maybe you could do a lot of these odd shapes, and put them together in a kind of patchwork, and it would look as if you meant to do them this way." He looked closer, at the random increases and decreases, the dropped stitches and yarnovers, and handed it back. "Or not," he concluded, getting to his feet. But he was still smiling.

Betsy looked up mournfully at his smiling face. "Oh, Goddy." She sighed. "If I'd known how much trouble breaking a leg could be, I never would have done it!"

Godwin began to think she was still taking a few too many pills, then he saw her smile, and the two laughed heartily.

"Okay," said Betsy, when they'd caught their breath, "what did you find out?"

"Lunch first." He opened the bag and brought out the sandwich, offering half to her and draping a big paper napkin across her lap. He waited until she had taken a bite of her half and nodded in pleasure before he said, "First, I found out that your advice on interviewing people was really good. Thank you, thank you, thank you — and Jill, too."

Betsy waved the sandwich half impatiently. "Yes, yes, you're welcome. But —"

He interrupted, "Second, Ramona thinks it wasn't Bob Germaine who stole the check."

Betsy frowned at him. "Who does she think stole it?"

"Some other man. I mean, she thinks the man who gave the thank-you speech at the banquet wasn't Allie Germaine's husband." He took a bite of his sandwich.

The frown deepened. "Does she have any idea who this man was?"

He swallowed and replied, "Not a clue. But she says she saw Bob Germaine at the hotel restaurant the day before — someone pointed him out to her, he was having lunch with his wife — and that the man up on the dais at the EGA banquet didn't look like the same man."

There were sparkles of interest in Betsy's eyes. "Now we're getting somewhere! I wonder if she could be right? But how would someone even think he could get away with a stunt like that?" Now she had that look she got when hot on the trail. "Wait, what we still need —" She leaned forward eagerly, then winced. But she waved the pain away to continue, "Who agrees with her about this?"

"Nobody. Ramona said she hasn't told anyone but her daughter."

"Why not?"

Godwin ate a potato chip thoughtfully. "I think because she's waiting for someone else to bring it up, and nobody has. So she isn't sure she's right."

Betsy was disappointed. "So it's not a rumor spreading around?"

"Nobody's come into the shop to tell me — and you know our shop is like a side room off Gossip Central." Godwin meant the Waterfront Café, where people met to eat lunch and dish.

Betsy, sipping milk through a straw, lowered her little carton to muse aloud. "But surely there were people at the banquet who know Bob. If the man who took the check wasn't Bob, how come nobody else noticed? Like, for example, the people who handed the check over?"

"Well, the woman who was supposed to hand the check over was at that meeting with Allie and the other officers of our local EGA — and with officers of other EGA chapters, plus the Regional officers."

Distracted, Betsy asked, "What was that meeting about?"

"I don't know, they haven't told us. Which means it's bad news, an increase in dues or something like that." Godwin swung back on topic. "Allie doesn't bring Bob along to many EGA events, you know."

Betsy took a pinch of potato chips. "Yes, that's right. So whoever took his place probably looked enough like him, height, coloring, build, that the people there just took it for granted it was Bob."

"But how did the imposter know Bob's wife wouldn't jump up and say, 'What did you do with my husband?' "

Betsy grimaced. "Yes, of course. That kind of makes Ramona's story a mistake, doesn't it?"

A little silence fell. Betsy chewed a bite of her sandwich moodily.

Godwin said, "But it's about the only

alternative we've got, isn't it? Either Bob Germaine is a crook or it wasn't Bob who accepted the check."

Betsy said, "And Allie has asked us to find out the truth. When we do, that may tell us where Bob is."

Godwin thought about that and felt a little stab of dismay. "No matter what, this doesn't look good for Bob, does it?"

Betsy sighed. "No." She dusted her hands onto her napkin. "All right, if anyone comes into the shop who was at the banquet, ask if they know Bob and what they thought of his acceptance speech at the banquet. Don't ask if they think it wasn't Bob at all, just see if they come up with that notion all by themselves."

They talked awhile more, then Godwin had to get back downstairs. Betsy had drawn up a grocery list and Godwin took it with him. Lots of fresh fruit and vegetables on it, he noted with a fond, brotherly interest. But he added "yogurt" and "calcium supplement" at the bottom; Betsy had probably just forgotten to write those down. She knew it was important to build strong new bone, but for him it was becoming urgent, too.

He had thought sleuthing would be fun. Finding out that a great deal of time was spent being flummoxed was a big disappointment. He wanted her to take that job back from him.

A total of three customers came in who had been at the EGA banquet. All of them were scandalized about the theft of the check, two of them already knew a stop-payment had been put on it, and none of them thought there was anything odd about the man who gave the brief, eloquent thank-you speech.

Godwin also wanted Betsy to come back to running the shop. Decision making was all right until it became important. For example, what to do about the costly hand-dyed yarn Betsy had ordered from a local woman whose samples had been gorgeous. A big box of it had come in while he was gone, and he had eagerly opened it, to find that while the colors were still gorgeous, the wool had been so carelessly prepared for dyeing that it still had little pieces of straw stuck to it — and maybe something worse; Godwin didn't care to inspect it too closely. He closed the box and set it aside. He'd tell Betsy about it tomorrow, when he had calmed down enough to refrain from shrieking. There were several customers all excited about buying the yarn. What to tell them? He'd much rather Betsy face them.

Then there were the "badgers." There seemed to be an unusual number of them the past couple of days. Badgers weren't customers from Wisconsin, whose state animal was that noble creature; these were customers who imitated the badger in its ability to dig fast and deep. They would disappear around a corner and pull things out of cabinets and baskets and off shelves, and leave the disorder for the help to discover. God knew what they were thinking; they seemed to root for the sheer joy of it, not in search of something.

It wasn't until Godwin restored order to a drawer of out-of-print cross-stitch patterns that he realized the motive of one badger: theft. It was only in putting things back that Godwin realized three patterns were missing.

And then he couldn't remember which badger it was who had gone pawing in that particular drawer. Betsy, he was sure, would have known. He felt incompetent, an unusual emotion for him.

At least his part-time help that afternoon was experienced and cheerful — and a real help in closing up. Marti ran the vacuum cleaner while he restocked; she straightened out the baskets of yarn while he ran the cash register; she even volunteered to take the day's money to the bank with a deposit slip Godwin made out. Godwin blessed her, told her to tuck the money bag inside her jacket to escape casual gaze, and sent her on her way, then went to the back to scrub out the coffee urn and set it up for the morrow.

Tony thought he should go to the bank before he went to his place of employment, but an old friend called and invited him to lunch. Tony thought it was time to see some friends. But Vicodin had made him sleep in and it took some time to make himself marginally presentable, so there wasn't time to hit the bank before lunch.

He made it to the restaurant only ten minutes late, where, despite his best efforts, Jeff said, "Well, I'm *shocked.* You look dreadful, simply dreadful, you poor thing." Tony didn't think he looked all that bad, but Jeff himself looked pretty good dressed all in teal, a great color on a man with red curly hair and large blue eyes. But, Tony reflected with a slightly malicious smile, Jeff's looks were spoiled by a heavy, petulant mouth, and Tony's wounds would heal.

But all Tony said was, "You'd realize how much better I look now, if you'd visited me in the hospital," his tone making the complaint light, because he planned to stick Jeff with the check.

Jeff's eyes widened. "Oh, hospitals! *Dreadful* places, I never go into a hospital, unless I'm in an ambulance, which hasn't happened yet, thank *God!* But I just know I'll keep my eyes closed the *whole time!* Ew, just the *smell* of a hospital gives me cold shivers!" Jeff twiddled his shoulders and lifted his hands, palms forward. "I don't know *how* you stood it!"

"Drugs," said Tony. "They give you lots and lots of lovely drugs."

"Well, yes," said Jeff, nodding. "Yes, drugs would certainly help."

They had a pleasant lunch until Tony refused to engage in a tussle Jeff clearly expected over the check, which enlarged Jeff's pout. Then Tony had to walk over to the Heart Coalition, because Jeff wouldn't drive him.

So he was a few minutes late. He clipped his ID badge to his jacket, nodded at the guard behind the high, round desk, and took the elevator to the basement.

He found Pissant Mitch in the mail room along with a man in a dark suit, whom he recognized after a couple of seconds as Colin Roose, Mitch's boss. And standing a little behind Mr. Roose was a very large man in a dark uniform who at first looked like a cop. There wasn't a gun on his hip, so he must be a rent-a-cop.

Still, Tony didn't like the looks of this *at all,* so he paused in the doorway. Then he slightly exaggerated the difficulty he had in managing on one crutch, and bit his underlip to show he was in pain, and came into the room. He'd almost forgotten how claustrophobic it was, windowless and much deeper than wide, with red-brown tile on the floor and tan walls harshly lit by four fluorescent fixtures hanging from the ceiling. The lights gave a sinister cast to the features of the three men waiting for him. Or maybe it was his suspicious mind, telling him he was in big trouble.

"Hi, Mitch!" said Tony, trying on a smile.

"Mr. Milan," said Mitch, not smiling back.

So Tony dropped the ploy like the dead thing it was. "Okay, what's the problem?" he asked.

"Well, for one thing, you're fired," said Mitch.

"What? You can't fire me for not coming to work, I was in an accident!"

"You're not fired for being absent, Mr. Milan," said Roose. And the rent-a-cop worked his shoulders — not like Jeff, shaking off a fake tremor of fear, but like a thug preparing to hit someone in the face.

140

Tony began to feel there was not enough air in the room. "What's this all about?" he asked, trying to sound calm.

"You're a thief, Tony," said Mitch.

Tony had to swallow hard before he could say, "No, I'm not." Then he had to swallow again before he could ask, "What do you think I stole?"

Roose consulted a small slip of paper Tony hadn't noticed was in his hand. "An iPod, a Chinese take-out order, various amounts of loose change, a gold ring set with a small garnet, a woman's purse containing three credit cards and sixteen dollars —" He paused and looked hard at Tony. "Shall I go on?"

Tony was so relieved he didn't know what to say. He cleared his throat and looked around. There was an orange plastic chair off to his left. He moved a few more steps and collapsed into it. "Um . . ." he said.

"We can continue this conversation down at police headquarters," offered Roose.

"No, no, that's not necessary," said Tony, finding his voice, but keeping his head down so they wouldn't see how relieved he was they didn't know about the check scam.

"So you admit stealing various items while picking up and distributing mail in the course of your duties?" said Roose.

141

"Well . . . what the hell. Yes, I did it. How did you find out?"

"You jerk, you left the iPod in your locker!" said Mitch.

"How come you went into my locker?" demanded Tony, raising his head. "That's my private space!"

"No, it isn't," said Roose. "If you'd read your employment contract, it says very plainly that your locker is subject to search."

"So you searched everyone's locker, I suppose," sneered Tony, hoping to catch them in a lie.

"No, of course not," said Roose, surprised. "But we noticed that the rash of thefts stopped after your accident, so that gave us probable cause to look in yours."

"Oh." Well, that was what he'd been afraid was going to happen anyhow. "So what happens now?"

"You will leave the premises under escort," said Roose, glancing over his shoulder at the thug, who did his shoulder trick again. "Since you are terminated for cause, you will forfeit your benefit package, including health coverage. However, I am obliged to inform you that there is a provision for you to continue the coverage at your own expense. You will receive a booklet in the mail explaining the program, called COBRA, how it works and the cost to you. The booklet will also describe other rights you have; for example, to appeal the firing. Mitch has the other contents of your locker in that grocery bag on his desk and will carry them out of the building for you. I'll take your Heart Coalition ID card, please."

Tony wordlessly unclipped it from his jacket and handed it to him.

"I'm sorry this had to happen, Mr. Milan," concluded Roose in a less formal tone. "We were looking forward to being a part of your finding a new structure for your life." But he didn't offer to shake Tony's hand before he left the room.

Nor did the pissant say another word as he carried the bag ahead of Tony, who was followed by the thug. They went up the elevator, across the lobby, and out the front door. Mitch set the bag down on the sidewalk, offered Tony an ugly triumphant grin, and walked back inside, the thug behind him.

TWELVE

Tony didn't like his job, but he didn't like getting fired, either. Especially since getting fired meant they'd cut off his health benefits. Oh, yes, there was COBRA; but he'd had a friend in the same mess, and paying for his own health insurance turned out to be very expensive.

So now Tony absolutely had to go close that Heart Fund bank account. He swiveled on his crutch to start up the street toward the bank, and someone called out to him, "Hey, you forgot something!"

He turned back and saw a short, thin man in jeans and dress shirt pointing snootily at the big paper bag. Tony nearly told the man what he could do with it, but realized he was in no condition to back up his attitude with muscle. So he went back, picked it up, and carried it half a block to a trash can where he stuffed it in.

He went down the street to the dark

granite façade of First Express Bank. He'd picked this big downtown branch of the bank for his scam for two reasons: First, it was close to where he worked, so he could drop in easily; and second, it was big, so he could remain anonymous.

He went in and paused just inside the second set of doors to reconnoiter. And was immediately nudged from behind by a tall, young, frozen-faced woman with a lot of magnificent red hair, a green silk suit under an open leather coat, and an attaché case that probably cost more than Tony's entire wardrobe.

"Pardon me," she said frostily, "but you're in my way."

"I beg *your* pardon," he said, matching her tone but moving a couple of yards sideways — this was no time to make a scene — "I'm still getting used to this crutch."

She sniffed unsympathetically at his crutch and went on her way.

He considered the row of windows along one side of the low-ceilinged, maroon-and-gray-carpeted room with its square pillars, fenced-off office section, and stand-up table with holders for deposit and withdrawal forms.

He had already prepared a withdrawal slip

at his apartment, so he got in line to present it at one of the four windows where a bank clerk stood. He wondered if there was ever a time when all ten windows were manned. Certainly he'd never seen them all open.

The pleasant-faced woman behind his window looked at the slip, punched some numbers into her computer, and said, "This will empty this account. Do you wish to close it?"

"Yes, ma'am," he replied, smiling, feeling that little tingle he loved when getting away with something. He could almost feel the cash in his hand.

"There's a separate form we'd like you to fill out to close an account." Noting his crutch, she added, "If you like, there's a place you can sit down while you work on it."

"Do I have to fill out the form?" he asked. "I'm in kind of a hurry. Doctor's appointment," he said, adding a plaintive note to his voice and drooping just a little on his crutch.

She gave him a look of compassion, but said, "I'm sorry, but we can't close an account without the form." She handed him a single sheet of white paper. "Both sides, I'm afraid," she said.

"All right." He sighed, wishing he'd decided to leave the account open with a dollar in it. Should he say he'd changed his mind? No, she might wonder at that, and his whole flimsy house of cards would come down if anyone started wondering. "Where can I sit down?"

"Over there," she said, pointing to a distant corner, where there stood a small wooden table and a pair of swivel secretarial chairs.

Tony made a pitiful display of traveling to it, which was not entirely faked. His leg was aching and the arm using the crutch was complaining of too-long use. He sat down and began filling out the form, which wasn't complicated. There was a little space for him to write, in his own words, the reason he was closing the account.

He frowned over it for a minute or two, then wrote, *Relocating to St. Paul.*

St. Paul was an inspired answer. Tony thought it was simply amazing how a lot of people living in Minneapolis treated St. Paul as if it were on the other side of the state instead of just across the river. Of course, he knew a lot of people in St. Paul who bragged that they had never been to Minneapolis in their life. Tony was an anomaly because he was not afraid to go back and forth, but the bank didn't know that. He was sure First Express would agree that if he was moving to St. Paul, he would not want to bank in Minneapolis anymore.

Still smiling at his clever ploy, he got back into line and soon was talking with the same bank teller.

"Oh, this is a business account," she said, looking over the form.

"Yes, is there a problem with that?"

"Are you an officer of the company?"

"Yes, ma'am, I'm chief financial officer." That was the title Tony had given himself when drawing up the phony company's organization papers.

"One moment, please." She walked away and he frowned after her. Were they going to make a fuss? It didn't matter — did it? He hoped not, but in any case this was taking more time than he had been prepared to give. His con artist sense was setting off alarms. He knew he should walk away now, right now, but he needed that money. *Stick it out,* he told himself. *It's gonna be all right.* He promised himself a dose of Vicodin if he stayed.

Which reminded him, he was down to his last four pills. He should have called in a refill of the prescription this morning, but how was he to know what his goddam lying boss was up to, telling him to come in for some "routine paperwork"?

He wondered what the full price of a month's worth of Vicodin was. A lot, probably. He'd have to go easy on them. Or maybe buy them off the street. But that was dangerous because sometimes you didn't get what you thought you were buying.

The clerk was gone for a long time, long enough that the nice little thrill was long gone before he saw her coming back. He smiled at her, but she wasn't going to give him his money just yet. "Do you have some identification?" she asked.

"Sure," he replied and leaned on his crutch while locating and bringing out his wallet. He handed her his driver's license.

She looked at it, then at him. "No, I mean some identification to show you work for the Heart Fund."

"Oh. Of course." He'd been asked for the identification card before, and generally a flash of it — too quick to let them see it read Heart Coalition, not Heart Fund — was all it took. But there was no card to flash today; it had been taken away from him earlier by the pissant's boss. He reached into his jacket pocket, pretending surprise when he didn't find it, and began poking around in other pockets. "I'm so sorry," he said at last, "we're packing up for the move and I guess I forgot to bring it along." He raised the ante on his smile from friendly to ingratiating.

She looked again at his driver's license and then at him. He said, "I probably don't look much like my photo. I was in a car wreck."

But the accident hadn't changed his hair from dark brown to auburn, or added twenty pounds to his once-buff frame — by-product of a job that let him sit a lot and turn his prison-built muscles to flab.

"I need to have you speak to one of our account managers," she said and walked away again.

Tony was blowing hot and cold by now and sighed heavily several times to help him keep his temper. He turned to watch the clerk go into the gated compound and speak to a woman behind a desk. And his heart sank: It was the cold-faced redhead who had complained about him blocking her way into the bank.

After a little conversation, the clerk straightened and gestured at Tony to come over.

Their conversation didn't take long; less than ten minutes later Tony was on his way out of the bank. He was in a rage, though he'd concealed it with all his con artist's skill. And, really, she hadn't been as shirty as she might have been. He had told her that he must have left his ID card at the office and inexplicably didn't have a business card on him, either. That was harder to explain — every business person carries business cards. He had to say they were making new ones up with the new address. She nodded as if that sort of thing happened all the time — and who knows? Maybe it did.

And maybe he just imagined there had been a steely glint in her eye as she listened to his lies.

Anyway, they had shaken hands and she had told him he could bring his ID back later today and she'd be pleased to close the account for him.

But for Tony, that opportunity had left the building.

Allie was on her way out the door to a Tai Chi class when Godwin came knocking that evening. "I think we may have a development," he announced. "But I'm not sure."

"Come in, come in," she said at once. "How can I help?"

"Do you have a better photograph of Bob than this?" He held out a newspaper clipping.

"I'm not sure what you mean," she said, looking at the photo on the clipping. "I mean, okay, this is cut out of a newspaper, but it's his official photo at work, and it looks just like him."

"Are you sure?" Godwin turned the slip of newsprint around and studied it. "I saw him at the banquet, and when I saw this picture, I thought the real Bob was a few years younger and a few pounds heavier than this photograph makes him look. And his nose — I don't know; somehow it just doesn't look a lot like him."

"May I see it again?" Allie took the clipping, which had a story attached to it about the theft and disappearance. "Well, maybe I'm just used to that picture. He had it taken two years ago, so I'm not sure how you can think Bob is younger than he looks in this photo."

"Do you have some other pictures of him I could see?"

"Certainly. Come in to the living room, sit down. I'll be right back." Allie tossed her jacket over a club chair and went off into another room.

Godwin sat on the very comfortable sofa in the beautiful living room and allowed himself a few moments of nostalgia. Not long ago he had been living with a wealthy attorney, and their home had been furnished in almost as costly a fashion as this, if in a more progressive style. The attorney was dead now, and Godwin was living in much more modest surroundings. Though far from poor, he sometimes felt the change keenly.

Allie came back with three scrapbooks of various sizes. The biggest had a green-and-tan cover of what looked like real leather. "This was our vacation in the Southwest this past summer," she said, and opened the album on the coffee table in front of Godwin. Its pages were beautifully decorated with ribbons, stickers, and fancy calligraphy, among which were pasted photographs and parts of photographs of Allie, their two teen-aged children, and Bob smiling, frowning, laughing, and looking solemn or silly at the Grand Canyon, Carlsbad Caverns, Meteor Crater, the Petrified Forest, and across the Navajo and Apache reservations.

Allie was about to open the next album when Godwin said, "No need, no need. I agree that the photograph in the *Strib* is a good one." He leaned back on the couch and continued, "The reason I was asking about a better photo is that Ramona Tinsmith thinks it wasn't Bob who accepted the check, but someone else."

"Who?" demanded Allie.

"Ramona Tinsmith. She was at the banquet."

"Yes, yes, I know Ramona. I mean, who was this other person?" Allie was staring at Godwin with frightening intensity, the scrapbook forgotten in her lap.

"I don't know. I didn't believe her at first, but the pictures you showed me make me wonder if the person I saw, and Ramona saw, might really have been someone else."

She closed the album slowly, frowning in thought, then turned toward him, gesturing sharply. "No, wait, that can't be right. For one thing, how could it happen? Where was Bob in all this? Are you saying he managed to talk Bob into changing places with him?"

"I don't know how it happened. He didn't sneak up to the microphone, he was introduced as Bob Germaine, and he gave a little thank-you speech." Godwin was struck with an idea. "Do you have a copy of it somewhere? The speech Bob was supposed to give?"

"No, not here, it would be at work, on his computer. He writes his own speeches, and spends a lot of time on them, even little ones."

"So you see, if we can find someone who remembers even part of the speech given at the banquet, we can compare it to the speech Bob wrote. That will help prove if it was Bob or someone who made up a speech of his own."

"But if it was someone else, *where was Bob?*"

"I don't know that, either. Maybe this other guy knocked him on the head so he could take Bob's place."

"And then — ?"

"And then I don't know. But we'll find out, I promise, we'll find out. Who knows about Bob saving his speeches on his computer?"

"The people he works with, I suppose."

"Anyone else?"

"Well, me. I think the children do — certainly they're annoyed enough by Bob's rehearsing the speeches all over the house." Allie thought. "I don't know who else does, really. Maybe a lot of people. It wasn't a secret or anything."

Godwin made a note in his pretty little notebook. He was almost trembling with excitement. He'd found a clue, a real clue. And even better, he'd drawn a conclusion based on the facts — and had an idea where to look for a solution!

Thirteen

Sitting triumphant on the couch, Godwin said, "I want to get a copy of the thank-you speech Bob was supposed to give at the banquet. People won't remember the whole thing, of course, but they'll remember parts of it, and we can compare what they remember to the speech Bob wrote. If the two are really different, then we'll have proof it wasn't Bob."

"So you seriously think it might not have been Bob Germaine up there accepting the check," said Betsy.

"Well, I must agree with Ramona, the man I saw looks different from Bob Germaine. And now there are more little things, like I asked Allie if Bob wore an ID bracelet with big flat links, and she said he never wore any jewelry but his wedding band."

Godwin abruptly cut himself off, struck by something, and Betsy guessed, "He wasn't wearing a wedding band."

Godwin made a face at her. "You're always a jump ahead of me, aren't you?"

"Not always. What I really am is jealous. You're doing such a good job, and you seem to be having a good time!"

"I am when I find a clue and draw a deduction from it, and you tell me I'm probably right." Godwin drew a breath that swelled his chest like a rooster about to crow and let it out through a broad grin. "You and Jill had me all nervous about it, but I tried hard to do what you said I should do, and it worked. It's like trying something you're not sure you can do, and making all kinds of mistakes, and then finally reading the instructions and finding you're not so bad at it."

Betsy nodded. She felt that way sometimes, though mostly about needlework. She remembered how frustrated she was when her head knew how to do a stitch but her fingers only halfheartedly acted on the knowledge. How she finally stitched a stack of frogs up a narrow piece of fabric and made a bell pull out of it. It still hung down in the shop, where stitchers would look at it and nod, ruefully, and sometimes buy Maru Zamora's pattern to make their own version, around a belt or dappled onto a sweatshirt or vest. Stitchers whose motto was the same as hers: Rip it, rip it, rip it.

But she was wandering from the point. She pulled herself back and said, "So what you'll need to do is contact the Heart Coalition for a copy of Bob's speech. Hey, wait a minute! *I* can do that! I can phone them and ask them to e-mail me a copy of the speech." Betsy was very pleased to at last have even this small part to play in the investigation.

"Yes! It'll be hard to wait till Monday to do that," said Godwin. It was only Friday evening.

"I'll call them first thing." Betsy, still smiling, leaned back in her chair. "So who do you think this imposter might be?"

Godwin shrugged. "We have a name: Stoney Durand. I was thinking it was a fake name Bob Germaine was using, but if the man isn't Bob . . ."

"Yes, if."

But I'm sure it has to be someone who is either in Embroiderers Guild of America or is married to a member. Because how else would he know about the money being raised? And that it would be presented to a Heart Coalition official at the banquet?"

Betsy nodded. "Good thinking."

Godwin swelled again, then let his breath out suddenly. "So what's the next step: Ask every person who came to the convention if he or she knows a Stoney Durand? There were over five hundred people there!" He was looking dismayed at the size of that task.

Betsy said, "You'll also want to talk to all the local membership, whether they came or not. But here's what may be a shortcut: Get a list of attendees, see if there's a Durand on it. And also take a look at regional membership lists."

"Oh, yeah," said Godwin. He was a bit deflated because he hadn't thought of that himself.

"And I am going to call Mike Malloy." Sergeant Mike Malloy was one of Excelsior's two investigators, and while he disapproved of amateur sleuths, he had experience with Betsy's previous efforts and was at least willing to listen to her. "He should know about this."

Officer Alan Johnson was tired, bone tired. He'd taken a second, part-time job after the birth this summer of his fifth child and was finding it tough to stay awake during the latter half of his graveyard shift, when things got really quiet. He'd heard that a good place to coop — sleep on duty — was the long-term parking lot at the airport, which was included in his patrol area anyway.

Right now he was so afraid of falling asleep behind the wheel that he decided to coop for just half an hour.

He drove up and down the rows of quiet cars until he found a space, deep in shadow and not near the end of a row. He pulled in and was about to shut his engine off when his computer beeped at him. He looked over at it and saw it indicating his in-squad camera had read a license plate on the hot list. Checking, he saw the plate was right in front of him, on the back end of a newish light blue Lexus. Which was the right car, too — there were thieves who stole just the plates.

He thought about ignoring it but then he saw that the car wasn't stolen, it belonged to the man who stole that check from some embroiderers' club. There had been a stink raised in the papers about that, because the check was for twenty-odd grand and made out to a charity. A lot of heat was being applied to find the man. And while Alan hadn't found the man, he'd found his car at the airport, which was a big clue to why they hadn't found the man. That alone would lower the heat on the cops.

Alan might even get a commendation out of this, which would be better.

Of course, it was not unknown for people

to abandon or be dragged out of their cars, and the cars subsequently be taken by thieves. Alan hoped this was not the case here.

Feeling much more wakeful now, he climbed out of his squad car. The November night air was cold and damp, smelling of snow. He walked all the way around the Lexus and found it undamaged — stolen cars were often damaged by the thieves, who were inclined to let their inner NASCAR driver take the wheel. The lights in the lot made bright spots on the car's pale finish and permitted a dim view through the darkened windows of its interior. Alan peered in but didn't see anything. Or anyone. He tried the driver's side door, and to his surprise found it unlocked. The interior was clean and empty, but a faint and unpleasant odor had wafted out when he opened the door.

Alan sighed. He had a very bad feeling about this. He reached for the trunk release, and walked back to take a gingerly peek, rearing back when the faint odor proved much stronger back here.

There was a white man folded up inside the trunk, naked except for underwear, nice dress shoes, and dark socks. His head was pressed up against a black Nike sports bag.

Alan pulled out his flashlight and, without touching anything, discovered an ugly dent in the man's temple that continued into the hairline. It was not bleeding, which was not surprising, as the man was dead.

FOURTEEN

Early Sunday afternoon, Betsy was standing in her kitchen waiting for the oven to heat to 350 degrees. On the counter was a half-thawed "hot dish" — casserole, to non-Minnesotans. This one had potatoes in it, and chicken, onions, peas, and mushrooms, all in a cheese sauce. Chicken, of course, was the all-purpose healing food, there was calcium in the cheese, and there was vitamin C in potatoes. The rest was mostly to make it taste good. Betsy smiled; her reasoning powers were coming back. Her self-justification powers, too. Because her appetite was also back, and she wanted something substantial.

The oven pinged to tell her it had reached its set temperature, and Betsy inserted the Corning Ware dish. She had barely straightened when her phone rang. She hobbled to it.

"Hello?"

"Betsy, it's me, Allie Germaine!" The woman sounded distraught.

"Allie, what's the matter?"

"Oh, Betsy, they found Bob!"

"Uh-oh." Allie's tone said this was not good news.

"He was in his car out at the airport. Someone . . . struck him, on his head, and, and pushed him into the trunk. He's dead. He didn't suffer, he died right away, they said."

"Oh, Allie! I'm so sorry. How terrible!"

"Yes, it's horrible, horrible!"

"Allie, is someone there with you? You shouldn't be alone right now."

"My children are here, but they're as upset as I am. I did call Peggy, she's known me almost all my life. She's coming right over."

"Good, good."

"I don't know what to do," she sobbed. "I'm frightened!"

"Of course you are. The first thing to do is nothing. Don't make any decisions, not about anything, for a day or two. You've had a really terrible shock. You may want to call your doctor, he can prescribe something to calm you down."

"Dr. Forman is out of town, he'll be back tomorrow."

"Well then, call Father Rettger, he's wonderful with grief. He was wonderful with me after my sister Margot was murdered."

"He was? Yes, I remember Jeannie saying he was a blessing when Jack had leukemia. All right, I will call him. And thank you for reminding me about him."

"I'm so sorry, Allie."

"Thank you, Betsy. I'm trying to think if there's anything else. Did I tell you Bob was undressed?"

"Undressed? What on earth for?"

"Nobody knows. He just had on his underwear — and his shoes and socks. Isn't that ridiculous?" Allie's voice had gone very high, as if she were going to burst into tears. "How — how embarrassing!"

"How *wicked!*" said Betsy angrily.

"Yes, yes, a very wicked man did this to him. But now, at least, the police will treat this as they should have from the start. And I guess — I guess, since he's found, this means you don't have a case anymore?"

"Of course I still have a case," Betsy replied. "Only now, it's murder."

Tony was lying across his unmade bed on Sunday afternoon, listening to a "classic rock" station, adrift on Vicodin. The top of the hour came up, and the music changed to the chintzy theme the station used to announce the news. Tony managed to ignore the national news — until the Muslims changed their attitude toward gays, he was *not* interested — but then . . . "On the local scene," said the plush voice of Rudy Randall, the KAGY reporter, "a blue Lexus in an airport parking lot became a crime scene when the body of a man was found in its trunk. While confirmation waits until next of kin are notified, the body is reportedly that of Robert H. Germaine, who is alleged to have stolen a check for over twenty-four thousand dollars last week. Police have been searching for Germaine — and now it appears they have found him."

Tony was suddenly wide awake. They had found Bob Germaine — dead! What did that mean? His heart began pounding, harder and harder, and his palms grew slick with sweat. Bob Germaine was found dead in the trunk of his car, out at the airport. Why was that the scariest thing he'd ever heard in his life?

He rolled over and put his good foot on the floor. Where was his crutch? What the hell had he done with his crutch? He found it half under the bed and used it to pry himself upright. He stumbled hastily to the door of his apartment. The touch of cold metal on his hand brought him back to himself. *Where did he think he was going?*

His mind swarmed with contradictory thoughts. Why did he feel this panicked need to run away? He was safe here.

Safe from what? There was no threat to him.

His suitcase, still packed, was by the door; he turned to look at it. But how could he carry a suitcase with only one hand — and it needed for his crutch?

And where could he go?

Why go anywhere? There was no need to run.

But Bob Germaine was dead!

He needed a drink.

He went to his tiny dark kitchen and opened a cabinet. His sole remaining bottle of liquor, a bottle of brandy, was half empty. Heedless of warnings not to drink alcohol while taking Vicodin, Tony poured a generous splash of brandy into a juice glass and drank most of it right there. He poured some more and sat down on the rocky stool beside the counter — he couldn't get to his couch with the glass — and took smaller sips while trying to slow his thoughts.

First of all, there was nothing to be scared of; he hadn't done anything. Sure, he'd *planned* to do something, but that wasn't the same thing. Germaine had gotten there ahead of him, stolen the check his own self.

And then someone had gotten to Germaine, killed him, and taken the check.

Not Tony, because Tony didn't have the damn check.

So who had the check? Where was it?

Dammit, that money was *his!* Twenty-four grand, as good as in his pocket, gone — but where?

Maybe Germaine had it, maybe it was on the body, tucked into the inside pocket of his suitcoat.

But he wasn't wearing a suitcoat. Or trousers. He was put inside the trunk of his car in his underwear.

Tony put down the glass. How had he known that? Was it true? Tony ran his confused mind back over the news announcer's words. He hadn't said that someone had taken off Bob's clothes before stuffing him in the trunk.

But Tony could close his eyes — he did close his eyes, and there it was, an image of a man in his underwear, kind of folded up in the trunk of a car. Blue boxers and a white T-shirt — oh, and black socks and shoes.

Tony had found a black suit and good

white dress shirt in the bag the hospital had given him on discharge. Tony didn't own a black suit, or a white dress shirt that needed cufflinks — nor a nice pair of real-gold cufflinks and a watch, also in the bag the hospital gave him. But Tony had been wearing those clothes when he got into the accident. Were they Bob Germaine's clothes? Why on earth would he be wearing Bob Germaine's clothes?

Tony hastily poured the rest of the brandy down his throat.

That vision of the car trunk and its grisly contents must be some weird dream the Vicodin gave him. There was not the least reason why Tony should think Germaine's body was unclothed. Or that he, Tony, had the missing clothing.

So why the vision?

He needed more information. The question was, how was he going to get it?

FIFTEEN

The Monday Bunch came out in force
Monday afternoon. From doll-size Idonis
to man-size Alice, there were nine women
in Betsy's apartment.

If there had been fewer, or if they had
been in less of a hurry, it would have taken
half as long to clean up the place. As it was,
they got in one another's way and issued
contradictory instructions. But somehow, in
a little over an hour, from kitchen to bath,
the apartment became spic-and-span.

There were two reasons they were in a
rush. First and foremost, they had read of
the discovery of Bob Germaine's body in
an airport parking lot and wondered if Betsy
knew more about it than had gotten into
the news. Second, they were quick to finish
any task standing between them and their
stitching.

Betsy, enthroned on the upholstered chair
in her living room, just smiled and smiled.

Gradually running out of things to do, the Monday Bunch gathered around her, bringing chairs from the dining nook and the two bedrooms, crowding onto the couch. The two youngest sat on the floor. Needlework projects were brought out.

"All right, girl," said Bershada, her glasses even lower on her nose than usual, "give!"

"Well, Goddy gets a lot of the credit, let's start with that."

"You mean Godwin DuLac, our own fair-haired boy?" said Idonis, who adored Godwin.

"He's the one who found out that it wasn't Bob Germaine who accepted the EGA check at their banquet."

There was a general gasp of surprise and indignation.

"What, you didn't know this?" asked Betsy. "I thought my telling Mike Malloy was what triggered the search for his car . . ." She ran down at that point, frowning. "That doesn't make sense, does it?" she asked, more to herself than the others. "They were already looking for his car."

"I thought they were looking for him," said Alice in her deep voice, looking around at the others, who nodded in confirmation.

"Well, they were," said Betsy. "But he drove off in his car, so they were looking for that, too. Allie was afraid he'd had an accident in it and was lying injured in a ditch somewhere."

There was an uncomfortable silence as the group thought of poor Allie, who had been living on a hope that grew fainter day by day, until she was told Sunday morning, when she was about to leave for church with her son and daughter, that her husband had been found murdered.

"So," said young Emily, drawing the word out, "it was the person who took Bob's place at the banquet, and who stole the check, who murdered poor Mr. Germaine."

"Well, that's the current theory," said Betsy.

"What, does Bob have a double?" asked Idonis. When the others looked at her, she said, "Surely someone would have noticed otherwise that it wasn't Bob up there, shaking hands and putting the check in his pocket."

"Everyone has a double, or so I've heard," said Shelly, an elementary school teacher with thick brown hair and beautiful eyes. She had taken a personal day from teaching to be here.

"He didn't look exactly like Bob," said Betsy. "What happened was everyone who really knows Bob was at that officers' meeting, so no one realized it wasn't Bob at the podium."

Rosemary was not a regular member of the Bunch, but she was well known to most of them, since she had taught knitting classes at Betsy's shop for years. Now she asked, in her dry, pragmatic way, blinking through her rimless glasses, "How did he arrange that?"

"What do you mean?" asked Alice, surprised.

"I mean," said Rosemary, putting down her knitting, "how did he either *know* about the EGA officers' meeting running long, or *arrange* for it to? I thought it was supposed to end before the banquet, so the officers could attend."

"It was," said Maureen, a soft-spoken woman who had been on the event planning committee of the local EGA chapter.

"So how did this crook know it would run over into the banquet and Bob's wife and others who knew him wouldn't be there?" Rosemary reiterated.

"There's no way he could have known," said Maureen. "Nobody knew, not even the officers at the meeting."

"What was it about, anyway?" asked Betsy, diverted.

"Redistricting," said Joyce Young, an

ardent needlepointer new to the group. "They're thinking about redrawing the borders of EGA regions and they ran into a whole lot of objections — which they should have anticipated."

"Of course they should have!" said Betsy. "How stupid! Didn't they think about running the notion past local groups first, just to test the waters?"

"What's that got to do with stealing the check?" asked Idonis, who was not a member of EGA.

"Nothing, nothing," said Betsy. "You're right, that's off topic. And you're right, too, Rosemary. There is no way anyone who didn't know the topic of that meeting could have guessed it would run over the time allotted for it."

"Or even if they did know the topic," said Patricia. "Because obviously the people who scheduled the meeting didn't know what a can of worms they were opening." Patricia was a beautiful, wealthy woman approaching middle age with great serenity, perhaps because she'd served time in prison for attempted murder, an experience that made her grateful for every blessing freedom brought.

"Then that means he didn't know," said Emily. "So why did he even try it?"

After a brief, thoughtful silence, Betsy suggested, "Maybe he didn't know Bob was Allie's husband."

"Of course, that must be it!" said Emily. "He didn't know anyone at the banquet had ever seen Bob, so why shouldn't he take Bob's place?"

"He was pretty good at thinking up a speech, too," said Bershada.

"What do you mean?" asked Betsy.

Bershada took off her little reading glasses to think. "It didn't sound made-up on the spot. He began with a statistic and a joke, saying, 'Heart disease is now the leading cause of death in women, especially women over sixty-five' " — Bershada paused to raise an eyebrow, imitating the speaker — " 'not that anyone in the room is anywhere near that age.' " The Monday Bunch laughed, as the EGA audience had, and Bershada continued, "He thanked the Embroiderers Guild of America for this significant gift, and the Minneapolis chapter especially for thinking of the Heart Coalition in their charity drive . . ." Bershada paused to recall what else he said.

"Did he thank anyone by name?" asked Betsy.

"Yes, he thanked the President of the Guild, I remember he said 'Karen Wojahn,' but he didn't mention anyone else, or if he did I don't remember it." Bershada looked around the room to see if anyone else remembered another name being dropped, but no one did.

"That's odd," said Rosemary. "If he didn't know whether anyone had ever met the real Bob Germaine, how did he know Karen's name?"

"I think Betsy has her work cut out for her on this one," said Alice.

"But she'll figure it out," said Emily loyally.

But Betsy was dismayed to think that what Bershada remembered of the speech was just what was contained in the speech Bob Germaine composed — Bob's secretary at the Heart Coalition had e-mailed her a copy of it. Suppose it was Bob Germaine who had set off Godwin's gaydar after all? Or had someone somewhere gotten a copy of Bob's speech in advance? She was less certain now than earlier that this was a puzzle she could solve.

"I wasn't as comfortable downtown as I usually am," said Patricia. "The hotel was very nice, but there are some odd people hanging out on the streets."

"Yes," said Bershada, with a nod. "And have you noticed that there are those check-cashing places opening up there, too? I mean, right next door to the hotel there was a PostNet place."

"What's PostNet?" asked Idonis.

"It's a mail drop," said Shelly. "If you're homeless, it's a way to have a mailing address. Or if you're a con artist, you can have a downtown Minneapolis address that isn't connected to where you really live."

"The things you know!" said Idonis, admiringly.

Betsy was glad no one wanted to talk anymore about Bob Germaine's murder, and she was glad to join the gossip — and the movement to unpack the needlepointing, cross-stitching, punch needling, crocheting, and knitting projects, which, after all, formed the real purpose of the Monday Bunch meetings.

Betsy was working on a counted cross-stitch model for her shop, showing a kitten and a puppy being friendly. She'd stitched that part and was working on the lettering, which read, "A Friend is someone who reaches for your hand and touches your heart."

Idonis was stitching a piece from S. P. Ink that featured a grand piano, musical notes, and the words, "Practice, Practice, Practice." It was for a great-nephew's birthday.

Betsy leaned forward to get a look at what Rosemary was working on. It was a scarf, done in squares, each square made of alternating narrow stripes of deep green and a twist of maroon and white.

Betsy frowned at the pattern: stripes running up one side, then turning to run down an adjacent side. It looked as if Rosemary had managed to knit around one corner of each square. Which was not possible; knitting went in a straight line, then came back again. Okay, you could take opposite ends of a row and join them and thereby make a circle. Build on that and make a tube, sure. But a knitter cannot come to the end of a row, make a ninety-degree turn, and continue.

"How are you *doing* that?" Betsy demanded and several heads turned.

"I call it mitered knitting," said Rosemary, handing the piece across to Betsy.

Betsy frowned over it a while, then, turning it over said, "Oh, there it is." She put a forefinger on a faint line going diagonally across a square. "It's a decreasing pattern, you decrease down the middle."

"Very good!" said Rosemary. "That's exactly the secret. You don't knit a square, you knit a diamond."

Betsy turned the scarf over to its right

side. "But that's not all there is to it, is there? How do you get that edging on it — and why put it there?"

"You slip the first stitch in a row, and purl the last one. It makes it easier to pick up the stitches you need. In this pattern you don't sew the squares together, you knit them right on."

Betsy nodded sharply. "Clever!" She frowned over the squares some more, then shrugged and handed it back. "I get the principle, I think, but not the details. Can you teach me? And can I make the squares any size? I'm making an afghan and I'm bored making ordinary squares, but they're bigger than the ones you're doing here, more like eight by eight inches."

"You can make a square using any odd number of stitches," said Rosemary. She reached into her rice basket and pulled out a finished hat, very Scandinavian in its style and in its white and blue colors. The squares it was made of gave it a boxy shape, and from the top came a tassel on a string. The squares were much larger than on the scarf, using just four to make a good-size hat.

"Oooooh," said Emily. "That would look adorable on Morgana Jean." Morgana Jean was Emily's daughter.

"I'd like one just for me," said Joyce.

"Maybe you'd better teach a class," said Betsy, laughing.

"All right. When you get back to the shop we'll start a sign-up list. These work up fast; people can make the hats as Christmas presents."

"Sign me up, too," said Shelly. "I have a friend who likes cross-country skiing, and that hat would be a great present for her."

"I have a friend, too," said Doris, not looking at anyone. She and a retired railroad engineer named Phil were dating, secretly they thought. But everyone else only pretended they didn't know.

"I'll work up a class and come back in a few days to try it out on you, if you don't mind," Rosemary said to Betsy.

"That would be wonderful," said Betsy. "Thank you."

Around two-forty, the last of them was packing up to leave. It was Alice, and she was deliberately slow in putting her crocheted baby blanket away.

When everyone else was safely out of earshot, Alice said, "Betsy, I have a favor to ask of you."

Since Alice was an elderly woman and had taken on the onerous task of cleaning Betsy's bathroom, Betsy did not feel in a position to say no, at least not without first hearing what it was. "You know I'm still confined to this apartment," she warned.

"Yes, I know, and that's actually one reason I feel okay about asking you. It's something you can do, but it's not hard and you don't have to go anywhere to do it." She drew a breath for courage and added, "But it's illegal."

Betsy stared at her. Alice was the widow of a Lutheran minister, and an extremely moral person. "What do you mean, illegal?" Betsy asked.

"Well, against the law — but I don't think it's a good law!" Alice burst out.

"What bad law are you asking me to break?"

"The one about injured wild animals that can't be rehabilitated." Seeing Betsy's confusion, Alice continued, "There's a law in Minnesota that if a wild animal is found so badly injured that it can't be restored to full health and released back into the wild, it has to be destroyed."

"I never heard of such a law."

"Most people haven't. It's a stupid law. And, there already are exceptions. Certain animals are kept for demonstration and publicity purposes; the Raptor Center has hawks and owls they show to school children to stir up interest in wildlife preservation.

But most seriously injured wild animals are killed. It's not altogether a bad thing; I mean if an animal is in terrible pain or would live a futile, unhappy life, seriously crippled, certainly taking its life is a mercy. But there are these other cases. For instance if a bird breaks a wing, it almost never can be mended, at least so it can fly again, but it's otherwise perfectly healthy. It can live happily in captivity if it has a good keeper. And that's what I'm talking about here."

"Are you asking me to take on a wild bird as a pet?"

"No. But there is this crow, an adult crow. Its wing was broken when it was clipped by a car, and so of course it can't fly, but otherwise it's perfectly healthy. We're trying to sneak it out of Minnesota, to another state where it will be safe."

"Who are the people doing this?"

Alice shook her head. "Well, one is a veterinarian, but I don't want to get her in trouble. The problem here is, the person in Iowa who can take the crow is out of town right now, a family emergency. And I can't keep it, it's my turn to host my book club and nobody must know about this." Alice was so earnest that her brow was dotted with perspiration.

"I don't know. Isn't a crow kind of big?"

"Yes, and it's not tame — you can't tame them if you don't get them before they leave the nest. But he's hardly any trouble, he feeds himself, and we'll supply the cage and the food. He's very quiet and he's all healed, so you don't have to doctor him or anything like that."

"But . . ." Betsy gestured. "Sophie."

"Oh, he's not afraid of cats. There were cats in the home where he was staying while he recovered from surgery to mend his wing. That is . . . we're not sure if he's a he. He might be a she. You can't tell just by looking at a crow. But anyway, Betsy, it's only for three days. Someone else will bring him — and the cage and food — and then will take him away again. He'll be no trouble, I promise. Only you mustn't tell anyone you have him, because it's . . . illegal."

Betsy would never in a thousand years have believed Alice would be do something actually illegal. "How did you become involved in this?"

"Well, I started doing volunteer work for a group that rescues and rehabs wild animals. One night a week I pick the animals up at the Humane Society and drive them to rehabbers. I've been doing it for over a year.

We're all volunteers and it's all legal; the re-habbers have licenses to have wild animals in their homes. But last week someone told me about this underground railroad for these otherwise doomed creatures, and I said I was interested. Only now they've come to me, and I can't help because of my book club. And I thought of you."

"Well, that's very flattering," said Betsy, "but I don't think I can."

"Oh, but, Betsy, you must! I can't ask very many people, because sooner or later someone might spill the beans, and then the program might be shut down. People might be arrested. *I* might be arrested!" Alice boggled at this. "So please, Betsy."

If it had been a sweet robin, or a lively little chickadee, Betsy would have said yes at once. But a crow? A thieving, wicked *crow?* Didn't they eat baby birds? Didn't they gang up on owls?

"They're the most intelligent variety of birds," said Alice, somehow out of desperation guessing Betsy's objection. "You can almost watch them figure things out. Tame ones can learn to talk, though of course this one will never be tame. But he'll be alive, and he'll have other crows for company, and he may even learn to be happy. Please, Betsy."

Betsy thought of her nice, clean bathroom and sighed. "Oh, all right, I'll do it."

SIXTEEN

It was a good thing that Alice was not afraid of the dark, because it was very dark in the empty parking lot behind a St. Paul library she had never been in. There was only one lamppost back there, and it was almost totally obscured by an oak tree holding stubbornly to its leaves despite their bone-dry, rustling state. The pavement also rustled, as leaves from less-stubborn trees were strewn in low waves across it. Alice pulled the collar of her brown wool coat up around her throat as a chill wind whirled through the lot, stirring up the leaves and ruffling her hair. As suddenly as it had come, the wind died, and the leaves settled into a new pattern.

A car swung around the library, its lights slashing across Alice and her own car, dazzling her, then leaving her blinded as it turned sharply into a parking slot near the back door. The engine shut off. A man got out, his attitude furtive. He turned toward her and seemed to wave. Alice tentatively waved back.

The man came to her. "You Alice?" he muttered, looking around.

"Yes," said Alice, relieved that this was indeed Andrew, a fellow member of the smuggling operation and not some random pervert. "Have you got the package?"

"Yes. Come with me." He walked to the back of his car and opened the trunk. Reaching in, he took hold of a box about eighteen inches square. As he lifted it, a scrabbling noise could be heard from inside. "He's a live one," he said, handing the box over. Its top was folded rather than taped shut and small airholes were punched along one side.

"Good," said Alice, who celebrated the return of liveliness in wild animals brought back from the dull misery of sickness or injury.

She put the box in her own trunk and drove away. In case of a fender bender or some other imperative reason to stop, it was better not to have to explain the contents of the box. It was after ten, and Excelsior was forty minutes away.

Betsy stood frowning at the immense cage

in her guest bedroom, which was also her home office. It was black, an empty three-foot cube made of heavy iron bars. It stood on a metal frame that raised the top to chest level. A perch made of a tree branch crossed it, and there were three openings that held ceramic bowls. "One is for water, the other two hold dog food and fresh vegetables or fruit," explained one of the two husky young men who had set it up. "Crows are omnivores, they'll eat just about anything."

Betsy, who had seen crows pulling at the innards of ran-over squirrels on the street, nodded.

"The cage seems very strong," she said.

The young man nodded. "It's a parrot cage someone donated to us. It's heavy, but we like it because it's almost indestructible." Seeing her eyes widen in alarm, he added, "No, it's because it gets moved around a lot, not because the birds we put in it are dangerous."

"Oh. That's good."

"Oh, one more thing: The latch doesn't work very well. We've used a piece of wire to reinforce it. Be sure to twist it around the bars and then around itself to secure the door." He pointed to the eight-inch length of gray wire bent into a long U and hanging from a crossbar.

"All right."

"Well, good luck, and I'll see you in three days. We'll call before we come over."

"Thank you."

The pair left and Betsy went into the kitchen to look in the paper bag they'd brought along. In it were three small cans of dog food, two apples, a browning banana, a tomato, and three hard-boiled eggs. More than enough, they had assured her.

Betsy went to sit in her chair and knit while she waited for Alice to bring her houseguest to her.

Godwin arched his back to ease an ache forming in his lower spine. He'd searched the membership lists for the three local EGA groups that formed the Twin Cities Chapter of the guild, but couldn't find a single Durand. There were two Corcorans, two Dolans, a Duranty, a Larent, a Tolland, and four Warrens, but not a Durand. And none of the others either were or had a spouse named Anthony or Tony.

The attendance at the convention, while much larger than the local membership, had been easier to search: it came on a computer disk. No joy there, either.

He thought of that Gilbert and Sullivan line: "A policeman's lot is not a happy one."

If this sort of thing was a regular part of one's duties — and, according to Jill, it often was — no, indeed.

Betsy was thinking that something had happened and she was not going to get a crow tonight. It was after ten, and she was getting sleepy. She began to put her knitting away, sticking the needles into the fabric, when there was a knock on the door.

"Come in!" she called and the door opened. A moment later Alice came into the living room with a good-size cardboard box in her hands. Something scrabbled inside it, and a faint, unpleasant odor wafted from it.

"He's either feeling lively, or he's upset at the confinement," said Alice. "Or both. In any case, here he is."

"Does he have a name?" asked Betsy, staring at the box.

"No. You can name him if you like, but it's likely to get changed when he gets where he's going. Where shall I put him?"

"His cage is back there." Betsy pointed, then followed slowly behind Alice. She heard the cage rattle and the door swing open before she got there.

"Oh, my, look at him!" exclaimed Alice.

"What's the matter?" asked Betsy, stopping in the doorway.

"Oh, he's dirtied himself rolling around in that box."

Betsy came closer. The crow certainly had. He also stank. "We can't leave him like that, can we?" said Betsy, stepping back.

"No, birds are very clean animals."

"How do you bathe a crow?" asked Betsy.

"Well, what I'd do is lower the shower head and turn on the water to just warm. Then draw the curtains around the tub and leave him alone for fifteen minutes or half an hour."

In her tub Betsy had a shower head that could slide up and down or even come off of a stainless steel rod — Alice had become familiar with the arrangement while cleaning the bathroom earlier in the day.

"All right," said Betsy, who really wanted to go to bed.

"Here, I'll set it up for him and put him in. All you'll have to do is get him out again and put him in his cage."

"Do I have to rub him dry with a towel first?" asked Betsy.

"No." Alice smiled. "For one thing, I don't think he'll let you do that without a fight. And for another, it'll give him something to do, smoothing out his feathers."

"All right. Thank you, Alice."

191

Alice re-closed the box and went out and into the bathroom. In a minute Betsy heard the shower start up, then the thump as the crow was dumped in, then the click and scraping of its claws as it moved hastily around the tub. Alice came back out, the box in her hand. "You won't be wanting this around," she said. "I'll toss it in the Dumpster and go home. Any questions?"

"No, I don't think so."

"If you have any problems, give me a call."

"I will. Thank you."

Betsy listened at the bathroom door for a couple of minutes, and heard the click of large bird claws behind the curtain, audible over the sound of the shower. She decided against going for a peek, and instead went back to her chair to pick up her knitting. She was working on a sweater that would be a Christmas present for Emma Beth, who was her goddaughter. It was a cheery red cardigan with cable stitching up the front and down the sleeves. Betsy was doing the tricky reductions as she neared the neck. She worked slowly, because she was tired and because half her attention was on the bathroom. She had closed the door, but if the crow got out it might lie in wait for her to open it and lead her on a merry chase around the apartment. If Sophie joined in, the crow might be severely injured.

That thought made her put her knitting away and go toward her bedroom. Sophie slept on the bed with her, and knew it was bedtime. As soon as Betsy went in, the cat joined her, leaping up on the bed and looking back over her shoulder at Betsy. Who promptly stepped back and shut the door, trapping the cat inside.

Then Betsy went to the bathroom and peeped behind the curtain to see a large — very large — black bird at the far end of the tub, wet but clean. When Betsy bent to shut off the water, the bird tried to retreat farther, flapping its wings and clawing futilely against the slope of the tub. Water off, Betsy straightened, and the bird stopped flapping. Betsy could see that one wing hung down a little while the other was incorporated smoothly into the side of the creature. It cocked its head to regard her with one shiny black eye. It was alert but did not look the least afraid. Betsy, herself, was a different story. It really was an extraordinarily large bird, with a frighteningly long, sharp beak.

Betsy went for a bath towel. She draped it over her hands and lunged through the curtain to wrap the bird in it. Grabbing blindly, she nevertheless got all the bird's body safely under the towel. As she lifted it up, careful not to let the head near her face, the bird calmly stretched its head over the towel and pinched her on the forearm.

"Owwwwwww!" howled Betsy, hopping backward and twisting her hands to make it let go. She nearly fell, but leaning against the sink saved her. The crow was still biting. She waved her arms in a sharp motion that threw the ends of the towel over the crow's head and, startled, it let go.

Betsy hastily secured the wrapping, tucked the whole bundle under one arm and, after standing there a minute to regain her equilibrium, and her temper, looked around for her crutches.

She took one and used it to get to the guest room. She shoved the towel and bird into the cage, holding onto one end of the cloth and pulling back until the bird rolled out of it.

It had not made a sound since it had arrived, but now it got to its feet, feathers all ruffled, looked up at her and, showing her its bright yellow tongue, released five short, angry caws at her. In reply, Betsy slammed the cage door and twisted the wire to make sure it stayed shut.

"Wow!" she said then, half in anger and half in awe. She looked at her arm. There was a nice red welt where the bird had pinched it, with a single dark drop of blood at one end.

The crow shook itself, scattering drops of water everywhere. Then it went to the farthest corner of the cage and stood there in silence, back to her.

"Humph!" snorted Betsy. Maybe by tomorrow it will have died of pneumonia, she thought; and on that happy note, she went to bed.

SEVENTEEN

Betsy was awakened early the next morning by Sophie tapping on her shoulder. Ordinarily the cat left her alone until she started showing signs of waking on her own, so this new behavior drew an angry growl from her mistress.

But the cat persisted. "Whassa matta?" grumbled Betsy, blinking her eyes open. Then she heard it.

"Caw-caw-caw-caw-caw!" came the rough-edged noise. The door to the guest room was shut, her own bedroom door was shut, but the noise was quite audible: "Caw-caw-caw-caw-caw!"

"Awww —" Betsy bit the next word off firmly. No need to waste good scatology on the cat.

It took her a few minutes to get out of bed, make that first, necessary trip to the bathroom, and pull on a robe. All the while, the crow kept calling.

"All right, all right, *all right!*" scolded Betsy, shoving open the door to her office.

The crow, dry, clean, and every feather neatly in place, was on the higher of the two perches, his head turned sideways so he could pin her down with that beady black eye.

"What's wrong in here?" Betsy asked. The crow did not reply, nor did it take its intent gaze from her. She walked to the cage. There were already several messes on the newspaper spread on the bottom. Did the creature expect her to clean up after every mess it made? Then the smell struck her in the face like a used diaper. It appeared that yes, indeed, she would be doing a whole lot of fresh papering of the cage.

Hampered by her need to balance on a crutch, it took a while to slide the old paper out on its tray and insert fresh. Good thing the cage was on a stand; she was not able to kneel. Meanwhile the crow kept cawing at her and once, when she got close enough to the bars, it reached through with its beak and pulled her hair. She took the messy paper to her kitchen, pulled a white plastic garbage bag from a box of them under her sink and shoved the paper in it, pulling the drawstring shut. Then she washed her hands thoroughly and went back to the bedroom, intending to boot up her computer. But the crow was waiting for her, and as soon as she appeared, it hopped from perch to perch, giving her hard looks and cawing.

Then she saw the empty dishes in the cage. Of course, it was hungry! It fell silent as she pulled the dishes, which were about the size of ashtrays, out of their holders, but it called after her as she took them out of the room.

Water was easiest, so she brought a filled dish of water back first. The crow came quickly to dip its beak and lift its head to allow the water to run down its obviously parched throat. Poor thing! Betsy hobbled to the kitchen to slice half a banana into one dish and half fill the other with smelly canned dog food. Sophie walked beside her, whining — she was hungry, too. Betsy brought the offerings back one at a time, one-handed because of her crutch. The crow abandoned the bananas for the dog food, and she left it to its meal to feed Sophie in the kitchen.

This was an angle she hadn't thought about. Birds rise with the sun, and apparently rise hungry. Alice had said the crow wasn't tame — but it wasn't stupid. It had learned that hollering made humans bring food. Meanwhile, Betsy was going to have to find a source of fresh newsprint. A single daily wasn't going to be enough, not if she wanted to do any work in the room she was now sharing with a crow. Thank goodness it was only for two more days.

Godwin was in Crewel World sorting through a shipment from Norden Crafts, a wholesaler in Chicago. There were some of the newest Kreinik silks, and boxes of DMC's Color Variations. Also there was an order of "wool rovings," soft, fat ropes of unspun wool in assorted colors. Spinners could use it, but Godwin had ordered it for a form of felting some of the shop's customers had taken to. They would draw an outline on felt or thick fabric, lay a thin layer of the roving inside it, then use a button-shaped instrument with a thin stem on one side and four needles on the other to punch the wool into fabric. The rovings could make a soft, almost abstract pattern of leaves and flowers or animals, or be blended in shaded and complex patterns or pictures. Bernina made an attachment for their sewing machines to speed the process — Godwin had an order of the attachments in another box waiting to be unpacked and put on display.

A customer, Laura Briggs, had taken a

plain, dull-green wool jacket and covered its lapels, sleeves, and bottom hem with a flowering vine that was startlingly beautiful. She had twisted green roving tight to make the vine, blended shades of green for the leaves, and used orange and yellow for the blooms. She had agreed to loan the jacket to Crewel World to display as a model. When the box from Norden had arrived, Godwin checked the packing list and phoned her, and the "bing-bong" of the shop's front door announced her arrival less than ten minutes later.

She was very young, barely out of high school, a pretty, slender blonde whose cheeks were pink with excitement. Wordlessly, she held out the jacket.

"It's even more beautiful than I remember," said Godwin, taking it and holding it out at arm's length. "*I* think it should go right in front," he said, walking over to an old, glass-fronted counter painted white that jutted out from one wall. "We can set it up on top of this," he said. "I've got a bust made of wire in back that we use for sweaters. That will be a real eye-catcher — you'll be famous by the end of next week!"

"All right," said Laura in a soft voice. She was a little in awe of being famous.

"We'll put some of the rovings into a

basket and one of these what-dya-callems
—" He held up one of the implements used
to punch wool into fabric. "Inside the cabinet."

"It's a felting tool. And I think that's a
great idea," said Laura.

"No, wait, let's put the basket and felting
tool up here on top beside the jacket." He
put a little wicker basket on top to try it
out.

"All right. That looks nice."

"Well, maybe it should go inside. Someone
might pick one of those tools up and forget
to put it back. Better to have the basket and
this gizmo behind glass."

"Yes, you're right," said Laura, starting to
look a little confused.

"And instead of one, let's put two of these
felting tools out." He glanced at her and
misinterpreted her expression. "Okay, one."

"Whatever you say," said Laura gamely.

They settled on two felting tools and a
small basket of rovings, inside the cabinet.
Laura said she'd think about teaching a
class and left.

A little later, Godwin was arranging coils
of wool rovings in the little basket — the
forest green twined around the deep orange
with the red showing here and there —
when the door chimed and Sharon, Ramona

Tinsmith's daughter, came in. "Hi, Goddy!" she said.

"Well, hello!" said Godwin. "I didn't think I'd see you for weeks and weeks, after you bought all those chicken patterns!"

Sharon giggled. "I know, I know — and I've only started working on them. I found the most incredible fabric print to use as an edging on the quilt: chicken wire! Can you believe it? But I was thinking: What threatens the chicken coop in song and story?"

Godwin frowned at her. "Chicken hawks?"

"Well, yes, but there's another reason for the chicken wire." He shook his head, baffled. "A fox!" she said.

He laughed. "You're right!"

"So my quilt needs a fox. What kind of fox patterns do you have? Remember, they have to be four inches by four inches."

"I thought some of the patterns you bought were bigger than that."

Sharon nodded. "Some are, they can make a square eight by eight. But most of the squares are four by four, and I want the fox to be kind of subtle. I want to place him along the edge. Top, side, or bottom, it doesn't matter, but he should be skulking, don't you think?"

Godwin was smiling along with Sharon. "I agree. Let's see what we can find."

There were quite a few fox patterns, but they were too small, or too cartoonish, or too big, or not "skulky" enough.

Godwin finally said, "I'm sorry, we don't seem to have one you can use. Maybe you should try Needlework Unlimited, or Stitchville USA."

Sharon sighed and started for the door, but Godwin called after her, "Hold on, hold on! Maybe I *can* help you!"

She came back eagerly, and Godwin said, "I have to make a phone call." He would have run upstairs but there was no part-timer in the shop. He dialed Betsy's number.

"Hello?" came the reply.

"What's that noise?" asked Godwin.

"There's a crow fight on the roof."

"Sounds like it's in the next room."

"Yes, I know, I have a window open. What's up?"

"Betsy, remember that class you took from Rachel Atkinson, the one where she taught that pattern of the fable about the fox and the grapes?"

"Oh, yes. But I didn't finish it. Why?"

"Sharon's here, and she wants to put a fox on her chicken quilt."

"A fox looking up at a grape arbor?"

"No, just the fox. Looking up at all those chickens."

Betsy laughed. "You told me about that quilt, all chickens. Now she wants to add a fox? That's great, that's funny! But don't we have fox patterns in the shop?"

"Yes, but we haven't got a fox pattern that's right for what she wants. Do you still have the kit?"

"Yes, I think so. Let me see if I can find it. I'll call you right back." She hung up.

"Who's Rachel Atkinson?" asked Sharon.

"She's a teacher as well as a designer," said Godwin. "That's about all I know. But this piece is what you're looking for, I think."

Sharon was looking at a book on crewel when the phone rang a few minutes later. Godwin picked up and said, "Find it?"

"Yes. Come up, I'll meet you at the door."

He asked Sharon to wait and to knock down anyone who came in, picked out something, and tried to leave without pay-ing — it had been a very quiet day, so there was small chance of that — and went out the back way and up the stairs. Betsy was standing in the open door with a clear, hard-plastic box in her hands. "Everything's in here," she said. "But be warned, it's not grafted." Meaning it wasn't designed as a counted cross-stitch pattern.

"Thanks," he replied, took it, and ran back

204

down the stairs.

Back in the shop, he opened it and found, folded in half, a sheet of paper with a color photo of the project: a red fox sitting before a grape arbor. The pattern was round, but the fox's tail ran off it onto what seemed to be the mat.

"Perfect!" exclaimed Sharon.

"Well, it looks great, but you'll have to copy it onto fabric and stitch it free style."

"Oh, I see."

"And, you'll need to contact Ms. Atkinson. Our policy is to never, ever violate copyright."

"Oh," said Sharon, in an even smaller voice.

"But it's perfect for you, and look, her e-mail address is on here."

Sharon brightened and said, "So it is. I'll contact her and grovel hard. Maybe she'll give me permission to use it."

Godwin waved good-bye to her as she went out the door, then frowned and looked thoughtfully after her as she went cheerfully up the street. Interesting, he mused, waiting for the idea that conversation had sparked to come out and explain itself: The chicken wire fence was to keep the fox out.

He was reaching for the phone when it rang.

"Crewel World, this is Godwin, how may I help you?" he answered it.

"Goddy, it's Betsy."

"Strewth!" he exclaimed. "I was in the very act of picking up the phone to call *you!*"

"You were? What about?"

"Well, I have this idea, it came because of the fox."

"The fox stitching pattern?"

"Yes, but the stitching part isn't it — and anyway, it's not all the fox."

"You'd better explain."

"What I mean is, EGA was in favor of that heart research charity. The officers got everyone excited about helping research women's heart disease, and they raised a lot of money. When they heard that the Heart Coalition was going to send a VIP down to pick up the check, they were all puffed up about it."

He could hear the smile in her voice as she replied, "Yes, I remember."

"So I think, like the fox comes in from the outside to prey on the chickens, that whoever stole that check isn't from the EGA, but an outsider.

"And once I started thinking that, I realized that if it *had* been someone in EGA or married to someone in EGA, then someone in the audience would have recognized him. But so far no one has said" — Godwin switched to a prissy gossip's voice to continue — " 'You know, that Germaine person looks *so much* like Ruth's husband, I thought it was him up there.' "

Betsy said, "If it wasn't someone from EGA, then where was he from?"

"Well . . . he could be from the hotel. Or maybe he's the newspaper reporter who wrote about the check. But I think he's from the Heart Coalition."

"So do I."

"You *do?*" Godwin was even more astonished than he was thrilled that she agreed with him. "Why do you think so?"

"Because I got an e-mail from the Heart Coalition, a copy of the speech Bob gave. Now, whoever picked up that check knew Bob was going to the EGA banquet to accept it. If it wasn't someone from EGA, it had to have been someone from the Heart Coalition. And it was someone with access to the speech, because this person gave Bob's speech, or something very close to it. Monday afternoon Bershada told me the parts of the speech she remembers, and they match up perfectly with the text of the speech Bob's secretary at the Heart Coalition e-mailed me. Bob always got the approval of the charity when he gave a speech, and copies of it got sent around in advance.

"But you know something else? You figured it out without the help of that fat clue of the speech matching. You are turning into a real sleuth. I'm proud of you."

When Godwin hung up, he did his famous Gene Kelly *Singin' in the Rain* circle dance around the table in the shop.

EIGHTEEN

Tony was in his little kitchen, heating soup. He was still upset about the cops finding Bob Germaine's body, though he could not think why that should be. He got these feelings every now and again, like in a bad dream when he was aware of approaching danger before he knew the name or shape of it. He wasn't always right about the feelings, but more often than not he was glad for the warning.

The soup, Campbell's Bean with Bacon, a favorite, began to bubble around the edges and emit steam. But Tony turned the heat down a couple of notches; he had lost interest. He hobbled into his living room, where a bar of sunlight from the high window — his was a "garden" apartment, meaning it was in the basement of the building — lay across his couch and coffee table, showing the worn fabric of one and the cigarette burns on the other. Tony was not a smoker, but he had rented the apartment furnished. What wasn't cheap was shabby, and the couch was both. It was depressing that the beautiful sunlight only highlighted the flaws.

He needed to get out of here.

Not only because he was afraid, but because this place was too depressing.

But where could he go? Madagascar was a quickly fading dream, and he really didn't want to cast himself on the kindness of his few friends. For one thing, he had very few friends good enough, and kind enough, to take him in.

Maybe this time the feeling of danger was wrong. It had been before. Maybe it was poking at him because he was in a tight place, low on funds and lacking a way to get more. But he'd been in tight places before. In a few weeks the casts would come off, his bruises would fade, and he'd be out there playing his games and sitting pretty. All he had to do was rein in his current panic and wait.

He sighed heavily, and then sighed again, deliberately, an attempt to settle his nerves. He remembered a friend who used to be a stoner, a heavy user of marijuana, who finally quit after a short prison term.

"Don't need it anymore anyhow," the friend had said. "I learned how to go to the place marijuana took me all by myself. I just lay back, close my eyes, inhale twice and hold it, and I'm stoned."

Tony swallowed an imaginary pill and let his head fall back against the couch. He imagined the heaviness, the sweet lethargy, the dimming of awareness only Vicodin could bring. Wow, it was working . . .

And suddenly he was coughing because the air was filled with smoke and someone was slamming really hard on his door and what was that damn whining buzz and his head was whirling because he couldn't catch his breath and now someone was in his apartment and had grabbed him and he was too feeble to fight him off, he was going to go to jail.

And then he was outside coughing his lungs out and that nice next-door neighbor was thumping him on the back and saying, "Breathe, man, breathe!" And sirens were howling.

Soon after that, someone was putting a plastic mask over his nose and mouth and he could feel his head clearing. Oxygen, that's what it was.

His coughing slowed to where he could swallow, and he looked around. It was dark out — so much for the lovely sunbeams — and there seemed to be around fifty cop cars and fire trucks and ambulances all over the street. And he was sitting on the hard, cold metal back end of an ambulance.

"What happened?" he croaked, pulling the mask off his face.

"Waaal," drawled the paramedic, replacing the mask and holding it there, "it seems you had a fire in your place, and your neighbor knocked down your door and saved your life."

"A fire?" asked Tony in a voice muffled by the mask.

"Were you by some chance cooking something on your stove?"

Tony hesitated. "Maybe. I — I don't remember."

"Well, somebody was, and they went away and left it, and the pot boiled dry and the residue started to burn. The cook — was that you?"

Tony coughed so hard he shook his head. Could he help it if the fellow took that as a no?

"Well, whoever the cook was, he left a potholder on a counter that touches the stove, and it caught fire, and it spread from there. Good thing your smoke detector is loud, that neighbor of yours heard it from out in the hall and broke your door down. You might've died in there."

Tony held out his hands, which showed no signs of burns.

"It's not the fire that gets most of them," said the paramedic, taking off Tony's face mask, "it's smoke inhalation. Now, take a couple of breaths."

Tony did, coughing some more, but not that horrible gagging thing he'd been doing earlier.

"You're going to be fine. No, stay where you are, I hear there's a representative from the building management company on his way. He wants to talk to you."

Tony did not doubt that. What he wanted to know was, could he get away before the management creep arrived?

As soon as the ambulance tech walked off, Tony got up and started moving around. Someone had brought out his crutch, so he leaned heavily on it, coughing and exaggerating his look of pain when anyone looked at him, and moving very slowly. Then, when he was sure no one was paying attention, he limped as quickly as he could around a corner and went down a block, to a bar, where one of the few pay phones left in the city lurked in a dim corner. He used it to summon a cab. He rode to a nearby cheap motel and told the truth to the woman behind the counter: his apartment had caught fire and he needed a place to spend the night. Since his clothes were reeking of smoke, she believed him, and since he had a valid credit card on him, she rented him a room.

In the room, which at least was clean, Tony took off his outer clothing and went to bed. Despite his long, if interrupted, nap, and being without his meds, he slept heavily and didn't wake until six the next morning.

Waking in a place that didn't smell of him made him realize how dirty he was. But what could he do? He washed his good hand and his face, blew his nose and was amazed at the amount of black stuff that came out. On the other hand, he was pleased to see that most of the swelling around his eyes and cheekbones had gone down. He rinsed his mouth thoroughly, wet his hair and combed it, then sat down with the Yellow Pages to look up Goodwill stores. He couldn't find one nearby, but since his neighborhood was one of the lower-class ones, there was a DAV — Disabled American Vets — secondhand store a couple of blocks away. But it didn't open until eleven.

He spent the waiting time by phoning friends, joshing and kidding and gossiping, telling about the fire, but making light of it — the cause, he said, was "some kind of electrical thing, but what do you expect of a place that was wired by Thomas Edison in person?" — before asking if he could crash with them for a couple of nights. But he kept getting turned down, even though this was a real emergency, not just some vague nervous feeling. So now he knew what they really thought of him, the bastards.

Though one of them said something interesting. "There was a good-looking young man asking about you, oh, less than a week ago, I guess — oh, yes, definitely one of us, but I don't think I've seen him before. Got a funny first name: Goddy."

Tony frowned over that briefly. He didn't think he knew anyone by that name.

"What does he look like?"

"Kind of a twink, with blond hair, nice blue eyes. Dressed preppy."

That described an awful lot of young gay men, so Tony shrugged it off and went on collecting turn-downs for places to stay.

Until Marc Nickelby. Marc was an older man, a semiretired antiques dealer. After Tony made light of his fire, but before he could hint-hint about needing a place to stay, Marc complained that he wished he could invite Tony out to lunch, but he had this great opportunity to buy some old Spanish furniture in Mexico, but only if he flew down there right away.

"What, you're flying all that way just to attend one auction?"

"No, it's not an auction, it's a tour of four towns plus a weekend in Mexico City. I'll be gone a week."

"A week? Have you got someone to stay in your place, look after it, water your plants, walk your dog?"

"After Fritzy died, I decided I wasn't going to have another dog," said Marc. "And our coalition hired a very proactive security company so I don't have to worry about burglars or other sneaky types."

"Oh," said Tony, who then wisely fell silent.

After what seemed eons, there came a sigh. "But I suppose it would be good to have someone in the place, if only to help carry out things if there's a fire."

"I wish I'd had someone in my place," said Tony, but lightly.

"All right. But no parties. Absolutely no parties."

"Oh, Marc, I'm not up to partying. I just want a quiet place to stay."

"I really hope that's true. And if it is, I guess I should count myself lucky that you called. Can you come right away? There's a three o'clock flight I can catch, if I hustle to the airport by noon."

"Well, I have some things to do. Is two all right?"

"I'll leave a key with the building manager and tell him to expect you. Don't disappoint me while I'm gone, Stoney."

"I won't, I swear." He hung up, lay back on the bed and waved his good arm in the air. He still had it!

Tony checked out of the motel and hobbled the three blocks to the DAV store on Franklin. It was a warehouse sort of place, with an acre of clothing hanging from pipes suspended from the ceiling. It had the odd smell common to all large collections of used clothing, and the people wandering the aisles looked as bleak as survivors of a tornado going through the rubble of their houses. Tony quickly found a long raincoat, a sweater, a pair of big-leg trousers he estimated would go on over the gear holding his leg together, a pair of socks and even some underwear, the last still in its original plastic wrap. He looked longer among the shoes before settling for a pair of suede boots he could shove his good foot into without too much effort.

The one dressing room was occupied by a large family quarreling in Spanish, so Tony couldn't try anything on, and the indifferent clerk behind the cash register wouldn't let him buy just one boot. Tony paid cash, put on the coat, and carried the rest of his purchases in a paper bag labeled Cub Foods. He took a cab to Marc's condo, which was in a luxury high-rise overlooking Lake Calhoun. The building manager sniffed at Tony, and Tony hoped that it was the smoke he detected, not the lack of a bath. "My place caught fire last night," Tony said. "I'm so grateful to Marc for letting me stay in his place while mine is repaired."

Marc's condo was on the ninth floor, facing the lake. Even this time of year, with no sailboats ornamenting the water, and the trees nearly leafless, it was a pretty view. Tony looked out the large window for a couple of minutes, before turning to admire the ambience of the place. It was big, three bedrooms, two and a half baths, a kitchen fit for a chef, a living room large enough to make the baby grand look lonesome. Tony had been here before, but it was still a pleasure just to stand and look, absorbing the peace, feeling the security. Everything was clean and in perfect condition. The walls were cream with dark green molding. The silk drapes were a lighter green and hung in elaborate folds and twists. The furniture was an eclectic mix of periods:

nineteenth-century Spanish, Art Nouveau, Art Deco, mid-twentieth-century Modern. There were paintings on the walls, statuary on the tables, silk flowers on the mantel.

The carpet was pale ivory — and though he'd taken his shoes off, Tony saw he'd left traces of his passage on it. He went immediately to the guest bath, shed his clothing, and spent the next hour soaping and rinsing. Marc not only supplied wonderful scented soaps and shampoos for his guests, he had toothpaste — and toothbrushes! Tony nearly wept with gratitude.

Clean at last, he went into the guest bedroom — Marc had done the second spare up as a library — and lay down gingerly on the bed, which was extraordinarily comfortable. He lay there for half an hour, letting the pain fade to a dull roar, then rose and dressed in his new things, which in the ambience of the beautiful bedroom look used and shabby.

He had some better clothing in his closet back home. And he wanted his meds. He especially wanted his meds.

But he didn't want to encounter his landlord — who was going to change the locks once they realized he was gone for good.

And he was gone for good, right?

Right. Even the thought of going back there to stay made him break out in goose-flesh. But he needed a quick trip, just in and right back out. He went into Marc's kitchen to find something to eat while he planned how he was going to do that without being seen.

Godwin walked into the Heart Coalition lobby in downtown Minneapolis. The floor was blue slate tile, the walls shades of gray and blue applied with a sponge. Bright posters of past Heart Coalition campaigns hung on the walls, with lights in the ceiling shining on them. There was a uniformed guard seated at the circular, light wood desk, who looked at him with a smile.

"I have an appointment with Mr. Erskine Morrison," said Godwin. "My name is Godwin DuLac."

The guard consulted his computer. "Yes, sir. One minute, please." He picked up a telephone receiver resting on a complex console and dialed four numbers. He waited a listening while then said, "I have a Mr. DuLac here in the lobby to see Mr. Morrison." He listened a bit more, then hung up and said, "Here, clip this to your lapel." Godwin, glad he had worn a sport coat, clipped on a white badge with a red heart and the word VISITOR on it. The guard then said to Godwin, "Take the elevator to four. Someone will be waiting for you there."

"Thank you," said Godwin in his most businesslike voice, and did as he was bid.

On four a young woman in a dark, modest suit was waiting. "This way," she said, and led him down a corridor to an open door. Inside was an office exactly halfway between totally chaotic and utterly neat. Stacks of files covered half the desk with a few more on a side table, but there was no loose paper. The two visitors' chairs were clear, and so was the thinly carpeted floor. Venetian blinds that were dusty but not dirty were pulled halfway up, revealing a window that had probably been washed this summer.

Standing behind the desk was a light-skinned African-American man with a close-cropped natural generously sprinkled with gray. He was slim and very handsome, wearing a white dress shirt open at the collar, his blue tie pulled loose. "Come in, come in!" he said in a pleasant voice, extending a hand.

Godwin shook it. "Thank you for seeing me," he said, and took one of the chairs when Morrison gestured at it.

"I understand you want to ask me about

the speech Bob Germaine gave at an Embroiderers Guild of America banquet last Friday night," said Morrison, coming to the point directly, the sign of a busy man.

"Yes." Godwin got out his beautiful notebook, opened it to a blank page and wrote down the date and Morrison's name. "Who wrote the speech Mr. Germaine was to give at the EGA banquet?" he asked.

"Bob did. He wrote all his speeches, he was very good at that. Of course, he sent them around for approval in advance."

"So you saw it?"

"Yes, of course. I was his immediate supervisor. He will be sadly missed." Morrison paused to consider his next sentence, touching the fingertips of both hands together. When he spoke, it was in the same ordinary tone. "He was a very good man, not just good for the Heart Coalition, he was a *good man.* What happened to him was shocking — and a disgrace to our city."

"Yes, sir," agreed Godwin, a little surprised at the strength of the words spoken with a minimum of emotion. "How long had you known Mr. Germaine?"

"Ten years — it would have been ten years in December."

"Was he generally well liked by everyone?"

Morrison thought about that briefly. "Yes,

I'd say so. Certainly everyone who knew him at all well liked him. He had a way with him, you know. He was very passionate about our mission, plus he was a gifted speechwriter, *and* clever and thoughtful about campaigns. Not a quiet man, however. Not one to keep his opinions to himself."

Godwin made a note. "Did this create problems here at the Heart Coalition?"

"Not really. I mean, you always get some people who think anyone who speaks his mind, especially if he can turn a phrase, is grandstanding. And others who don't know sarcasm when they hear it." Morrison smiled. "His riff on Why I Can't Give to Your Charity Today was very amusing."

"But it wasn't a problem, you say."

"Not a problem."

Godwin made another note. "Now, here's a different topic. Has there ever been a problem with a thief at the charity?"

"That depends on what you mean by *thief.*"

"You know, stealing."

Morrison smiled. "You mean stealing funds? Embezzlement? Or stealing a wallet?"

"Well, any of that, I guess."

Morrison leaned slightly forward and said very seriously, "There has never been any malfeasance among the executives here." He leaned back. "On the other hand, we had to fire an employee very recently for such misdeeds as stealing an employee's take-out Chinese lunch."

Godwin smiled. "Hardly the same thing as stealing a twenty-four-thousand-dollar check."

Morrison smiled back. "Hardly. But it was part of a series of small thefts."

"How did you find out it was him? Or was it a her?"

"A him. The big clue came when he was taken to the hospital after a car accident. The series of thefts immediately stopped. A look at his employment record showed they began a few months after he started working here. And, he was on parole for theft by fraud. Under our Rules of Employment, employees' desks and lockers are subject to search without notice, but we rarely invoke that. Still, in this case, we thought we had good reason — and it turned out we did. His locker was opened, and in it was an iPod with a dead battery that had gone missing."

"Did he admit to the thefts?"

"Rather surprisingly, he did. In fact, I heard that he appeared relieved at being caught."

"Interesting," said Godwin, writing that down. "I suppose he was part of your maintenance team?"

"No, he worked in our mail room. One of his responsibilities was delivering mail, which is how he found several opportunities to take things that were out on peoples' desks."

"Did you find any evidence that he took bigger things? I mean, for example, since he was in the mail room, might he have stolen money coming in as donations?"

"People don't send cash anymore, or very rarely. And a check made out to the Heart Coalition is hardly something Mr. Milan could cash, is it?"

"Oh. No, I guess that's right." Godwin felt abashed at not seeing that obvious flaw in his question. He hid his embarrassment by making a rather lengthy note. Finishing that, he rose. "I think I've taken enough of your time. Thank you very much." He stood, then thought of something.

"Just one more question, please, Mr. Morrison," he said. "What did this Milan fellow look like?"

Morrison looked surprised at the question, but answered readily enough. "A little over average height, I think, dark hair and eyes, strong looking, as if he worked out, or used to. He was polite, smiled a lot, but was just a little standoffish." Morrison shrugged. "Or, maybe he was intimidated by the executives on this floor. The mail-room supervisor says he was developing a bad attitude — but I think that's hindsight illuminated by his turning out to be a thief."

Godwin smiled. "Yes, hindsight is pretty generally twenty-twenty. Well, thanks again."

Down in the lobby, he unclipped his badge and handed it to the guard, turned, and nearly walked into the side of a wheeled cart with four shelves on it loaded with mail.

"Oh! Sorry!" said Godwin.

"No problem," said the man pushing it, a burly fellow with straight brown hair. He wore a dingy white dress shirt, dark green trousers, and an impatient expression.

"Say, you work in the mail room, don't you," said Godwin.

"Say, you must be a detective or something," retorted the man.

"Something like that. Actually, I'm involved in an investigation of Robert Germaine's disappearance, and now his death. This is probably nothing to do with the case, but could I ask you some questions about the man from the mail room who got fired?"

"What's Tony Milan got to do with anything?" demanded the man loudly.

Godwin lifted a hand in a shushing gesture. "Like I said, probably nothing. But you never know, you know? Now I can see you're busy, so can I meet you outside of work? I can buy you a cup of coffee or something."

The man tilted his head a little to the side and half closed his eyes. Godwin recognized the look as that of a straight man taking the measure of a man he suspected was gay. So Godwin gave him a bright smile and brought out the flowered notebook. "I'll write down anything you want to tell me," he said in his most dulcet voice.

"George!" the man appealed to the guard, asking in that single word if this odd person was for real.

"Unwind that kink in your tail, Mitch," drawled the guard. "He's been up interviewing Mr. Morrison, so he's the real deal."

Mitch said, "How long is this gonna take?"

"Five, ten minutes," estimated Godwin.

"All right, let's do it now." He wheeled the mail cart to a place behind the guard's desk. "I'll be back," he said, making it more of a threat than a promise. "Come on," he said to Godwin and pushed through a door on the other side of the lobby from the elevators. Godwin snatched up the clip-on visitor badge and followed.

The door led to a set of metal stairs thinly coated with a cement-like substance stained gray-blue. The stairs resounded loudly under their feet as Mitch hurried down, Godwin right behind him. A corridor at the bottom of the stairs led to a long, narrow room, mercilessly lit with hanging fluorescents. The front portion was much smaller than the back, set off by a plywood counter. There were three orange plastic chairs. Mitch took one and waved Godwin to another.

"Now, what do you want to know?" Mitch said.

"Who was this man who got fired for stealing?"

"His name was Tony — Anthony — Milan. He was an ex-con, on parole, so I guess we shouldn't've been surprised that he didn't work out."

"I understand he was in a car accident?"

"Yeah, I visited him in the hospital."

"When did the accident happen?"

"Oh, around eleven p.m. Friday before last."

Godwin made a note of that. He asked, "Is it possible that Mr. Milan knew about the big check coming from the Embroiderers Guild of America?"

"Sure. A lot of us did. In fact, we got a request from Mr. Germaine to keep an eye out for the check coming in the mail — then he called the next day to say 'Never mind.' He was going to go pick it up in person, because it was bigger than expected."

"Did he say how much bigger?"

Mitch frowned at Godwin. "What does all this have to do with Tony?"

"That depends."

"On what?" Mitch was definitely looking suspicious now.

"On what Tony looked like. Do you have a photograph of him?"

Mitch stared at Godwin for a long few moments, then sighed and pushed himself up from the counter with both hands to show how tiresome all this was. He went through a door to the back part of the mail room, then pawed through the center drawer of a big green desk until he came up with a sheet of paper.

He brought it back out and handed it to Godwin. It was a good-quality photocopy of an ID badge. The man staring out of a corner of it was Stoney Durand.

NINETEEN

"I even got his address!" crowed Godwin on the phone. "But I simply *had* to get back to the shop. Marti has a class to get to. But I *recognized* him, Betsy! Mitch Wilson, his former boss, showed me a copy of his ID card and I'm *sure* he's Stoney Durand, the man who is *well known* among a *certain set* in the gay community. And Stoney Durand is really *Tony Milan* — See how *right* you were about *choosing a phony name* that sounds like your *own*, you're so *clever!* He used to work at the *Heart Coalition,* in the *mail room* — isn't it *brilliant* that we were both right about that! But we know *more* than *who he is,* we know *where he lives!* His former boss gave me his address, he lives in an apartment near Uptown. He's the man who took the *check* at the *banquet,* so *obviously* he's the man who *killed Bob Germaine!* I just *wish* I'd had time to *pay a call* on him!" When excited, Godwin used a

lot of italics.

"No, you don't!" exclaimed Betsy sharply. "Oh, Goddy, I'm so relieved you came back to the shop, and bless Marti for having a class so you had to relieve her. If Tony Milan murdered Bob Germaine, he certainly wouldn't hesitate to murder someone who comes knocking on his door to accuse him of it."

"Oh, p'shaw, as Fibber McGee would say, puh-*shaw!* I'm no idiot, I wouldn't have *accused* him, not to his *face!* Besides, he was in a bad car accident, he's got a broken *arm,* a broken *leg,* and a *skull fracture!* He couldn't harm a *flea!*"

Betsy drew a shocked breath. "When did this happen?"

"The same night he murdered Bob Germaine and stole the EGA check."

"Wait a second, wait a second, maybe that's an alibi? Could he have been like me, in the hospital when the check was stolen?"

"No, no, the accident happened *after* the banquet. *Hours* after. Mitch says he visited Tony in the hospital and they talked about that. He says it was really late, going on midnight, when the accident happened. Some drunk ran a red light — not Tony, the other guy. Tony was in intensive care for a

231

day and a half. He took a big knock on the head, he doesn't remember anything after leaving work around five on that Friday."

"All right. And that could explain why the check wasn't cashed, couldn't it?"

"I hadn't thought of that," said Godwin, without any italics.

"And how do you know he's at his apartment? If he's so badly injured, why isn't he in the hospital?"

"They sent him home — you know how they are, they tossed *you* out on your ear while you were still dizzy from the *anesthetic!*"

Betsy chuckled. "Well, not quite. But almost. So he must have been there about the same time I was. In fact . . ." She frowned in thought.

"What?"

"I was just remembering that they were bringing someone up on the same elevator Jill and I came down on, a young man who had a lot of injuries. He looked awful, I remember feeling so sorry for him, it made me feel less sorry for myself. I wonder if that was Tony Milan. No, wait, it couldn't have been, that was two days after the banquet." She shook her head at her silliness.

"Well, if they were bringing him up from

intensive care, that might be him you saw. Did the man you saw have dark hair?"

"I think so, but his head was all wrapped up. And his face was so bruised I don't think his own mother would have known him. But that's not what we're talking about here. Goddy, you've done great work, I think you've solved it, and I'm going to call Mike Malloy and let him go talk to this Tony Milan."

"What if he doesn't?"

"He will," Betsy promised. "Or some member of the police department will. I'll call you back after I've talked to him."

She dialed the nonemergency number of Excelsior's police department and asked for Sergeant Malloy. "One moment, please," said the woman who answered, in a very professional voice Betsy didn't recognize. It gave her a little pang that Jill wasn't there anymore.

"Sergeant Malloy, how may I help you?" Malloy's flat tone took any warmth out of that query. Though, of course, he rarely had someone call him at work with good news.

"Mike, it's Betsy Devonshire." She waited for the usual deep sigh — which didn't come. "Mike, are you there?"

"Sure I'm here, where do you think I am?"

"I think I may have some important

information about the Germaine case."

"Oh, yeah?" This was not said sarcastically, but in a tone indicating real interest. "Have you talked to the investigator in Minneapolis PD?"

"No, but Jill says his name is Omrick or something like that."

"*Oh*-mer-nik, Sergeant Stanley Omernic. But why don't you first try it out on me?"

"Thank you, I will." Betsy hid her surprise at this sign of respect for her opinion — Mike had long considered her a pest and an unnecessary complication in his cases, and only grudgingly would he have acknowledged that she had been helpful in the past. "You may know that Godwin DuLac took my place at the EGA banquet the night Bob Germaine disappeared. Well, he says the man who accepted the check set off his gaydar."

"Oh, sheesh! Godwin! I might've known!" Now that sounded much more like the old, familiar Mike Malloy.

"No, now listen: Bob Germaine is not gay. And we have talked with someone at the banquet who says the man who accepted the check was not Mr. Germaine, but someone else."

"Just one person says this?"

"Yes, I know. But this person volunteered

the information, we didn't go looking for her. She says she had Bob Germaine pointed out to her the day before, so she's sure it wasn't Bob Germaine up there making an acceptance speech, but someone who looked vaguely like him. And Godwin has run Stoney Durand to earth. His real name is Tony Milan — and he was recently fired from the Heart Coalition's mail room for theft. Godwin saw a photograph of him, and he looks to Godwin like the man who carried a great big check out of the banquet room. Godwin has been complaining that the photo of Bob Germaine he's been shown doesn't look much like the man he saw. So that's two people who don't think it was Germaine."

There was a studied silence on Malloy's end of the line. Then a faint sound of someone clearing his throat. "Those are interesting tidbits, *if* they're factual."

"Do you think Sergeant Omernic would listen to me? I think this should be checked out. After all, someone stole Germaine's clothes. Maybe it was so he could impersonate him better."

"Any ideas on why the check hasn't turned up?"

"Because he got into a car accident that same night. He was seriously injured, a concussion and broken bones. He's out of the hospital now, but we have his address. I told Godwin the police would check him out; otherwise, he wants to do it himself. Mike, would it be too much to ask you to speak to Sergeant Omernic, tell him I'm not just thrashing around carelessly, playing sleuth to amuse myself?"

The silence this time was longer. "I tell you what. I'll call Omernic and say that we have an intelligent civilian who may have pertinent information about this case. I'll give you his phone number and you can call him in about an hour. Okay?"

That was more than she expected. "Thanks, Mike."

Erskine Morrison was elbow-deep in reports from area reps on the new fund-raiser campaign when his phone rang. Answering it, he heard, "I'm so sorry to interrupt you, Mr. Morrison, but we got a little problem here and maybe you can help me to handle it."

The caller was Janice Hamilton, head of accounting, she of the soft Southern accent and the mind like a steel trap. If there was a problem Janice needed help with, it was a serious problem.

"Can you come up right now?"

"Yessir, I can."

She came in a few minutes later, a heavy-set black woman in a red pantsuit with white trim and low-heeled red shoes, limping on her bad leg, waving several documents in one hand. "I think we have us a serious problem here," she said, coming to a stop and falling heavily into one of the chairs against the wall.

"What kind of problem?" he asked.

"We may have another thief here at the Coalition, and it ain't just take-out Chinese he's stealin', but contributions."

"Oh, Lord."

"You mean, Lord have mercy, and you got that right. If this gets out, we're likely to lose our jobs, if not the whole Minneapolis branch. Now here's how it came to light." She held up a thin collection of pink phone slips. "This lady, Miss Elena Bedford, called last week to say she sent us a two-hundred-dollar check in honor of her mother, who passed this past spring of congestive heart failure. Miss Elena sent it in to us in July, and now she's pulling together her records for taxes and she couldn't find any acknowledgment from us for her gift. So she's been calling us and I've looked everywhere and can't find any record of receiving it. But the check has been cashed, according to her bank statement. Now you know how nowadays banks don't send your cancelled checks back to you, so Miss Elena wrote her bank asking for a copy of the front and back so she could claim it. An' what she sent me is a photocopy of the bank's printout copy, so it's kinda hard to read. But it's clear enough." She rose awkwardly, handed the top sheet to Erskine, and fell back into the chair again.

The front of the check showed that Ms. Bedford — or Miss Elena, as Janice's old-fashioned Southern ways would have it — had bought her checks from a mail-order company, because after a moment he deciphered the squiggle pattern ornamenting the face of it into morning glories being visited by a hummingbird. The check was handwritten in schoolgirl cursive to the Heart Coalition in the amount of two hundred dollars. The back of the check bore the imprint of a stamp as endorsement. It looked at first glance like the one the Heart Coalition used but then Erskine grunted. The name of the payee was the Heart Fund. And the second stamp below it indicated the bank was not one the Heart Coalition had an account with.

Erskine looked up at Janice. "What do you think?"

"I think this is probably not the only check intercepted and paid into this account."

Erskine sighed. He agreed with her. The degree of effort it had taken to set up this fraud would hardly be worth it for just one check.

"On the other hand, I think I know who we should look at first for this."

"Who?"

"That man we fired for theft, what's his name, Tony something — Milan, that's it. He worked in the mail room, and one of his jobs was opening mail."

That was actually a cheering thought. Only one crook in the company, not two. And Janice was right, Tony Milan had been in a perfect spot to divert incoming contributions. Someone in Personnel should have thought of that when they found out Milan was a thief and investigated further before firing him. Though wait, if there had been no complaints of missing checks — and there wouldn't be, because Milan could get them out of the system before anyone else even saw them — there had been no reason to spend time and money looking further. So give 'em a pass on this one.

"Meanwhile, what do we do about this check?" Janice asked.

"There isn't anything we can do — well,

belay that, there is one thing: Contact Elena Bedford and instruct her to contact her bank. Her bank can start an action; it's called 'an affidavit of bank fraud,' I believe. I note that this check has the account number set up by the thief, so the bank can identify him — or her, let's not get too hasty here — as the person who set up the account and deposited this check." He handed the papers back. "Is there any way we can determine if and how many other checks were detoured into this account?"

"No, because we never got a chance to run them through our system."

"So that lets us off the hook, except for the fault of hiring a thief to work in a place where he got to handle money."

"And that's a serious fault, don't you think?" asked Janice. " 'Lead us not into temptation.' "

"All right, yes. We should have known better. But I think the First Express Bank would be glad to open their records on this account if they can find a legal reason to do it."

Suddenly Janice grinned and cawed, "Hah-heeeeee!" — her high-pitched laugh. "We may not have been too smart at first, but we learn fast, and Mr. Tony is going to be sorry he thought he could play us!"

■ ■ ■ ■

Sergeant Stan Omernic was five-eleven and one-eighty, broad-faced with narrow, gray-green eyes, a twice-broken nose, and dirty blond hair. Minneapolis was going through a bad patch, and he had more homicide cases than he could readily handle, so he performed a kind of triage. The cases involving gang members killing one another went to the bottom and got the least attention, because bad guys killing bad guys was, as far as he was concerned, not altogether a bad thing. The deaths surrounding domestic violence were in the middle, because they didn't take a lot of effort, and so were easy to solve. The kind involving stranger on stranger were often difficult and took a lot of effort, and so were near the top. On the very top were the hot ones that caught the attention of the press and/or the government. These, fortunately, were few. Ones in which a child was the victim were the worst, the most heartbreaking to work, but happily right now he didn't have a child murder. On the other hand, the mayor, the city council, *and* the press had been following the Robert Germaine case before it even became a homicide. That a respected man, an executive in a reputable charity, would steal a check representing funds gathered by a sweet group of women needleworkers was odd enough all by itself to get the attention of the press and the chief of police. Now that the suspect had been found in the trunk of his own car, a murder victim, everyone was howling. How could the police have been so wrong in accusing him of theft?

And they had been wrong. Worse, they were two weeks behind in investigating the real crime.

The phone rang. Omernic groaned as he reached for it. What fresh hell was this? He didn't know it was salvation in the person of a woman with a broken leg and a secret crow.

TWENTY

Omernic drove to Excelsior, about thirty minutes away from downtown Minneapolis. The sky was clear overhead, though clouds were approaching from the northwest, dark gray ones that promised rain, sleet, or snow in a couple of hours. Temps were in the middle thirties, and the wind shoved his car around a bit as he came up Highway 7. The trees, he noted, were mostly bare, though some bushes still glowed a deep red, and the oaks held onto their brown leaves. Here and there, a shrub that hadn't gotten the word at all was still defiantly green.

Excelsior had redesigned the exit so it no longer lunged to the left and crossed to the right up and over the highway and some old streetcar tracks. Instead, it contented itself with leaning right and crossing up and over some restored streetcar tracks, coming down alongside a nursing home. The street came to a halt at an intersection that had

five corners instead of four, and he picked
the one that went off to the upper right and
curved around past a tall clapboard condo
building that overlooked the lake. On the
other side of the street was a dark redbrick
building, two stories, whose ground floor
held three businesses. The upper story was
apartments. The first business was a deli,
the third business was a used-book store
with the clever name ISBNs, and the middle
store was Crewel World.

As he pulled to the curb, he saw a young
man standing in the big front window, hanging miniature tree lights across the top. The
window itself had clear plastic suction cups
stuck all over it and hanging from them
were elaborately colored Christmas stockings ranging in size from too big for Omernic's own outsize feet to small enough for
his brand-new granddaughter to wear.

Omernic got out and crossed the street.
As he drew near, he could see that the
stockings weren't printed in colors, but
embroidered. Some had simple designs —
one was two leafless trees standing in snow
— and some were very complex, featuring
Santa Claus and reindeer or Santa and a
Christmas tree or Santa and young children.
Two were religious, one with the Three
Kings in gorgeous apparel stacked up the

leg of the stocking and the other with an angel whose wings had very detailed feathers hovering over a sleeping babe. Another stocking, middle size, had chickadees and cardinals resting on branches of holly. Another . . . Omernic looked up and saw the young man looking back at him, a smile playing around his mouth. Omernic raised a disapproving eyebrow at him to show he was here on serious business and went into the shop. A two-note electronic alarm sounded as he opened the door.

The store was carpeted and there was a lot of yarn around, some hanging from pegs on a wall, some piled in baskets. The effect of all that fiber was very restful, as if God had said, "Hush a minute," and put a stop to the cacophony of the world. There were a few sweaters and shawls, so few they were probably examples of what customers could make themselves from the yarn. And there were pictures of Santa Claus and castles and game fish painted on unframed canvases. Some were pinned to a strange contraption comprised of thin canvas doors on a single hinge fastened to the wall. There was a good-size table in the middle of the room with a tall lazy Susan holding scissors and knitting needles and rulers and crochet hooks in its center. Track lighting on the ceiling. Classical music playing softly. An attractive place.

A young woman with red hair — a deep, rich auburn not like that Kool-Aid color the young affected — and Harry Potter glasses came out from behind a glass-fronted counter. "May I help you?" she asked.

Omernic dug for his ID folder. "I'm Sergeant Stan Omernic, Minneapolis Police."

Her face went from friendly-helpful to dismayed surprise. "Is something wrong?" she asked.

"Not in here, as far as I know," said Omernic.

"It's all right," said the young man from behind them, climbing off the step stool. He wasn't quite as young as he'd looked through the window, Omernic could see he was probably twenty-six or -seven. "I think Sergeant Omernic wants to talk to me," he said. "I'm Godwin DuLac." He held out his hand.

Omernic shook it. "Is there someplace we can talk?" he asked.

"Certainly. Follow me." Mr. DuLac sashayed — there was no other word for it — toward the back of the shop. Ceiling-high box shelves displayed books with titles as varied as *Stitch 'N Bitch, Helen M. Stevens' Embroidered Animals,* and *Needlecrafters' Travel Companion.* There were pyramidal stacks of knitting yarn and gadgets he could not guess the use of. The box shelves divided the front from the back, with an opening in the middle. Omernic followed DuLac through the opening, where he stopped to take in the scene. There was a second store back here, with specially designed upright-angling shelves holding thin booklets, and spinner racks dripping scissors, packets of needles, and lots of embroidery floss. The walls were covered with framed examples of embroidery that were, in some instances, elaborate and startlingly beautiful.

"What is this, a kind of museum?" asked Omernic, looking up and around.

"No, these are models of patterns we sell. The patterns themselves don't look like much, so models inspire our customers or help them decide what they want to stitch next. The front of the shop is for needlepoint and knitting, mostly; back here is for counted cross-stitch and punch needle, mostly."

Omernic nodded, not too surprised that all this might be called something other than embroidery, there being subgenres in everything. But there was no need to have it clarified; he was not here to interview Mr. DuLac about the intricacies of needlework. "I received a very interesting phone call from a Ms. Betsy Devonshire this afternoon," he said. "She told me you have been interviewing people who might have helpful information about the death of Robert Germaine."

Godwin gave a pleased smile. "She told me she was going to call Mike. But you talked to her, not him?"

"Who's Mike?"

"Mike Malloy, he's our own investigator, with the Excelsior Police Department. Betsy has helped him before, lots of times. He didn't like it at first, but I hear he's come to accept that he can use her help with some of his cases."

Omernic had, in fact, spoken to Sergeant Malloy and was amused at this glib put-down of a very competent investigator, though he was careful to hide it. He got out his notebook and took Godwin through an examination of all his actions in finding out about and locating Stoney Durand, also known as Tony Milan. His first impression of Mr. DuLac as light not only in the loafers but in intellect underwent some revisions along the way. He was no airhead.

DuLac insisted that the real credit for all he'd discovered lay with his boss, Betsy Devonshire, owner of the store. Ms. Devonshire, he said, normally did her own sleuthing in addition to working in her shop, but she was currently confined to her apartment upstairs, having suffered a badly broken leg a few weeks ago.

It was Ms. Devonshire who had phoned Omernic earlier, and he closed the interview with DuLac by saying he would go up and see her now. Mr. DuLac asked if he might warn Betsy she had company coming, sweetening the request by saying he'd show Omernic a back way up the stairs so he wouldn't have to go back outside and ring the bell.

Omernic agreed and two minutes later was upstairs knocking on Ms. Devonshire's door.

"Just a minute!" came a call from well back in the apartment, and it was just about that long before the door opened and a moderately plump woman with streaky-blond hair and nervous blue eyes stood there on crutches looking up at him. She was wearing a loose-fitting dark blue dress and using two crutches to stand up. Her lower right leg was encased in a buff-colored hard-plastic boot with a rolled-down bright blue sock covering her toes. The other foot was sensibly shod in a walking shoe.

"I'm Sergeant Stan Omernic, Minneapolis Police," he said. "We talked earlier on the phone. Is something wrong?"

"Wrong?" she said, trying to quell her nervous look by opening her eyes wide and smiling falsely. "No, nothing's wrong."

"What you said on the phone to me earlier, do you now want to revise that in some way?" he persisted.

"Oh, gosh, no!" she said. "Not at all. Come in, come in, Sergeant." She stepped back, turned and moved away, and he came into the narrow little hall. A door to his left opened into a galley kitchen, but straight ahead was a spacious, low-ceilinged living room done in lots of red. She led the way into there, moving well on the crutches.

The red was mostly in the carpet, but the chintz curtains on the windows had red as well as cream flowers on them. The walls were cream colored, and the room's cozy look was completed by the knitting left on the seat of an upholstered chair and a large, fluffy cat staring complacently from her basket under the window.

Omernic knew the cat was a female because she was three colors: mostly white with gray and red-tan blotches down her back and up her tail. Tomcats can never be more than two colors. Omernic liked collecting esoteric little facts like that.

"Here, won't you sit down?" Betsy said, gesturing at the couch, which was gray with bright red in the embroidered cushions, moving to take the upholstered chair for herself. "Can I get you some coffee?" she asked, turning without sitting down. "Or tea? The water's hot, it won't take a minute."

"No, thank you," he said, sitting down, his cop antennae vibrating toward her.

"I've got some cookies, too," she continued. "I'm glad you came out so promptly, it was good of you to take me seriously."

She was anxious about something, but trying to conceal it by talking a little bit too much, nodding at him on the couch while she took the chair, ostentatiously putting the knitting into a carpetbag beside the chair, then smoothing the skirt of her dress with both hands. They were shapely hands and the curve of her cheek, while mature, was sweet. She looked at him with a direct stare out of keen blue eyes.

And while she was worried, she seemed to want his attention on her, which was odd. Normally, people nervous about having a cop in their apartment wished to become one with the furniture. Unless they were

dope dealers with a pound of something illegal hidden on the premises. But dope
dealers were only very rarely middle-aged
women who owned small businesses. What
was it she didn't want him to see?

He looked around the apartment, which
was tidy and nicely furnished. The couch
looked freshly upholstered, the chair was
done in a gray, red, and white chintz
that echoed the drapes. Across the room,
near the kitchen was a dining nook with
two chairs and a round table that held a
small vase of silk flowers. In the other direction —

"What is it you wanted to ask me, Sergeant?" Betsy said abruptly.

So whatever it was, was back there, in a
bedroom or bathroom.

"May I wash my hands?" he asked, rising
and heading that way.

"Certainly — it's the door on your *left*,"
she said, so he went straight ahead and
opened that door.

He found himself in a bedroom — a big,
beautiful, iron-framed four-poster bed stood
to the right, with a lacy comforter and lacy
pillows on it and on the left a small but
businesslike desk with a computer on it.
Crowded between the bed and desk with a
computer was something very large and

cube-shaped, covered with a hastily tossed dark blue blanket. There was a smell of chicken coop in the air. He hooked two fingers in the edge of the blanket to lift it upwards and was immediately rewarded with a sharp pain.

"Ow!" he shouted and dropped the blanket.

"I *said* the bathroom was the door on your left," came a chilly voice from the door.

"What the *hell* do you have in that cage?" he said, turning on her, pointing a hand at her — that he suddenly realized was bleeding. "Oh, Christ, look at my hand!"

"It's a crow. And he bites." She turned away. "This way."

He bent for a look into the cage — for it was in fact a heavy-duty cage on a sturdy stand — and caught a movement in the dim interior that suddenly morphed into a large, black bird, whose sharp beak was reaching for his eyes. He jerked backward, dropping the blanket.

Betsy had opened the bathroom door, and stood aside as he went in. There was a dispenser of liquid soap, the orange kind that meant it was antibacterial. He scrubbed thoroughly, wincing as the soap stung the two small wounds in his middle and ring fingers.

"What kind of a pet is it that bites when you get anywhere near it?" he demanded.

"He's not a pet, he's not even mine. He's a wild bird, and he's going to go live in Iowa in a day or two."

"If he wants to live in Iowa, why doesn't he fly there his own damn self?"

"Because he can't fly. He broke a wing and avian wings rarely heal properly. He's otherwise perfectly healthy, so he's going to live in a great big cage in a state that doesn't demand that damaged wild animals be destroyed."

She said it defiantly, and suddenly a light went on inside Omernic's head. "So you're sneaking him out of Minnesota."

"That's right."

"And you're stuck with him until your own broken bone heals and you can drive." He smiled, and grabbed a towel to dry his hands.

"Something like that." She was lying again, he was sure of it. Protecting others in the chain of this scheme, he thought.

"Well, good for you," he said, because he'd heard of that law and disapproved of it, and thought it commendable that a group of outraged Minnesota citizens had organized a sneaky way around it.

"Don't let him out of the cage," he advised.

"Of course not. He's not housebroken."

"And you have a cat."

She smiled wryly. "He's not afraid of the cat."

He smiled back. "Yeah, they're even bigger than they look. But another reason to keep him caged is that they're thieves."

"What could he steal? I don't think he understands money."

"My uncle had one as a pet, and he had to climb up a tree every month and retrieve the spoons, necklaces, coins, bottle caps, buckles, pens, and anything else shiny left where Blackie could get at it and carry to his nest. And he could open purses, and even drawers. Or so my uncle said."

She was smiling broadly now. "Thanks for the warning. But he's confined until he leaves, which will be tomorrow or the day after. If you open the medicine cabinet, you'll find a box of Band-Aids."

"Thank you."

Omernic found the box and while he applied a Band-Aid to each of his injuries, he wondered briefly how widespread this movement was to sneak crippled wildlife out of Minnesota. Then he decided he didn't want to know. He didn't approve of killing one-eyed deer, three-legged raccoons, or flightless birds, especially if the effort to save them didn't cost any taxpayer dollars.

He came out of the bathroom to find Ms. Devonshire again seated in her chair. A lamp with a cocked shade stood behind the chair, looking over her shoulder like a kibitzer. She had gotten her knitting out.

"I want to apologize," she said on seeing him approach, "for trying to keep you from learning about the crow. But I was actually a little afraid you'd arrest me for harboring a felon." She cocked her head in a gesture that was a little birdlike itself. "No, that's not right. Let's see, aiding a convicted felon to escape justice? Except, of course, he's not a felon, and I don't think it's justice to kill a crow because he broke his wing."

"Unless he was doing it in the course of committing a crime?" suggested Omernic.

"Oh, well — but you'd have to prove that was the case, wouldn't you?"

"To some people, just being a crow is a capital offense."

"Yes, that's true." She looked toward the back room. "Poor thing."

"He doesn't seem to think he's lost the game just yet," said Omernic, displaying his bandaged fingers. "And you seem bent on helping make that be true."

"Guilty as charged."

Omernic sat down and took out his notebook, growing serious. "But let's talk about Mr. Tony Milan."

Twenty-One

Betsy discovered that Omernic was an excellent interrogator. She was impressed with how he led her, with simple, clear questions, through the whole tangled mess. She told him about how the Embroiderers Guild of America had given the Minneapolis chapter the responsibility of hosting its national convention, and how the chapter had decided to sell a heart pattern and give most of the proceeds to the National Heart Coalition in support of research into women's heart diseases. About how the sale was more successful than anticipated, raising over twenty-four thousand dollars.

About how Crewel World had been fortunate enough to be chosen as the sole vendor of needlework products for the convention and her strenuous efforts to do the honor justice. About how she had gone horseback riding with a friend just before the convention and how her horse had fallen, tearing tendons in her ankle and breaking both bones in her lower right leg. About how Godwin had set up and run the booth, found employees to help, and gone to the banquet using Betsy's ticket. And how he later reported that the man who accepted the check to the Heart Coalition had returned Goddy's flirtatious smile on his way out the door.

Omernic asked, "Is Mr. DuLac inclined to see flirtatious smiles when they are not there?"

"No, I don't think so. He will initiate the flirtatious look — in fact, he did in this case. And he says his 'gaydar' went 'ping' when he first saw the man step up to the lectern. But in this case, he also claims the look was returned."

"What conclusion did you draw from that?"

"I thought he might be mistaken, if the man was Bob Germaine. But perhaps it wasn't. His wife didn't believe he stole that money, and when he disappeared she was frightened for him and asked me to find out where he'd gone — and to prove he wasn't a thief. Godwin came up with the notion that Bob was a closeted gay man and used this opportunity to break with the straight world. He even went to various gay bars and

259

coffeehouses and found some people who said a person matching the description Goddy gave them frequented those places. The man goes by the name Stoney Durand."

"And you think it is possible these people were talking about another individual than Mr. Germaine?"

"Yes, I'm sure they were. I think this 'Stoney Durand' murdered Bob, changed into his clothes, and took his place on the dais at the banquet in order to steal the check."

"How would he cash the check?"

Betsy gave him a look. Was he testing the depth of her knowledge? "Anyone who reads mystery fiction, or watches crime shows on television, knows that stolen checks can be sold. At a deep discount, of course, but still. What was odd in this case is that no one made an attempt to cash the check."

"Have you any idea why?"

"Yes. Goddy and I think Stoney Durand is actually Tony Milan, who worked in the mail room of the National Heart Coalition until very recently. And who was in a serious car accident the night the check was stolen. He was in the hospital for over a week, so by the time he got out, the Embroiderers Guild had put a stop payment on the

260

check. So it was useless. I think Tony knew about the check because he worked for the Heart Coalition, and so put himself in a position to intercept —" She stopped, a thoughtful look on her face.

"What?" asked Omernic.

"I think perhaps the original plan wasn't to take Bob Germaine's place at all. That would be a terribly risky thing to do. This Tony wouldn't know how many people in the place knew Bob, after all. What if someone stood up and wanted to know who this stranger was, and where was Bob? I think that Tony went there to steal the check from Bob — you know, mug him. And after he knocked Bob in the head, he searched the body and realized Bob didn't have the check. But he did find the speech — *that's* why people are remembering the speech right, Tony just read Bob's speech!" The idea had obviously just come to Betsy and it fit her theory so well!

Omernic was taking some swift notes, nodding as he wrote. "Say, hold on a minute!" he said, lifting his pen and staring into her eyes. "Aren't you the one who broke the case of that museum curator who was replacing Chinese artifacts with fakes — and who murdered that woman —" It was his turn to stop suddenly.

"Yes." Betsy nodded, her face gone sad. "The murdered woman was my sister, Margot Berglund."

"You did some good work back then," he said, looking at his notes. "You seem damn sharp at this kind of thing."

"Thank you. I only wish Allie Germaine could have gotten her husband back. I wonder . . . Was Bob beaten to death?"

"No, he was killed by a single blow to his temple."

"Ah, then perhaps Tony Milan really didn't mean to murder him. How awful, what a terrible waste!"

Sergeant Omernic had barely left when Godwin called. "Betsy, Alice is down here and wants to know if she can come up."

Betsy smiled. Doubtless Alice was coming to arrange to take the crow away. Wonderful! "Yes, of course."

"What do you think of Sergeant Omernic?" asked Godwin. "Odd name, Omernic."

"Yes, I wonder what nationality it is. He looks kind of Slavic, except he has green eyes, and I think Slavic people have gray or blue eyes. Anyway, he seemed extremely competent. What did you think?"

"He asked a lot of questions, but they

were all easy to answer." His voice faded as he turned away from the receiver. "She says come on up," he said, obviously to Alice.

"A good technique, I think."

"Yes, it's easier to answer when the question is like that. I think that's the way I ask questions." In an unexpected show of humility, he added, "Or, if it isn't, it will be from now on."

"Why, what are you going to investigate now?"

"I don't know, I was going to ask you what we do next."

"Nothing, Goddy. We've done our part. We found out who murdered Bob Germaine — no, *you* found it out — and now it's up to the police to arrest him. I assume you gave his address to Sergeant Omernic."

"Yes, of course. So we're done?"

"Yes — excuse me, I think Alice is at my door."

"Then why don't I feel like this is over?" persisted Godwin.

"Because this time we're not going to have that wonderful moment when we watch the culprit confess. But Omernic will go see him, and probably get a confession, sometime in the next hour. Now I have to go let Alice in." Betsy cut the connection and went to the door.

Alice, tall and mannish in her mud-brown overcoat, was not smiling when Betsy opened the door.

"Uh-oh, is something wrong?"

"Yes, I'm afraid so."

"Oh, dear. Well, come in and tell me about it." Betsy stepped back, turned, and went dot-and-go-one back into the living room.

Alice stopped just a step or two into the living room, and stood there rubbing her hands together and not looking at Betsy.

"What is it, what's wrong?" asked Betsy.

"It's about the crow."

"Oh, no, is someone from DNR coming to take it away?" The Department of Natural Resources would be the government agency enforcing the law about crippled wildlife.

"No, no, that's not the problem. It's Annie Spence, the woman in Iowa who is going to take the crow. Her family emergency was her mother, who had a heart attack. She had another, right in the hospital, and died. Annie is stuck in Arizona for at least another week, helping her brother straighten things out."

"So it looks as if you get to babysit a crow after all," said Betsy, hoping that was true, even though she could see by the look on Alice's face that it wasn't.

"No, I can't do it, at least not right now. I

264

have workmen coming in to remodel my bathroom. It'll take four or five days, probably. Betsy, I'm so awfully sorry about this. I've asked around, but no one else involved in the rescue project can take the crow, and I really don't want to ask someone who's not, because once word starts getting out . . ." Alice saw the look on Betsy's face. "Oh, dear, who did you tell?"

"A police investigator from Minneapolis."

"Betsy, no! How could you!" Alice looked and sounded much more frightened than angry.

"I didn't tell him about you! He came up here to talk to me about the Bob Germaine business, and he asked to use the bathroom and opened the wrong door." Betsy smiled grimly. "Mr. Crow drew blood on two of his fingers, which served him right!"

"Oh, no — was he mad?"

"More surprised. I told him the crow was going to live in Iowa, and let him think it was all my own doing. And anyway, he approves of the mission to rescue it. I'm sure he won't tell anyone. But, Alice, you can see how this isn't going to work. People are going to come up here — the Monday Bunch is coming back, and Jill is coming over — and she'll bring Emma Beth. I don't want Emma Beth poking her little hand through the bars — she gets into everything."

"Why did you invite — Oh, you were thinking the bird would be gone."

"Yes, and Goddy's up here a lot with questions about the shop. I don't want to explain to all these people why I have a crow in the apartment."

"All right, you're right. I'll see what I can do."

Omernic drove to the address Godwin had given him. It was a three-story brick apartment building, probably a hundred years old and looking every day of its age. The basement was built up several feet above ground and had good-size windows, so technically it had four stories of apartments.

And one of the basement windows was broken and there were smoke stains around the cement facing and surrounding bricks. There was only cardboard over the broken panes, so there had been a recent fire — a deduction confirmed as he approached and caught a whiff of the ugly, unmistakable stink of house-fire smoke.

He went up the four steps to the main entrance, found the button for the building manager, and pushed it.

The manager was barely medium height, but with broad shoulders and a belligerent air. His work boots were paint-spattered, his dark work pants were rumpled, and his old green pullover was badly pilled. His scalp shone through his greasy, lank brown hair, and when he saw Omernic, he ran a heavy palm across it. "We're full up," he said, "though we're remodeling a garden apartment, and it'll be available in about a week."

"Was the previous tenant named Tony Milan?" asked Omernic, reaching for his ID folder.

The manager froze at the question, then grimaced when he saw the badge. "Yeah, but he took off while the fire department was still here, didn't say where he was going, and hasn't come back to give us a forwarding address."

"When did this happen?"

"Night before last. The idiot was cooking something on the stove and decided to take a nap while it cooked. A neighbor heard the smoke alarm and broke in, hauled him out before he got burned."

"The fire spread to other apartments?"

"Nah, and it's mostly smoke damage to the one apartment — but smoke gets into ever' damn thing. We have to replace the carpet and furniture and paint everything."

"Who was the person who saved Mr. Milan?"

"A kid name of Gary Schulz. He helped out after Milan got hurt in a car accident, went to the drugstore for him, and grocery store, too, and didn't get anything but one thin 'thank you' for his trouble. His apartment is right across the hall from Milan's."

"Is he home?"

"I think so. He works odd hours, I know that."

Schulz was at home — asleep in bed, unfortunately for him. Omernic gave him a couple of minutes to go splash water in his face to get his brain unclogged.

He was young, just twenty-two, working in a bakery. He'd graduated from the Le Cordon Bleu School of Culinary Arts — the one in Minneapolis, not the one in France — last spring, and was hoping to get work in a restaurant someday soon. He and Milan weren't friends, exactly. Milan was gay, but that was okay with Schulz, who wasn't. Milan had told Schulz he was moving out soon, but then got into a car accident just before the move was to happen.

"He was banged up pretty bad, he had a cast on his whole left arm and one of those black canvas things, like a really serious brace, on his left leg, covered the whole leg so he could hardly bend his knee. And his face was all bruised, and he had a big bandage on his head — I think he said he had a skull fracture. He was in a lot of pain, one of the two prescriptions I picked up for him was Vicodin. I recognized the name because I fractured my elbow in high school, and they gave me Vicodin. Sweet —" He cut himself off.

Omernic only nodded. "I had a bottle of it once. It surely does kill the pain." He made a little note. "Tell me about the fire."

Schulz shrugged. "Not much to tell. I heard this sound, and I thought, 'That sounds like a smoke alarm.' I went out in the hall and didn't see flames or smell smoke and then I saw the sound was coming from Tony Milan's apartment. I just bumped up against it a couple of times and it opened. It didn't seem to be all that smoky in there, but I took one breath and started coughing and my eyes watered and I fell over a suitcase he left right near the door and over his coffee table getting to him on the couch. He was coughing, which helped me find him. I got him out as fast as I could."

Schulz began by talking fast, then slowed when he saw Omernic taking notes. He continued, "Next thing I knew squad cars and fire trucks and ambulances are all over the street."

"Did you see Mr. Milan go back inside the apartment building?"

"No, last time I saw him, he was sitting in the back door of an ambulance with an oxygen mask over his face."

"Could he have gone back inside?"

Schulz thought about that for a little while. "Not while the firefighters were there; they pretty much took over the entrance. Did you know they set up fans to get smoke out of a building? Big honkers." Schulz made a very large circle with his arms. "Cleared the air fast."

Omernic went back over his notes. "What's this about a suitcase?"

"Well, he'd packed one to leave, then he had the accident and didn't go. And I guess he was too banged up to be bothered unpacking."

"So you'd seen it before."

"Yes, when I brought him his prescriptions the day after he came home from the hospital. He must've been going out of the country."

"Why, was it a big suitcase?"

"No, but there was a passport on top of it. I just forgot it was there when I came into his place."

Omernic thanked him, and wondered if

270

that passport was still there. If not, perhaps
Milan had gotten on that plane after all.

TWENTY-TWO

Omernic went to talk some more to the building manager who said there was no suitcase in the apartment when he went in to start cleaning up. No, not just none in the living room, there wasn't a suitcase in the apartment. Yes, he opened the two closets. No passport lying out in the open, either. Of course it could have been put into a drawer; he didn't open any drawers.

"Anything gone missing?" asked Omernic.

"I didn't notice anything — but I wouldn't, would I? Except if he took the couch or the bed or the stove, and he didn't."

"I was thinking like toothbrush, underwear, aftershave," said Omernic. "And maybe there's a notepad by the phone with an address on it, telling us where he's gone."

The man rubbed his jaw while he thought. Then he shook his head. "Nope, I didn't notice anything missing in particular, or a note with an address on it. But I wasn't looking, either. Want to go in yourself?"

"Not right now," said Omernic, thinking of the rules about admissible evidence. "But could you lock the door and keep it locked? I may be back later with a search warrant."

"So the fella was a crook, was he? I kinda wondered."

"You did? Why was that?"

Here the manager became a little vague, perhaps because Omernic's tone was sharp.

Omernic asked, "Have you changed the locks?"

"I'm about to do that right now."

"Good. If Mr. Milan comes to you asking to get back inside his apartment, let him, and call me right away." He gave the man a card with his office and cell phone numbers on it.

Omernic came back a few hours later with a search warrant and a small crew. The warrant described Tony Milan, aka Stoney Durand, as a murder suspect and possible fugitive, and stated that the police were looking for evidence of flight and evidence relating to the murder of one Robert Germaine. The search took longer than Omernic thought necessary — but searches generally did — and afterward Omernic asked the manager some more questions.

Though it was past quitting time when all was done at the apartment building, Omernic went back to his office and sat down at his computer terminal to write up his notes.

Milan was last seen outside his apartment that night with only his crutch. He'd been fully dressed, so he also had, probably, his wallet and keys. No, obviously he had his wallet and keys, since he'd gotten clean away — meaning a cab or other transport he'd paid for — and since he'd gotten back in without breaking down the door. (The manager had repaired the damage done by the neighbor in breaking in.)

But now a suitcase, a passport, and the two prescriptions Schulz had picked up for him were missing. An airline ticket, unused and still in its little folder, was found in a wastebasket. It was issued to a passenger named Ronnie Moreland and was budget class to Antananarivo, the capital of Madagascar, via Paris. So he'd been thinking of skipping the country — evidence of guilty knowledge. Also of some preplanning, since the flight was to have left the day after Bob Germaine was murdered.

So why hadn't he gone? Omernic wondered. He was out at the airport, that's where he stashed Germaine's body. Why hadn't he just gone to the main terminal and spent the day there, safely away from his apartment, to take the evening flight out of the country?

He'd come all the way back into the city — how? By light rail, possibly. Why? To collect his car — where had he left it? And been driving — where? Home, probably, to pick up his suitcase and ticket — why hadn't he put them in the car? — when a drunk ran a light and rammed him.

He saved the file and shut off his computer, wondering if that woman with the keen brain and broken leg out in Excelsior had any ideas.

Before he could leave, Lieutenant O'Bryan, Omernic's boss, came in. "I've got some more information for you on that Tony Milan case you're working," he said.

"Yessir?" said Omernic, sitting back down and pulling out his notebook.

"I had a meeting today with the FBI, a Heart Coalition executive named Erskine Morrison, and a couple of bank representatives from First Express and Wells Fargo," he said.

"Why the fed?" asked Omernic.

"Bank fraud," explained O'Bryan.

Omernic took notes as O'Bryan told the sad story of how the Heart Coalition was defrauded of contributions by means of a phony bank account set up by Tony Milan at First Express, and how it came to light when a contributor complained her check went astray. Bank fraud is a federal crime, so now the FBI was also after Mr. Milan.

"How much did he steal?" asked Omernic.

"Fifteen thousand two hundred and sixty-three dollars, over a period lasting just over a year. Not enough to jiggle any alarms at the Heart Coalition, he was pretty clever about that. He drew on the account, so there's only a little over four thousand left. He made an attempt to close it the day he was fired, but questions were raised — he didn't have his Heart Coalition ID anymore, and he was acting pretty hinky. He said he'd come back, but of course he didn't. I take it you busted him while I was at the meeting."

"No, sir," said Omernic, and explained about the fire, and how it was a pity that this minute he wasn't sitting in an interrogation room across from Tony "Stoney Durand" Milan. Godwin DuLac and his backer, Ms. Devonshire, were pretty damn clever figuring it out.

"Oh, this won't do, Sergeant," said O'Bryan. "I want this man found. I want him found right away." When O'Bryan was upset, a faint Irish accent showed in his voice. It was currently present.

"Yessir," said Omernic.

So without a break for supper, Omernic went to a leather bar called the Eagle near downtown Minneapolis. He didn't envy O'Bryan, doubtless having a conversation with the chief about this.

The Eagle smelled of hard liquor, oiled leather, and cigarette smoke (Minneapolis was "smoke free" but no one wanted to be the one to tell the Eagle's customers not to light up). The bartender had a shaved head and an eye that didn't track.

Omernic could feel waves of hostility coming off him and the customers, most of whom seemed addicted to both weight lifting and tattoos. But he maintained his cool, which warmed the chill enough to get an answer or two. Some acknowledged they knew Stoney. But no one had seen or heard from him since he was hurt in a car accident.

Omernic next tried the Gay Nineties on Hennepin, where dropping Godwin's name elicited several confessions from people who had heard from Stoney. He had wanted a place to stay after being burned out. But no one had granted his request, and none knew where he was staying.

Omernic then went to Vera's, a coffee bar

over on Lyndale. Here the atmosphere was much more pleasant. Mostly young people sat at tables in a comfortable room overseen by a large color portrait of a woman with the dress and hairstyle of the 1930s. They looked ordinary enough, drinking coffee or eating sandwiches or salads, some poking at laptops. But men sat strictly with men, and women with women. There was a nice deck outside, festooned with strings of lights, but they were waving hard in a driving wind that was whipping the boards with sleet, so it was unoccupied.

Omernic asked the young man behind the counter if he knew Stoney Durand. The response was somewhat elliptical — but when he dropped Godwin's name, the young man unbent. And the purchase of a big, gooey cinnamon roll and a large café latte made him almost friendly. Yes, he knew Stoney. No, he hadn't seen him in a while, maybe two or three weeks. Well, yes, he'd heard from him, got a phone call from him. Stoney said he'd been burned out of his apartment and was looking for a place to stay. No, he hadn't invited Stoney over, Stoney was inclined to invite third parties over without permission, to borrow money without paying it back, to poke through drawers and pockets when no one was looking and take things that weren't his. And while he could dish the dirt and was a great cook, sometimes that just wasn't enough.

Two other men in the room also knew Stoney, and one had also received a request for a place to crash for a couple of days, a request turned down for pretty much the same reasons. "What goes around comes around, you know," said the man with an air of being original. None of them knew where he was right now. None of the women had ever heard of Stoney Durand.

Omernic went back to his office downtown to turn his notes into a report. And leave an e-mail message for O'Bryan that he hadn't located Tony Milan.

Twenty-Three

Betsy was in the back bedroom the next morning, working on her computer. She had long ago discovered that the only way to get her data entry stuff done — hours worked, sales taxes collected, bills paid, etc. — was to do it before she gave herself permission to check her e-mail or read RCTN or the ANG list, or cruise the Internet.

She muttered to herself as she worked. "Is that a five or a six? Marti has the worst handwriting!" She was trying to read a pair of sales slips, which in her shop were still filled out by hand.

The crow made a comment in a quiet gurgle, and Betsy looked over at the creature, which was looking back at her with one shiny black eye. "Hello, crow," she said, but it did not reply.

She continued muttering and entering figures, and again the crow made the soft sound. "You talkin' to me?" Betsy said, looking at it. "What do you want? You've been fed, your water is fresh, your cage is clean."

The bird cocked its head from side to side, turned around on its perch in a single hop so it could look at her with its other eye, and made a long comment that sounded like a dog choking on a bone fragment and ended on a squeak.

"*Argher-gurgle, bek, bek, eek* to you, too," said Betsy, and went back to filing numbers.

The crow flapped its wings, and Betsy looked over yet again. "Is something wrong?" she asked. "What is it?"

The bird looked down at the floor near the china cup that held its dinner. On the floor was a bit of orange that it had dropped or flipped out of the cup. Betsy said, "Oh, is that it?"

Betsy could not get down on one knee — or rather, if she did, she would not be able to get up again. Having dropped a pen and a tablet of sales slips yesterday, she had taken a pair of hinged salad spoons from her kitchen to keep on her desk. She used that to pick up the tidbit and put it in the cup. The crow went immediately to it and ate the treat.

When she had worked about ten minutes

longer without hearing from the bird, she looked over to find it crouched on its perch, regarding her with its eyes half closed.

"That's right, crow," she said. "You think about that."

While Betsy was at work upstairs, Godwin was unpacking and stocking an order in the shop, occasionally pulling an item for himself. One was a packet of tapestry petites, blunt needles, shorter than usual, used for counted cross-stitch or needlepoint. These petites were about an inch long, which would allow him to use floss down to near the very end. Godwin liked silk floss, a costly indulgence, and less waste of expensive floss makes a happy stitcher.

He was humming a pleasant tune to himself when the phone rang. Part-timer Shelly was closer, so she picked up. "Crewel World, Shelly speaking, how may I help you?" She listened briefly, then called, "Godwin, it's for you. Someone named Larry Thao."

Godwin put down the Tweezer Bee he was hanging on a spinner rack — he'd decided his own tweezers would do a while longer — and came to the phone.

"Hello, Larry, what's up?"

"Goddy, my dear boy, did you know

there's a big, ugly policeman taking your name in vain at Vera's?"

"Whatever do you mean? Oh, wait, is he tall, with light blah hair, a nose like an Indian, and green eyes?"

"I was too intimidated to look into his eyes, but that nose — ! You don't mean he's one of us?"

"No, of course not! He's investigating a murder."

"Well, how does he know you?"

"Because I've been investigating it, too, and I found a suspect my very own self, and now he's looking for him. Tony Milan is the suspect's real name, though he goes by Stoney Durand, too."

"Oh, my God, Stoney is a *murder suspect?*"

"Didn't Sergeant Omernic say so?"

"He did not! Fancy that, our Stoney a murderer!"

"Do you know Stoney?"

"Yes. Not well, but yes. He's awfully butch and he has a taste for leather, but he also knows his way around a kitchen. I went to a party where he spent the entire evening in the kitchen, turning out hors d'oeuvre after hors d'oeuvre, all of them different, all delicious, and the presentation was beautiful, simply dee-vine! I thought I was falling in love — did I mention that he's *awfully* good looking? — but someone told me that he — Stoney, that is — stole his — my informant's — diamond earring at a hot tub party. So when he — Stoney, that is — phoned me a couple of days ago to beg for a place to stay because his apartment had caught on fire, I said I had company already staying with me and had no more room. I guess that was a better decision than I knew at the time, because he might have murdered me in my bed!" Godwin could hear the shiver Larry gave right through the phone.

Godwin said, "If he calls you again, see if you can find out where he's staying and then you call me or Sergeant Omernic *immediately,* all right?"

"Well, all right. But I don't want him mad at me, do I? Stoney, I mean."

"I'm sure someone as clever as you can get Stoney to talk without him suspecting a thing."

Larry purred, "You sweet thing! When this is over, you must come to my place and tell me all about it."

Godwin agreed and hung up. He stood a few moments, hand on the phone.

"Something wrong?" asked Shelly.

"Oh, no, I guess not. I just thought this person would be in jail by now. I don't like the thought of him running around free."

In the early afternoon, Rosemary Kossel — she of the fresh complexion and advanced knitting skills — was sitting beside Betsy on her couch. Betsy was holding a square of mitered knitting in her hands. "Okay, where do I begin to pick up the twelve stitches on this to do the second square?" she asked.

"Where was your ending point?" asked Rosemary.

Betsy turned the square around, looking for loose ends, which were on opposite corners. She had worked the square in yellow and maroon yarns and, as promised, it appeared she had knit around one corner of her square. The corner where the yarn turned was uppermost; Betsy turned the square around so it formed a diamond. There was a loose end of yarn sticking out of what was now the top. "I started here," she said, and reached down to the opposite corner, which also had a tag end of yarn. "So I ended here." She put a big safety pin into the square near that corner.

"Good," pronounced Rosemary. "Now, turn it one more time, so that ending corner is on the bottom right." Betsy gave it another half turn, making it a square again. "Using your main color yarn, the color you started with, pick up twelve stitches along the top row. Remember, what you're trying to do is end up with a square of four mitered squares, with all four turning points aimed at the center."

Betsy did as instructed, noting that it was easy to pick up the stitches with Rosemary's clever instruction of slipping the first stitch of every row and purling the last. After a minute she said, "Okay — but I need twenty-five, not twenty-four stitches for my next square."

"That's right. So pick up a thirteenth stitch on the point. Then cast on twelve more."

After a minute, Betsy said, "Done!"

"Very good. Now do what you did with the first square, row one: Knit twenty-four, purl one, still using your original color."

Which in Betsy's case was maroon.

"Now, using your contrast color, slip one knitwise and knit ten."

"Got it," said Betsy after another two minutes.

"Good. Slip one, knit two together, pass the slipped stitch over the stitch you made knitting the two together, then knit ten, purl one, and turn." Betsy, tucking the tip of her tongue into the corner of her mouth, made the row as instructed.

"Very good. You're knitting much faster than you used to, you know."

"It's all that practice. Which I don't mind, because I love to knit. Let's see, for row two, I just knit my way back in the contrast color, purling the last one."

"Don't forget to slip the first stitch."

"Oops, that's right! Okay, here we go." Without that pause for a complication in the middle, this row went fast.

Then, using the maroon yarn, Betsy slipped one knitwise, knit nine, slipped one, knit two together, slid the slipped stitch over, knit nine, purled one. Then she starting knitting her way back with yellow.

"How are you getting on with your broken leg?" asked Rosemary, who had taken out a project of her own, a piece of fine lace she was knitting in number 10 thread with size 0 needles.

"All right, I guess. The doctor's happy with my progress. I'd skip doing the exercises, but if I do the muscles will lose their tone, and I'll have to go into rehab, which will keep me out of the shop another couple of weeks. It's already driving me batty staying away this long. I miss it. What do retired people do?"

"You know, I don't know when I found the time to go to my job," said Rosemary, who had retired last year. "Classes, projects, shopping, volunteering — the day just fills up from start to end."

By row ten, the knitting was definitely bending in the middle, the decreases pulling it down — Betsy was down to knitting just six before slipping and knitting two together. It was fun to watch it happen. When she got to row twenty-two, the rows had decreased in length so much that all she could do was slip one, slip another one, knit two together, pass the slipped stitch over, knit one, purl one. Then slip one going back, knit three, purl one. Turn, and for the final row, in maroon, slip one, purl two together, and slip the first stitch over the second to end.

There was a sound from the back bedroom and Betsy quickly said "Ha!" to cover it.

"What's that?" asked Rosemary.

"I said 'Ha,' because I finished the next square," said Betsy, pretending she hadn't heard the curious gurgle. It was a sound the crow made when it found something tasty in its food dish. The cage was heavily covered; the crow should be thinking it was night and be asleep, not up and chuckling to itself over a forgotten dab of dog food.

Rosemary said, "No, I thought I heard —"

Fortunately, just then the phone rang, and Betsy lunged for the cordless sitting on the coffee table. "Hello?" she said, a trifle too loudly, in case the gurgle sounded again.

"Betsy, it's me, you don't have to shout," Godwin said.

"What's up?" asked Betsy, not quite as loudly.

"Have you heard about Tony Milan?"

"No, what about him? Has he confessed?"

"He isn't even under *arrest!*"

"He isn't? Why not? Doesn't Sergeant Omernic think he's guilty?"

"Oh, he certainly does! But Tony's apartment caught fire two days ago and Tony took that opportunity to disappear!"

"What do you mean, disappear? Did he catch a plane to somewhere?"

"Nobody *knows!* He could be *anywhere!*" Godwin was lapsing into italics again.

"Calm down, calm down. Remember, if he's still in town, he won't be hard to find — there aren't many people walking around with a broken arm, a broken leg, and a head wrapped up in bandages. And if he's found a place to hole up in town, he is certainly going to stay there, not go out where he might be seen. Anyway, there's no need for either you or I to be afraid; he has no idea we even exist."

"Oh. Oh, that's right. So I guess we just go on waiting. Right?"

"Right. Now excuse me, I've got to start square three of this four-part piece Rosemary is teaching me how to do."

As soon as Rosemary left, Betsy went to the back bedroom to check on the crow. The double cover on the cage was pulled half off — and the door to the cage was open. And the crow was not in the cage.

He was up on the very top of the beautiful iron framework that rose above the bed, teetering back and forth as his claws wrapped themselves around it.

Even worse, the bird had shown — twice — that it was not housebroken. The beautiful lacey duvet cover on the bed was spattered.

"Caw-caw-caw-caw-caw!" the bird shouted at her from its high perch, ducking its head and slightly opening its wings at each caw.

"Get down from there!" Betsy shouted, waving a crutch at its head. Startled, the bird fell backward. Its good wing flapped strongly, turning it sideways in the air, but the crippled wing opened only part way and kept it from whirling down on its head. It landed on the bed breast first, then hopped to its feet, head turning every which way as if confused by its inability to fly. It hopped three times across the bed, away from Betsy, turned to look at her and showed that, so far as loose went, a crow is the equal of any goose.

"No, no, no! Don't do that!" shouted Betsy, waving the crutch again. "Get down, get off, you filthy bird! The bird hopped to the edge of the bed, fluttered to the floor — and started to run. Barely in time, Betsy got to the bedroom door and shut it before the bird could get out.

But that was as good as it got. She could not herd the bird back into its cage — it simply would not hop up to the door, but when driven to the cage, went around it or, once, over the top. It couldn't fly like an ordinary bird, but could use its wings to make amazingly high hops.

She chased it around the room, across the bed — twice — and into and out of the closet.

And then it fluttered clumsily up onto her desk. Both paused, breathing hard. The bird stepped up on, then slid around on the keyboard, finding only poor purchase on the keys, and, just before hopping off, made a mess that went from the R to the P and down to the space bar.

Betsy shrieked and the bird fled to the

floor and went under the desk. If Betsy had been able to kneel, she would have captured it, but she couldn't.

Then someone started banging on the door to her apartment. The noise was so urgent that Betsy abandoned the chase and, careful to close the bedroom door behind her, went to see who it was.

Godwin. His face pale and his expression anxious, he asked, "Are you all right?"

"Of course I am," said Betsy, irritated. "Why shouldn't I be?"

"Oh, Betsy, I heard sounds as if you were being chased, and then I heard this scream, so I came dashing up to see if you needed rescue." Godwin had a sturdy wooden embroidery frame in his hand, an impromptu weapon brought from the shop. When he saw Betsy looking at it, he tried to hide it behind his back. "But you, you're all right?"

"Yes, I'm fine. Well, no, I'm not. Come in, I want to tell you a secret and ask for your help." She explained quickly and briefly about the crow, careful to not name any names.

"Wow," said Godwin. "And it's gotten loose?"

"Yes. Can you help?"

Half an hour later the bird was back in his

cage, and Godwin was in the bathroom applying Band-Aids.

When he came out, he asked, "How did he get out of his cage?"

"I don't know. I was told the latch didn't work properly, but they gave me some wire to twist around the bars to hold it shut. I guess he figured out how to untwist it, and now it's gone — I wouldn't put it past him to have hidden it somewhere."

"You better buy a padlock. And hide the key."

"You're right, he'd probably learn the combination if I got that kind of lock."

"Or, why don't you just toss him out a window and say he escaped?"

"Because I don't want to. I kind of like him."

"*Like* him? How can you possibly like him?"

"Because he's smart and proud and not grateful for the good we humans are doing him. Oh, don't get me wrong, I like gratitude. I remember us taking in a starving puppy back when I was married to my first husband and that dog was the most loyal and loving pet I ever knew. Every day he reminded us of our kind deed by his grateful behavior, and I loved him dearly. But — I don't know — here's this other creature, as dependent on the kindness of humans for his existence as that dog. Humans took him in, healed his injury, and we're feeding him good, balanced meals. And his reaction? 'What-ever!' " Betsy laughed. "There's something refreshing about that."

"I think it's mean of him."

"He's not being mean on purpose, he just doesn't understand how helpless he is. I think he's sure he'd be fine if we'd just turn him loose. Though maybe not. I've been reading up on crows, and I've found that they're about the smartest birds on the planet. There are crows who have learned to put unshelled nuts on the road for cars to run over and crack for them. This one pays attention, too; he's seen me twist that wire a dozen times, and I really do think he learned from me how to undo it. Just this morning, he asked me very politely to pick up a piece of food he'd dropped outside his cage. I think it was an experiment, to see if I would do it, because he's never spoken to me in that gentle tone of voice before. Later I saw him watching me very carefully, trying to figure out more things about me. Maybe he thinks I'm some new kind of crow — they live in mobs and they do look out for each other. They're outlaws, pirates, thieves, oh, yes, and not ashamed of it. They eat the eggs of other birds, and eat the young of any species small enough for them to attack successfully. But they're very loyal to their tribe. They're interesting, arrogant, intelligent, noisy, messy, independent creatures who will look a human right in the eye without a trace of fear."

"Wow!" said Godwin, taken aback. "Looks like this particular crow has made a conquest."

Betsy sighed. "Which is not to say I won't be relieved when he is *gone* from here. But now listen, what I'm doing is illegal, so you mustn't tell anyone, all right?"

Godwin grinned broadly. "That's the part I find hard to believe. *You* doing something illegal!"

"Oh, it's not all that illegal, especially if a cop catches me red-handed and thinks it's okay."

Godwin, still grinning, said, "All right, if you say so. Anything else I can do for you?"

"Yes, two things: Put that duvet in a plastic bag and take it to the cleaners tomorrow, and so long as you're out, buy me a new keyboard. We cleaned this one off pretty good, but I don't know if it can survive what happened to it — and meanwhile, it still smells."

"Yet you're not mad at the crow."

Betsy shrugged. "It was just doing what nature tells it to do. They're bright, crows, but I don't think I could explain keyboards or duvets to them."

Much later, before she went to bed, Betsy changed the papers at the bottom of the crow's cage again — she was going through several copies of the Minneapolis *Star Tribune* every day, trying to keep ahead of the creature's output — and found not only the wire to hold the cage door shut but her antique, heart-shaped gold locket and chain tucked under several layers in a corner of the cage. She hadn't even missed it.

She glared at the bird, who cocked his head at her, merely interested. "And you were making believe you couldn't get back inside when we were chasing you!" she scolded. "I bet in another couple of days you'll learn how to refasten the wire so I won't even know you've been out!"

She stormed out of the room, and so she didn't see him make that thoughtful gurgling sound and go to peck at the wire holding shut the door to his cage.

Twenty-Four

Tony had broken his resolve to stay strictly in the condo. He'd taken that watch he couldn't remember acquiring to a pawn shop in a nearby strip mall and had to use all his con artist skills to keep from showing how astonished he was when the man behind the counter offered him three hundred dollars for it. Three hundred bucks for a *Bulova?* That meant it was worth fifteen hundred, maybe two grand. Tony didn't know Bulovas could be worth that much. And he didn't know anyone who owned a watch that costly. Except Marc, and Marc's watch was a Rolex, thank you very much. He decided to keep the pawn ticket; maybe he could redeem it someday.

Meanwhile the money meant he could refill his Vicodin prescription without stealing any of the fifties from the stack he'd found stashed in the condo. He called his pharmacy, then took a cab over to pick it up. The pills cost about two bucks apiece.

The good news was he'd reached that point where he wasn't in a great deal of pain even without the pills, and so was cruising on them recreationally.

But after two more days he needed something else to do. When he'd first arrived, it was wonderful, so quiet, so secure, so clean and everything beautiful and expensive. He'd lain the first morning in his comfortable bed, thinking what a great thing it would be to stay here permanently. Surely that wouldn't be a hard thing to arrange. He'd be sweet and neat and very careful of all Marc's beautiful things. And when Marc got home, Tony'd be nice and welcoming and as helpful as he possibly could be. He'd cook some of his wonderful dishes and impress Marc with his gentle ways, and Marc would fall in love and Tony would never have to steal or con anyone ever again. And Marc would take him to interesting places, and buy him nice things, and they'd have such great fun!

It was easy to be honest with all that wonderful stuff hanging in the balance.

So that's what he would do.

That was the first day.

But now, on the third day, he was bored. This damn condo was starting to feel like a prison. Nothing on cable he wanted to watch anymore. And with his arm and leg still messed up, he couldn't use Marc's Jacuzzi. And he'd eaten all the fun snacky things. Luxurious? Absolutely, but still a prison.

Pretty soon he'd need to see a doctor about a walking cast. But he couldn't afford a doctor's visit, especially since he hadn't paid the deductibles. But in another few days Marc would be back and Marc would pay for a doctor's visit, surely. All he had to do was wait.

Why was waiting so hard? Why was he feeling this way? Here he was, going stir-crazy in a palace. It didn't make sense. Life was such a gyp.

Hold on, maybe he wasn't so much bored as lonesome.

Well, sure! He knew what he needed to fix that: a couple of friends over. Not really a party. Marc had said *No parties,* and Tony had agreed. Just having a few friends over wasn't a party, it was a visit. And surely Marc hadn't meant for him to sit here all by himself till he got back from Mexico.

Just three friends, that wasn't a party. What did he need to host a visit? There was plenty of alcohol left, but no chips or olives or fancy crackers. So that meant he'd have to do some cooking. Three or four friends — and he'd ask them to bring ingredients so he could make some of his famous hors d'oeuvres. Artichoke and goat cheese bruschetta, of course. And, with Thanksgiving on the horizon, something with cranberries. Ah, meatballs in cranberry and pinot noir sauce! And pumpkin hummus with toasted pita chips, yes! And, of course, chocolate-covered strawberries. *Lots* of chocolate-covered strawberries.

He could feel himself coming to life just thinking about it.

Suiting action to the thought, he rolled to his feet. Whoops, hold on just a minute: He only had one hand. He couldn't make hors d'oeuvres one-handed.

Travis. Travis Dash was pretty good in the kitchen. He'd make a fine assistant. It would enhance his reputation as a cook, to learn some of Tony's secrets. He'd be grateful for that. So — just as a backup, it wasn't going to happen that Marc would come home and not want Tony as a permanent guest — but just in case, Tony would have another place to move into.

Sweet!

Tony picked up the phone, thought briefly, then recalled the number and dialed. "Hello, Travis, how's it hanging?" he asked cheerily.

"Have I got a great idea for a get-together!"

"Who is this?" Travis asked. "Is this Sto-ney?"

"None other."

"Well, well, well, how are you?"

"As well as can be expected, considering. But I'm out here all by my lonesome, and I am lonesome, so I want to have some people over. Not a big party, but a get-together, just a few friends, for food and fun."

"Where are you?"

"In Marc Nickelby's condo."

"Oh, my God! How did you manage to land in such a pot of jam?"

"Marc is in Mexico and needed someone to watch his place. Take in his mail. Water his plants. So here I am. And I thought I'd share the wealth a little. Are you in?"

"But naturally, naturally!"

"Also, I need your help."

Travis's enthusiasm faded about halfway. "For what?"

"In the kitchen. I want to cook for my friends, and I'm one-handed."

The enthusiasm came back. "Will you make tape-ade?"

"What in the world is tape-ade?"

"You know, that black-olive stuff with garlic and, and, what-are-they — capers! Olive oil, capers, and black olives all mushed

together and you spread it on little squares
of bread or crackers. Better than caviar, in
my opinion."

"Oh, tapenade! Certainly — if we can find
someone to bring capers. Marc hasn't any
capers in the place. Or black olives."

"Ask Milky, he's got a few dollars in his
pocket. In fact, make that the theme of the
party! If you want your favorite hors
d'oeuvres, you have to bring at least one of
the ingredients."

That seemed a perfectly delightful idea,
and soon Tony was talking to more people
about the hors d'oeuvres party. He was up
to eight before he remembered it wasn't
supposed to be a party, but a small gathering. But what the heck, he could handle
eight, and if ten showed up — people
brought friends, after all — that would only
make more ingredients for the hors
d'oeuvres. The gathering was going to be
tomorrow evening, it was going to be splen-
did, he was in much better spirits already.

All right, it was a party — fourteen people
showed up instead of Tony's original plan
to invite four, but some of them brought
liquor or wine, and most of them brought
something that could be used in hors
d'oeuvres.

The party got louder as the drinks went around, a few spills happened, a statue got broken. But everyone was having a great time, and the statue's pieces were quickly picked up and thrown away. Tony cooked and cooked, his friends ate and ate. Travis got really drunk, and Tony drank more than he meant to himself, but by the time their hors d'oeuvres started turning out sloppily, everyone else was too drunk to notice. Someone turned up the music, and a quarrel broke out about it. Then the phone rang. "Stoney, Stoney, it's for you!" shouted the man who'd answered it.

Tony picked up the extension in the kitchen. "We're full up!" he announced, laughing.

"Excuse me, sir, but I've been asked to inquire: May I call a cab for some of your guests?"

"What? Oh. Oops, sorry. Sure, I'll send some down right away." Because Tony understood the real message: The party better be over; the neighbors were complaining. He hung up, checked the clock on the microwave, and was amazed to see it was after two in the morning.

He shouted against the noise until someone turned the music off. "Okay, boys, time to wind it down," he announced. "There's a man downstairs who will call you a cab if you don't feel able to drive home."

"I'm a cab!" shouted Winston, and such was the general inebriation of the guests that they found this hilarious, and there were several shouted repeats of it.

"The neighbors will call the police if we don't shut it down," warned Tony. "Anyone here care to spend the rest of the night in jail?"

"No, thank you!" said Donni. "Where's my coat?"

That started a general exodus, but somehow three of the guests stayed on. They were very quiet and sat sipping wine amid the ruins — Tony had used every single plate, bowl, and glass in the condo to feed and ablute his guests, and those that weren't broken were stacked all over the place. There was considerable spillage, as well. "Wow," he said reverently to his remaining guests.

Travis said, "Wow, indeed. That was quite an affair." He looked around at the mess. "Is there something we can do to help you clean up?"

Milky shook back his flaxen hair and said, "I think we should bring in a fire hose, open a couple of windows, and let 'er rip." He gestured with a half-empty wineglass, adding another stain to the carpet. "Sorry," he said and drank the glass dry so it wouldn't happen again.

Plump Winston said, "Say, I heard The Man is after you."

"Me?" said Travis.

"No. You, Stoney. That's what I hear."

Tony came with his own refilled wineglass to sit on the dais and lean against a leg of the piano. "What? What man?"

"The heat — the cops."

"After *me?* What for?"

"I dunno."

Milky said, "I don't know, either, but it's a man in a suit, not a uniform. We were talking about it earlier, but you were in the kitchen making delicious things, so we didn't want to bother you. But I bet it's not a traffic ticket. He asked me some questions."

Tony was suddenly feeling stone-cold sober. "About what?"

"Mostly about where you'd got to. Nobody'd seen you in a while and you weren't in your old apartment, and he wanted to know if you'd left town."

"What did you tell him?" asked Tony.

"The truth," said Milky. "We didn't know where you were."

Travis winked and looked muzzily around

the room. "Well, we do now." His wine was in a tumbler and he took a big swallow. "But not for long. Ol' Marc isn't gonna like what you did to his place."

"Never mind Marc, I can clean this up so he'll never know. Winnie, what else did this cop say?"

"Not too much. When he first came in — this was at the Eagle — we were like, 'Who are you?' Then he said he was a friend of Godwin DuLac's. Some of the men had heard of him. Do you know him?"

"Never heard of — But hold on, wasn't someone named Goddy looking for me not very long ago?"

Travis said, "Thass right, I remember that, he was in Vera's. No, wait, he was lookin' for someone else, first, name of Bob German — no, Germaine. Wanted to know if Germaine was gay. But in the closet, like."

Milky said, "Yeah, Godwin was in the Gay Nineties, too, looking for this Bob Germ."

"Germaine," corrected Travis.

"Whatever. But then he came up with a description that sounded like you, including that ID bracelet you wear all the time, so Pauly gave him your name. We hadn't seen you in a little while, I think that was while you were still in the hospital."

Tony glanced at the bracelet on his wrist

but didn't say anything.

Winston raised his glass. "Welcome out of the hospital, man, 'cause you sure know how to throw a party!" The other two cheered and raised their glasses to that.

"Do you know a Bob Germaine?" asked Milky. "I mean, why would he be looking for Bob Germaine and end up with you?"

Tony shifted a little and said, "Beats the hell out of me. I never talked to this Godwin. Who is he, anyway? Do you know him?"

"I do," said Travis. "He runs a needlework store. Calls himself the President, or CEO, or Commander of Opra — Operations, something like that. And Editor in Chief of a newsletter, too. Nice li'l store, if you like that kinda thing." He took another big drink.

"Where is this store?" asked Tony.

"Asselsior." Travis's speech was growing more slurred by the minute. "Th' owner of the store owns the whole buildin' —" Travis gestured a big circle with his glass to show it was a very big building. "And lives in a 'partment on the second floor. *And,* this lady was s'posed to be in charge of selling embroidery things at this embroidery convention, only she broke her leg, so he took over. Made a big pile of money." Travis stopped to look back at what he'd just said, then nodded sharply and said, "That's right, that's 'zactly how it was. Made a whole big pile of money."

Travis didn't say "a whole big pile" of money, but used a more vulgar expression. The idea was the same, however.

"Do either of you two know this Godwin fellow?" asked Tony.

"Not me," said Winston.

"I've seen him around," said Milky. He smirked. "I think he's cute."

Travis said, "Well, *you* wouldn't think he's all that, Stoney. He's kind of a twink." He winked and nodded.

"He knits his own socks," offered Milky, in support of that statement.

"Yes," said Travis, "and he teaches knitting classes, in his store. Cute as a button, can dance like nobody's business. But he don't do drugs or go to raves. Specially now he's a big-shot businessman."

"And he lives in Excelsior," said Tony.

"Yeah. He drives a hot little sports car. But: *He made his bones,* as the gangsters say."

Tony stared at Travis, whose nod started in again. "He says an ex-lover *gave* him the car, it's an Audi, I think. But it was this same *rich* ex-lover that got *murdered.* And guess who murdered him? Our cute-as-a-button li'l twink, Godwin."

"He *murdered* someone?" said Tony.

Milky gaped at Travis, and Winston said, "No!"

Travis was still nodding. "Yep, got arrested for it an' ever'thing. But he got away with it, never got convicted, never went to prison. One day he's sitting in jail, and the next he's home free."

Winston raised a finger and said, "Wait a second, I remember that! It was a man named Nye who got murdered — he was a lawyer. Someone else was convicted of murdering him."

Travis stopped nodding and said, "Someone Goddy set up, I bet. *I* say, 'Is the lover dead?' Plus, who's driving around in the dead man's flashy sports car?"

Tony said, "I thought you said he's a twink."

"He is. If he likes you, he'll knit you a sweater."

"Cute," sneered Winston.

"And if he don't like you, he'll *kill* you."

"Well, may I never run into this twink," said Tony. His heart was racing, suddenly he understood this whole thing. He yawned hugely and announced, "I am *bushed.* I think we should call it a night. Travis, you are the best left hand a cook ever had."

"Yeah, that was fun. Maybe we should do it again."

"No, I think the next time I cook for a crowd I should be all healed up." He staggered to his feet, a little surprised at how uncertain his feet were, because his head felt very clear. Milky came to steady him while Travis picked up his crutch and handed it to him.

"You sure you don't want some help cleaning up?" asked Winston, looking around at the chaos.

"No, no, I'll hire a crew. The carpet's going to need professional handling. I think someone dropped at least one of every single hors d'oeuvre recipe I prepared."

"An' someone else walked in it," agreed Travis, nodding at one particularly ugly stain. "Well, if you say so. Less leave you to it."

The trio gathered their coats and gloves and scarves, went out the front door and trailed down the hall. Tony watched to make sure they got on the elevator, then closed the door.

He went back into the once-beautiful living room, groaning at the wreck his party had made of it. God, he had so loved living in this place! Why hadn't things worked out so he could go on living here?

Not that he was sad about it. No, he was beyond sad, well into scared, almost as scared as he'd been when he learned they'd found Germaine's body out at the airport.

But this time he knew why.

A police detective was after him. After this party, enough people knew where he was that, if he stayed here, the detective was going to find him, arrest him, and charge him with murder.

And it was *wrong!* He hadn't *done* it! If he'd committed a murder, he'd *know* it! It would be in his bones, in his fists, the knowledge would be in his whole body! And he had absolutely no memory of killing Germaine. None.

Okay, he'd meant to go to the hotel, meet him, hit him, knock him down, steal the check. But he hadn't done it — or where was the check, huh? Where was the goddam *check?* He didn't have it, did he? So he *wasn't guilty!*

But this Godwin person was trying to convince everyone Tony was a murderer. Hold on, hold on, not Tony, but Stoney. Stoney Durand. Every person who came to the party tonight thought his name was Stoney Durand.

Hold on again. Travis and Milky and Winston agreed the cop had come looking for

Stoney, and they said Godwin was told about Stoney, and Stoney was the man living here on Lake Calhoun, so it all came down to the same damn thing. The cop would come and arrest Stoney. And the minute they ran his fingerprints, they'd know Stoney was Tony Milan.

Tony went to the liquor cabinet and found half a bottle of scotch among the empties. He poured some of it into a glass that looked clean enough and went back to the couch. He slumped deep into the suede leather and took a big swallow. So here was this Godwin — what was it? DeLake, duPont. Something. Who had gotten away with murder some time ago — and so had gotten away with it again, right there at that EGA convention. He took another swallow, feeling the warmth of the alcohol flood his stomach, like the warm wrath that fumed into his brain.

Because it all fit. This Godwin creep had stolen the money *himself.* Money that should have gone into *Tony's* pocket and left *Germaine* with nothing more than a headache. Germaine was *dead,* Godwin had the *money,* and they were going to blame *Tony!*

And Godwin might get away with it, the big-shot businessman. Just because the creep owned a building and knit his own socks — ! Tony frowned and waved that thought away. It was because he got away with it once, this Godwin, he thought he could kill anyone any time and get away with it. Tony finished the scotch in a final, angry swallow, then tossed the glass onto the carpet.

He couldn't go to the cops, not with his record. And they'd investigate and find out about the bank scam and fall right in with Godwin's scheme to frame him.

Jeez, what could he do, how could he get out of being set up like this? He was going to go back to prison! Gyp, big time!

Tony looked for the thrown glass, thinking about another trip to the scotch bottle — then changed his mind. No more drink. He needed a clear head if he was going to thwart the evil plans of this Godwin person.

How satisfying it would be to go out there and beat on him till he told the truth! But he couldn't, not like this, all beat up himself. Like this, he couldn't beat up a little old granny lady. Though the thought of a granny lady quailing under the thumping of his crutch made him smile.

Then he thought of something that would make things equal — more than equal — between him and this Godwin person. He had, of course, gone poking around in Marc's drawers and cupboards. He'd found a key taped to the underside of a desk drawer. He'd already found a very heavy steel box that Marc had hidden in his bedroom closet, and sure enough the key opened it. But Tony very honorably hadn't taken a thing from it, not the gold ring with a ruby the size of his fingernail, not the beautiful gold chain whose links had been carved to make them twinkle, not even a single bill that Marc probably would not have missed from the nifty stack of fifties.

But now things were very different, and this was an emergency. Tony really had to go back to that box because he needed the one other thing in it: the equalizer, in the form of a snub-nose revolver, dark and deadly, and already loaded. He could fire one shot to show this Godwin person he meant business and still have five bullets left in case he needed them. Shoot him in the foot, then the knee and so on, until he confessed. Good plan.

Tony couldn't remember under which drawer Marc had stashed the key to the box, but after pulling out drawers all over the condo, he found it. He dragged the box out of the closet and over to Marc's bed, where he sat down and opened it.

He took the gun out first, then after a few seconds' thought, took all the money as well. He told himself he was coming back and would need the money to have the place properly cleaned up. But in the back of his head he knew he couldn't come back here. He needed that money to get out of town after he took care of that Godwin person. He'd just go, but cops got persistent when the charge was murder — and Tony would be easy to spot. There weren't many fugitives with a broken left arm, a broken left leg, and a bandage on his head. He counted the money and found there was an even thousand dollars. He could go pretty far on that. And if Godwin had the twenty grand, he could go even farther, and dig himself an even deeper hole.

He closed the box, then opened it again. In its velveteen box was the ruby ring. He took it out. No, too gaudy, no one would believe it was real. So he put it back. But the gold chain was lovely. He put it on over his head and it was just heavy enough to announce its presence, but not so heavy that it looked silly, or fake. The carved links twinkled when Tony moved, and they had an interesting texture when he ran his fingers over them.

What the necklace called for was more

gold — no, not the ring, dammit! Marc could wear the ring; it looked okay on him, an older guy who somehow made the ring look as real as it was. But Tony was too young for a stone that size.

Hold on! He knew what it needed. Tony went back to his bedroom and found the white dress shirt. Someone had told him once how to get bloodstains out of cotton — and the shirt was 100 percent cotton, though of a smoothness Tony had never known cotton could attain. The secret was shampoo. Soak the stain in shampoo, wet it with cool water, scrub a bit, then rinse. Repeat as necessary. Okay, it was kind of wrinkled; Tony had never gotten any good at ironing, and with only one hand he was not now ironing anything at all.

He had to rip the seam of the left sleeve to get it on over his cast. And put one of the beautiful gold cufflinks on the right cuff first and then work the sleeve over his hand. But laying the beautiful gold necklace over that lovely smooth fabric on his chest was just perfect.

The black suit hadn't been washable and so Tony had thrown it away, so he put on his best jeans that already were ripped up the left leg, and shoved his good foot into a deck shoe. He needed a shave, but after he looked at himself in the mirror, he realized the bristles only added to his cool look. Getting dressed had made his broken bones ache a little, and he had work to do, so as long as he was in the bathroom anyway, he took a Vicodin just to keep the pain away.

Then he went back to Marc's closet, to take out and hang Marc's artfully-antiqued aviator's jacket over his left shoulder to hide the ripped sleeve, then pulled the shirt a little loose so it covered the gun tucked into his waistband. And just for fun, he also took down the matching pinch-brim leather hat. He tried it several ways, and almost decided to leave it behind — but it covered the bandage on top of his head. He finally wore it backward, which sort of gave him an air.

He thought about writing a note to Marc, then thought, Why? Marc would get the message as soon as he walked in on the disaster Tony was leaving behind.

TWENTY-FIVE

Tony went down to the lobby of the condo. The night concierge was not someone he recognized, which was perfect. "May I summon a cab for you?" the man asked.

"Yes, please," replied Tony — soberly, of course.

"What is your destination?"

"St. Paul," lied Tony. If he was asked afterward, the concierge could say that the man with the broken leg went to St. Paul, not Excelsior.

To avoid further conversation, he went out of the lobby into the big covered portico. The outside wall of the lobby was a curve, and the portico followed the curve around it, then plunged downward, into the underground parking area. Tony followed the curve a little way on foot. There was a biting wind whistling into the portico, and he wanted to get as much away from it as he could — he couldn't put the jacket on over his broken arm, and he'd forgotten to put a sock over the bare toes on his broken leg. But a person always had to suffer to look good, and he was happy to look terrific.

He caught movement outside the portico and looked to see if it was his cab, but it was someone coming out of the underground parking — the exit was on the other side of the building, but curved around to meet the same street as the entrance came off. He watched the beautiful car slow then turn onto the street, the people inside mere shadows behind the dark windows. Probably off to the airport, Tony thought enviously, warm and comfortable in the car, going to warm and happy Hawaii or expensive Singapore or exotic Bangkok for Thanksgiving and Christmas. Not a care in the world. And here Tony stood freezing!

Another car pulled up, and its driver got out and hurried into the lobby. Tony turned and watched him wave at the concierge as he hustled past, bound for the elevators.

Tony turned back and saw the car, an older Cadillac in beautiful condition, standing at the curb. Its color was cranberry or black cherry, not a hint of rust. The engine was running; Tony could see the faint trail of exhaust whipped away by the wind. He moved out from the wall to see the license plate: Florida. Naturally.

Some rich couple, or rich biddy, or rich geezer, lived here in the spring and summer, and then went to Florida when the weather turned sour. And kept Florida plates on the car, in part because Florida plates were cheaper than Minnesota plates and in part to rub the noses of the poor in their good fortune.

Gyp.

But hold on a second: Big car, all warmed up, doubtless an automatic — did these cars even come with a stick shift? — sitting there at the curb, like it had pulled up on purpose to take Tony anywhere he wanted to go.

There was danger in taking a cab. The driver might remember — of course he'd remember Tony, handsome, chic Tony, and all banged up like he was! What had he been thinking, ordering a cab to take him to a crime!

So for cripe's sake, go get in the car before the man came back with old Mrs. Gotrocks and her luggage!

Tony moved as unobtrusively as he could over to the car and, after a struggle with a leg that didn't want to bend much in the middle and a huge and useless arm, with a coat wrapped around it besides, he managed to get behind the wheel. He adjusted the seat back a few inches, pulled the seat belt down and fastened it — no need to get stopped for that minor offense and blow the whole deal — and drove sedately away.

Whoops, turn the headlights on! Adjust the mirror at the stoplight at the top of the street. Flip the turn signal on to go right, no need to draw the attention of a patrol car by doing something ticketable. Comfortable, comfortable car, seats real leather, a dark red to match the exterior. No wonder old folks kept buying these great old road yachts, so easy on fragile bones. And look at this: The gas tank was almost full!

Two blocks later the street forked, and the left fork was Highway 7, which led to Excelsior. This time of night there was almost no one else on the road, which was a good thing, as it was a little hard to stay in one lane. But Tony rejoiced to be on his way. Steering with one hand, he felt for the gold necklace with his other. It was just long enough to reach down to where his hand could get it. The texture of the links was soothing, and he let it slip over his fingers again and again.

Sometimes things like this happened, things suddenly turning right, coming into focus, becoming effortless. Tony knew with all his being that he was doing right, following the correct path, making the choices that would lead to success. When things started going his way like this, he would come out on top. That likely meant that not only would he neutralize — hopefully not kill, but kill if necessary — this Godwin person, but he would also regain that twenty-four grand. Then he could get out of — Uh-oh.

He was almost all the way to the Excelsior turnoff by then, when he remembered he hadn't packed anything, and had left the fake passport behind, too. It was far too late to go back. But so what? When he got his money, he could buy some new clothes, and a new passport, too.

Crewel World wasn't on the main drag, but Excelsior wasn't a big town, so Tony drove at random until, coming up a street, he drove past a two-story, dark brick building that had Christmas stockings hung in one of the three big front windows. And there was the sign, Crewel World — ha, he'd found it! Tony pulled to the curb right in front, then decided that wasn't a good idea. What if a cop drove by? Because after all, the owner of the car hadn't meant to leave it sitting more than a couple of minutes, and so probably had already reported it stolen. And Tony was pretty sure Excelsior was still in Hennepin County and so word would reach even out this far right away.

He'd just started to pull away when he noticed something: a narrow driveway going up beside the building. He turned into it. At least the car would be harder to spot here. To his surprise the driveway went around back, to a small parking lot. See? His luck was still in.

He steered over to a big Dumpster, bumped it lightly, and shut the engine off. It took a couple of minutes to get himself out of the car and his crutch under his arm. A low-watt light gleamed over a back door to the building. A back door! Smiling, he made his way over to it.

The door was wood, with a window in the top half made of thick glass with chicken wire embedded in it, hard to break. But his over-the-limit credit card served his purpose one more time as, with some effort, he slid it in to move the tongue of the lock back.

At first it was as dark as the inside of a black cow at midnight — an old jest he remembered from grade school. He stood there a while, waiting for his eyes to adjust. His hand strayed to the gold necklace. The feel of it under his fingers was soothing and kept him occupied until, finally, he could see by the outside light dimly pouring through the top half of the door that he was in a narrow, uncarpeted hall. Turning away from the door, there was a wall to his left, and — was it? Yes, it was, another door down the longer way to his right. He moved as stealthily as he could down to the door. It was unlocked.

On the other side was a big wooden staircase. He came out and there it was, just a few feet away, painted a shiny light green color. Then he saw he was in a much bigger hall. The front door was to his left, and there was an open tiled space in front of it, better lit, with one of those bristly things to wipe your feet on. He went in that direction. Apartment on the second floor, Travis had said. Tony turned and looked up the broad, uncarpeted stairs, which were made of some kind of stone or marble with a nonskid edge on each step. At the top was a big landing. He looked around. No elevator. He would have to climb those stairs to that landing, and then there would be as many more stairs to climb to the second floor. A long and painful journey — but Godwin lived up there, and was probably peacefully asleep in his bed, unaware that justice, or doom, or something equally fearful, with a gun in its waistband, was coming up the stairs after him.

Tony, who would have admitted to being

a little tipsy, wanted to emit a wicked laugh, but was not so drunk he yielded to the impulse. He was content to silently recite the chant from an old ghost story, about a ghost coming after a wicked man, as he started up the stairs: "Old man, I'm on the first step; old man, I'm on the second step; old man, I'm on the third step . . ."

Around the landing, and up again. Finally, at the top, "Old man, I'm on the sixteenth step." He paused then, to catch his breath and look around. He was in another broad hall, this one carpeted. A light glowed beside a window on the wall nearest the street, and another lit an old red glass EXIT sign on the wall beside the top of the stairs. There were three doors up here, meaning three apartments. No name or number on any of them.

Tony stood awhile, uncertain which door to try first. Then he remembered what Travis had said: He lives over the store. And the apartment most nearly directly over the store was . . . that one.

Tony walked to the door and simply tried the knob. To his immense satisfaction, and in furtherance of his belief that he was acting in accord with his karma, the door opened.

He found himself in another hallway, this

one narrow and short. There was a pleasant smell of cooking — basic cooking, like a hot dish — and then a trace of perfumed soap. Was he in the wrong place? He couldn't tell, but this was no time to hesitate.

He closed the door silently — and found himself in utter darkness. He felt his way down the short passageway until he was in a much bigger space. There was a vague lighter rectangle on the wall to his right — that was probably a window with the shades down. He took a few steps forward and bumped into something that was substantial but soft when touched. A couch.

"A-row?"

"What th— !" He managed to stifle the exclamation as he staggered back. He stopped himself from falling with his crutch, and came forward to put a hand on the couch again. By then he realized what had spoken in that tiny, high-pitched voice: a cat.

The thought was immediately followed by something landing on the couch, he could feel the shock of it. Must be a damn big cat. "A-row?" it asked again.

"Here, kitty, kitty," he whispered, and it came to him, to sniff the fingers sticking out of his cast and rub its face on them. A big cat, yes, but friendly and — he stroked down its back — long-haired.

He heard a sound from across the room, in another room. Bedroom. Godwin was awake.

Tony stepped back from the couch and drew his weapon, braced for the light that would come on. And it did.

And there was a woman standing just outside the door over there. She wasn't pretty, or even young, despite the tangle of dyed-blond hair.

"Who are you?" They asked the question in unison.

"Where's Godwin?" growled Tony. "Get him out here."

"Godwin doesn't live here," she replied in a surprised and sleepy voice. Then, in a more awake one, "Oh, my God, are you Tony Milan?"

"How d'ya know that?" he demanded.

"Because . . . because of several things," she said. "Godwin told me Tony Milan broke his arm and his leg in a car accident, and you have about the same build and coloring as Bob Germaine. But how do you know about Godwin? Or me?"

"What's that — Never mind any of that! Where is he?"

"Home, I suppose."

"No, no, don't you lie to me! *This* is his

home! Unless he's in one of the other apartments?"

"No, he doesn't live in this building."

"But that's his store downstairs, right? The embroidery store?"

"He's my store manager, yes."

"No!" he shouted, waving the gun, pleased to see fright drain what little color there was from her face. "I told you not to lie to me! Godwin owns the embroidery store and he lives in an apartment over it! *This* apartment!"

She did not reply.

"He's here, isn't he?" He let his rage show in his voice.

"N-no," she faltered. "I told you, he doesn't live here."

"Liar!" He raised his voice even louder. "You bastard, stop hiding behind a woman! Godwin, come out here!"

She looked behind her, into the bedroom she'd come out of. "There's no one in there," she said.

He shifted the gun to his left hand, barely able to hold it there with his imprisoned fingers. "Move out of the way," he ordered, and she obeyed, moving slowly. He suddenly realized she was on crutches. "Freeze!" he barked, just like a cop, and again she obeyed. She was wearing a flowing nightgown of some pink material, cotton or thin flannel, and had a flimsy robe over it of the same stuff. The combination had hidden her crutches and the hard-plastic boot on her right leg.

"Who are you?" he demanded

"My name is Betsy Devonshire."

"What are you doing in this apartment?"

"I live here."

That had to be a lie, Godwin lived here. He asked a question he already knew the answer to, so he could compare how she looked and sounded when telling the truth. "What's wrong with your leg?" he asked.

"It's broken." Either she really did live here, or she was a damn good liar.

"Move a little more," he said, waving the gun and she came away from the door — doors, he saw now. Three of them, in a kind of alcove. He went to the door she'd come out of. The light was on, and the bed was empty. And by the look of it, she'd been sleeping in it alone. He went to the second door, moving so as to keep an eye on her while he groped for the door and slammed it open. The room was in darkness. He felt around with his hand on the wall and found a switch. The room had a desk, a great big box with a blanket tossed over it, and a four-poster iron bed stripped of sheets and blankets. The closet door was open, and inside it were office supplies. No clothes.

"What's behind that other door?" he asked.

"It's the bathroom."

This was stupid, crazy — was it possible Godwin really wasn't here?

"You say this is your place."

"Yes."

"Where does Godwin live?"

"About five blocks from here."

"But he owns this building, right?"

"Well, no. I do. And I live in this apartment. Alone. Godwin is my store manager."

"I'll kill you if you keep lying to me!" he raged, and pointed the gun at her, with his finger on the trigger.

"What do you want me to say?" she asked, breathless with terror, her eyes enormous in her white face.

"I want you to tell me Godwin owns a store called Crewel World."

"Godwin owns a store called Crewel World," she said, as if reciting a lesson — and suddenly he knew that was the lie, that *she* owned Crewel World, she owned this building, Godwin was a manager, not an owner.

"He lied!" he shouted.

"Who did?" she asked stupidly.

"None of your business! I need to get to Godwin! *Now!*"

She was near tears, he could see that, which would render her useless to him, so he took a breath and then another, to calm himself. "All right, all right."

"Do you want me to call him?" she asked.

"Yes!" he said, then, "No, no. He'd call the cops before he came."

"Yes," she said, "very likely. He told me he was afraid of you."

"Well, he should be, setting me up like he did. What did he think I was gonna do? Lay down and take it?"

"I don't understand. How did he set you up?"

He felt his throat start to close. He was perilously near tears himself. This was not going his way at all. He grabbed for his anger to give him courage. "He *framed* me! He set me up! *He's* the murderer, not me!"

She stared at him. "Godwin — you think *Goddy* killed Bob Germaine?"

"You're damn right I do! It won't be the first time he's murdered someone!"

Something flickered behind her eyes, and he thought, *She thinks I'm crazy.* "I'm not crazy! I heard how he killed his lawyer boyfriend and got away with it. He set up someone else to take the fall, and now he's

331

doing it again!"

"No —" she began.

"Shut up, just shut the hell up!"

"All right," she said.

He tried to think. What should he do? She was no good. And she knew who he was. Christ, was he going to have to kill her, too?

TWENTY-SIX

"May I sit down?" she asked in a humble voice. "My leg is starting to hurt."

He nearly decided to say no, but his own leg was aching and he wanted to sit down, too, so he said, "Okay, but move slow," and waved the gun at her to get her started moving — he had taken it back into his good hand.

He watched as she started for the upholstered chair sitting at a right angle to the couch. Then he saw the big soft bag in a wooden frame beside the chair and called, "Hold it!" She froze. "On the couch, on the couch!" he ordered. Because who knew what she had in that bag?

"All right." She went to the far end of the couch and sat down heavily. The cat, which had jumped down and gone somewhere when she turned on the light, reappeared and jumped back up to lie down beside her, reaching with a forepaw to touch her on the leg. She stroked it once, then looked at him, and put both her hands in her lap. Being the good little girl, he thought with cruel satisfaction.

He moved to the chair himself and sat down in it, easing his own leg. He'd banged it around some getting in and out of the stolen car and climbing the stairs, and it was really hurting. His arm was, too. He wondered if she had any painkillers. Probably, they gave girls medicine more often than boys, even though they needed it less. Probably something better than his damn no-good Vicodin.

But if he took one of hers, he might be slowed down to a dangerous degree. He was already having trouble holding on to the high his rage at this Godwin person had produced. What if he got so relaxed she figured she could charge him and take the gun? That was so alarming a thought that he stirred himself to talk, asking, "Who lives in the other apartments?"

"Doris Valentine lives in one, the other is empty right now."

That answer came with a convincing carelessness. He tried to think how to get Godwin over here. If he asked her to phone him and tell him to come over, Godwin would want to know why, and even if she told some kind of story, he might not believe her — after all, it was a scary hour of the morning; there probably wasn't much she could say that he would believe — and if he didn't believe her, he might call the police. *I'll ask her for his address,* he thought. But then he'd have to leave her here. He couldn't tie her up, not with only one hand. And the woman across the hall might hear him if he shot her. Damn, this was stupid, this was ridiculous!

Without conscious thought, his left hand went to the necklace. Though he'd only owned the thing for a couple of hours, it felt as if it had always been his, soothing his stress with its texture moving under his fingers. And soothing his stress helped him think.

"Who told you Godwin lived here?" He started at her voice.

"What's it to you?"

"I just wondered why someone would lie to you like that."

"It was a fellow named Travis," he said, because he was angry with him and so didn't mind naming him.

"Travis Dash?"

"You know him?" Good!

"I've heard of him. I think I've even met him once. He and Goddy know each other.

335

But he knows Goddy doesn't own Crewel World."

"But he said . . . he said . . ." Tony was trying to think of what Travis said. "He said Goddy — he calls him Goddy, too — he said Goddy ran a booth at that embroidery convention and made lot of money."

"That's true. He had to run it because I was in the hospital with a broken leg."

"So he *was* there, at the convention."

"Yes, of course."

"So he's the one who murdered Germaine."

"No, of course he isn't!"

"Well, then, who did?"

She looked frightened at the question.

"See? You think so, too!"

"No, I think you did."

"No, I didn't!" he shouted.

"Well, Goddy didn't, either," she said in a very humble voice.

"How do you know that?"

"Because he wouldn't. And anyway, he saw the man who murdered Bob walking out of the banquet hall," she said.

"Germaine was murdered in the banquet room?"

"No, out in the parking garage."

Tony blinked at her. Echoing voices, a smell like automobile tires . . . Was that a memory? "I didn't," he said. "I couldn't've."

She said gently, "Perhaps you don't remember. Here's how I think it happened. Bob Germaine was supposed to pick up the check at the EGA convention. I think someone found out about it and decided to steal it from him. This person went to the hotel and waylaid Bob in the parking garage next to the hotel. I think he was scared and hit Bob harder than he meant to, and killed him." Tony felt his whole attention fastened on this recitation. Apart from the bit about hitting him too hard, she was right.

She went on, "But Bob didn't have the check. The killer didn't know Bob was going to pick it up at the banquet, which hadn't started yet. The killer went through Bob's clothes, looking for the check, but what he found was a speech Bob was going to give, thanking EGA for the check. What was he going to do? Maybe he should just run away. But he'd killed a man, and if he ran, it would be for nothing. Then he had a very clever idea, but one that would take enormous nerve."

Trying not to sound too interested, Tony asked, "What was that?"

"He took Bob's place. He undressed Bob, put his black suit and white dress shirt on himself. He hid Bob's body in the trunk of his car. Then he very boldly walked into the banquet room, read the speech, and was presented with the check."

Though he was sure this wasn't how it happened — Tony never got the check! — Tony nodded at her to continue.

So she said, "The killer wanted to walk out and drive away in his own car, but several officers of the local EGA chapter walked him to Bob's Lexus, so he had to drive off in it. But then he had another clever idea: He drove Bob's car out to the long-term parking lot at the airport and left it there. Cars can sit out there for weeks."

Tony nodded, he knew that. But so what? A lot of people knew that.

She said, "He came back to town on the light rail, picked up his own car — and got into a serious accident on his way home."

"But if that was me, where's the check? Where's the goddam *check?*" demanded Tony.

"I don't know. Maybe it got lost during the accident."

"No, it didn't! I got everything back, my clothes, everything! The hospital sent me home with everything! I did mean to intercept that check — it was mine, I had plans for it and everything. But I never got my hands on it. So see? See? Your story is cute, it may even be true, but it's not about me, because I don't have the *check!*"

She was looking nervously around the living room, trying to think what to say next, but he waggled the gun and her attention came back to it. She blinked at it, as if she'd never seen a gun before.

He taunted her, "Any more ideas, lady?"

She asked, "Did the hospital send you home with a black suit and a white shirt with solid-gold cuff links?"

His left hand went to the necklace. "What about it?"

"That's what Bob Germaine was wearing when he disappeared. When his body was found, the suit, shirt, and cuff links were missing. And his watch, a nice Bulova —"

"I didn't pawn it!" he said, but his voice came out too high, and he moved his good arm to hide the cufflink, but it was too late, she'd already seen it, that's what caught her eye, not the gun. He pulled the necklace away with his left hand to distract her, but she just kept on looking at his right cuff.

So he wriggled the gun some more, to bring her attention to it, to the danger she was in, to make her begin to promise not to tell anyone. Because he knew that, somehow, she knew more than he did about what happened that night at the hotel.

That was it! She was Godwin's *partner* in this frame-up! He really was going to have to kill her, even though he'd never killed anyone in his life. But he could do it. And now he could see that she was aware of it, too, gesturing at him, opening her mouth to beg —

Suddenly something black and feathery was smacking him on the face, blotting out his vision, and biting the fingers of his broken arm, and pinching his shoulder. It was the woman, he tried to punch her with the gun. But he kept missing her somehow. The flapping was like the wings of a big bird, and now there was a bad stink. Was she whipping him with a dirty cloth? It had fishhooks in it, his fingers were being seriously torn, and his face was being scratched — the cat!

He tried leaning back and sideways while yelling and thrusting it away, but it was fastened to him and he fell out of the chair, he was on the floor, and she had tipped a lamp over on him, his arm and leg hurt, his face was being bitten, and the woman was shouting something — and then the flapping stopped and he could hear, real near and loud, a crow cawing. The gun was gone — where was the gun? He started to roll over, even though it hurt, groaning and feeling for it. Then he saw she had the gun and was pointing it at him.

Twenty-Seven

"It was that gold necklace," Betsy said. "It twinkles and the crow came after it."

"God bless the crow!" exclaimed Godwin.

"Amen," said Betsy. "May it live long and happily in Iowa. I wish I could nominate it for that animal hero medal, but its existence has to retain the tattered remnants of a secret."

"Did you think it would attack Tony?" asked Detective Omernic.

"No. I noticed it coming into the living room — Tony left the office door open and the light on. I never got a padlock for its cage, so it was always getting out. I tried not to look at it, but it kept coming closer to the chair. I could see it had its eye on the necklace he was twiddling. I thought about warning him, because I didn't want it to startle him into shooting, but then I saw it was coming up to him from behind and I hoped it might distract him enough so I could run out of the apartment."

"On a broken leg?" scoffed Godwin.

"When you're really scared, you can run on a broken leg," said Sergeant Omernic with the air of one who knows. They were sitting around Betsy's table in her dining nook. Omernic had kindly come by for a wrap-up.

"Why didn't you sic Tony on Godwin?" asked Omernic. "It was Godwin he was mad at."

Betsy stared at him. "I couldn't do that!"

Godwin, moved beyond words, touched his mouth with his fingertips, then went in another direction. "Anyone want coffee? It's already made."

"Thank you, black," said Omernic.

"No, thank you," said Betsy.

Godwin stood and asked over his shoulder, "Does Tony still say I'm the murderer?"

"He's not saying much of anything," said Omernic. "He's an old hand at being arrested, he knows better than to say anything more than he has to. Besides, he honestly doesn't remember what happened that night in the parking garage. That skull fracture he suffered in the car accident wiped about thirty-six hours of memory from his brain."

"Can you convict a man of a crime he

doesn't remember committing?" asked Betsy.

"Certainly," said Omernic. "If you can prove he did it."

"Still," said Godwin, coming back with a mug in each hand, "it would be weird and awful to go to prison for something you don't remember doing."

"I think he already halfway believes he did it," said Betsy. "If only — I wonder where the check got to? It was never cashed or deposited in that fake account he set up. He was very firm that he never saw it, and he thinks that's proof he's innocent."

"Well, Germaine's shirt and cuff links were in his possession. Plus these two clues." Omernic put down his mug and reached into a pocket to pull out a folded sheet of paper. Unfolded, it proved to be two sheets, photocopies. One was of a small key, the other of a photograph of a watch. Each item had a big evidence tag attached to it.

"Where did you find that?" asked Betsy, touching the picture of the watch. It appeared to have a lizard- or crocodile-skin band.

"It was pawned just a few blocks from Marc Nickelby's condo, where Mr. Milan stayed after his own apartment caught fire.

We found a partial of Milan's thumbprint on the band, and the pawn ticket was in Milan's possession. Also, the pawnbroker's description of the man who pawned it for three hundred dollars matches Mr. Milan, though he used a different name."

"Three hundred dollars for a *watch?*" said Godwin. "But it's not a Rolex."

"No, it's a Bulova."

"My father wore a Bulova," said Betsy. "But I can't imagine he paid even a hundred dollars for his. Of course, that was a long time ago."

"You don't understand," said Omernic. "This is a very high-end Bulova, valued at close to two thousand dollars."

"Oh!" said Betsy, bending for a closer look. "Oh, I see. Well then . . . is it Bob Germaine's?"

Omernic took a drink of coffee. "His wife says it is. She bought one for his birthday about eight weeks ago, and he was not wearing a watch when he was found in the trunk of his car. Tony at first said he picked it up at an estate sale a couple of weeks ago, and had no idea it was an expensive watch. Now he says he didn't say any such thing and since we aren't listening to him, he's saying nothing further."

Betsy shook her head. She had no further

thoughts herself about it. She turned to the other sheet, the one with the picture of the small brass key. She and Godwin leaned forward to look at it. The key had a small piece of white paper taped to it, or maybe it was just a strip of white adhesive tape on which was neatly printed the number *36*.

"Where did this come from?" asked Betsy.

"Tony's apartment. He says he doesn't know where it came from. It's listed on the items returned to him by Hennepin County Medical Center, so it was in his pocket when he was brought there after the accident."

"It looks like a key to a mailbox," said Betsy.

"It doesn't open his mailbox in his apartment building," said Omernic.

"Maybe he has a post office box," suggested Godwin. "You know, at the post office."

"No, it's not a post office box key," said Omernic.

Betsy recalled a conversation from a Monday Bunch meeting. "I bet I know. There's one of those mail-drop places right next door to the hotel. Patricia was complaining about 'those kind of places' opening up downtown. I bet he took the check there. He didn't want to keep it on him, his bank was closed — anyway, I'm sure he didn't have a deposit slip with him — or an envelope and a stamp, either, so he couldn't mail it to himself. He had to put it somewhere while he figured out what to do with the body. So he went up the street and put it in PostNet." She was looking brighter. "If the check is there, it will have his fingerprints on it. Then even he would have to admit he's guilty."

"I saw that place," said Omernic. "I went and had a talk with them, and while they agree the key looks like one of theirs, no one named Tony Milan — or Stoney Durand, for that matter — has ever rented a mailbox there."

Godwin thought while he drank some coffee, then said, "Anyway, when would he have done that? He had to drive right off from the hotel, remember?"

"When he came back from the airport —" began Betsy. "No, wait, he would still be wearing Bob Germaine's clothes."

"Maybe he changed," offered Godwin.

"No, he was wearing Germaine's clothes when he got into the accident," said Omernic. "The hospital sent them home with him."

"There, then!" said Betsy, with an air of stating the obvious.

"What?" said Omernic.

"If he was wearing Germaine's clothes, then he was carrying Germaine's wallet and ID. You go back to that mail drop and see if Bob Germaine rented a mailbox."

Omernic looked at her for a long few seconds, then he began to smile. He reached into a different pocket and pulled out yet another photocopy. He unfolded it, bumped it with a forefinger so it spun around and across the table toward her. It was of a commercial-size check all black and smeary — "Fingerprint dust!" exclaimed Godwin. "You *knew!*"

"And those are Mr. Milan's fingerprints, all right. I brought it along to show off with, but I see Ms. Devonshire is just as clever as Sergeant Malloy thinks she is," he said, smiling at Betsy.

"Of course she is! Strewth, she's cleverer than that!"

Omernic's green eyes twinkled. "I think you're right, Goddy, I think you're right."

Alice had brought a new cardboard box for the crow. And, somewhere, she had acquired a pair of heavy leather gauntlets that came well up her forearms.

"I'm surprised you don't want to keep him, now," she said. "He's a hero."

"That doesn't lift his sentence of death in Minnesota," said Betsy.

"True," said Alice. "But he at least deserves a medal."

Betsy held up the Crewel World keychain she was going to give the crow. "I hereby present you . . ." she intoned, and its shimmer and faint clatter drew the crow's attention. It sat more upright on its perch, like a soldier at attention. ". . . with this medal for courage beyond the call of duty."

Alice, taking advantage, reached into the cage with one hand to crowd the bird into a corner, then brought the second in to clamshell the creature and lift it out. All it could wiggle were its feet, which it did, industriously.

"Of course, there are other considerations that make me celebrate his departure," admitted Betsy.

"Like the fact that you about doubled sales of the Minneapolis *Star Tribune* in Excelsior all by yourself?" Alice put the crow in the box and Betsy held it partly closed so Alice could get her hands out without freeing the bird.

Betsy said, "That, too." The box was closed and Betsy pulled off a length of clear mailing tape from the big roll and bit it so it would tear. She taped the box shut. "I hope he has a long and happy life in his new home." She touched the box as if blessing the bird inside it. "He was about the worst houseguest I've ever had in my life, but I was sure glad to see him come sneaking out of the back bedroom that night. Almost as glad as I am to see him leaving this morning." She handed the trinket to Alice, who put it into a pocket.

Alice said, "I take it you would not be willing to be a stage on our secret passage out of state for some other crippled wild animal?"

"Maybe, if the animal were a bluebird, or a possum."

Alice smiled at this partial victory and left.

Less than an hour later two burly young men — the same as the original pair? Betsy couldn't tell — arrived and went to work dismantling the cage and its stand, hauling the pieces down the stairs and into an old gray van.

Sophie watched all this from the safety of Betsy's bedroom. When the apartment was quiet again, she slipped into the back bedroom and very thoroughly sniffed the hardwood floor where the cage had sat on its platform. Betsy came in a few minutes later with a mop and bucket to find the cat circling a small black pinfeather on the floor, one forepaw pulling inward as if burying it.

"I take it you are telling me, 'No more crows'," said Betsy.

The cat looked up at her in eloquent silence and left Betsy to her work.

MITERED SQUARE
BY ROSEMARY KOSSEL

Materials
Worsted weight cotton in 2 contrasting colors
Size 5 knitting needles
Size G crochet hook

Abbreviations
MC: main color
CC: contrast color
WS: wrong side
RS: right side
KW: knitwise, slip right needle into next stitch as if to knit
psso: pass slip stitch over

Note: The first stitch of every row (except for Row 1) is slipped knitwise and the last stitch is always purled.

Note: When picking up stitches, place the needle under a whole stitch, which will give a neat and clear appearance to the row below the pick up.

Square One

With MC, cast on 25 sts using knit cast on.

Row 1 (RS): K 24, P1.

Row 2 (WS): With CC, Sl 1 KW, K 10, Sl 1, K2tog, psso, K10, P 1.

Row 3 and all RS rows: With color of the previous row, Sl 1 KW, knit to last st, P 1.

Row 4: MC; Sl 1 KW, K 9, Sl 1, K2tog, psso, K 9, P 1.

Row 6: CC; Sl 1 KW, K 8, Sl 1, K2tog, psso, K 8, P 1.

Row 8: MC; Sl 1 KW, K 7, Sl 1, K2tog, psso, K 7, P 1.

Row 10: CC; Sl 1 KW, K6, Sl 1, K2tog, psso, K 6, P 1.

Row 12: MC; Sl 1 KW, K 5, Sl 1, K2tog, psso, K 5, P 1.

Row 14: CC; Sl 1 KW, K 4, Sl 1, K2tog,

psso, K 4, P 1.

Row 16: MC; Sl 1 KW, K 3, Sl 1, K2tog, psso, K 3, P 1.

Row 18: CC; Sl 1 KW, K 2, Sl 1, K2tog, psso, K2, P 1.

Row 20: MC; Sl 1 KW, K 1, Sl 1, K2tog, psso, K 1, P 1.

Row 22: CC; Sl 1 KW, Sl 1, K2tog, psso, P 1.

Row 24: (RS); Sl 1, P2tog, psso.

End off yarn and cut.

Square Two

Place a pin in Square One for identification. Hold Square One with ending point at the bottom right and with MC pick up 12 stitches along the top cast row on of Square One, another stitch from the corner point, and then cast on 12 stitches. Work mitered square through Row 24.

Square Three

Cast on 12 stitches, pick up one stitch from the corner point of Square One holding

Square One with the ending point at the bottom left, and then pick up 12 stitches on the remaining stitches of the cast on of Square One. Work mitered square through Row 24.

Square Four
Pick up 12 stitches from the side of Square Two, another stitch from the corner point of Square one and 12 stitches along the cast on edge of Square Three. Work mitered square through Row 24.

Finish off the completed Mitered Square with a row of single crochet around, working 3 stitches in each corner. Weave in all ends.

ABOUT THE AUTHOR

Monica Ferris is the *USA Today* best-selling author of several mystery series under various pseudonyms. She lives in Minnesota.

We hope you have enjoyed this Large Print book. Other Thorndike, Wheeler, and Chivers Press Large Print books are available at your library or directly from the publishers.

For information about current and upcoming titles, please call or write, without obligation, to:

Publisher
Thorndike Press
295 Kennedy Memorial Drive
Waterville, ME 04901
Tel. (800) 223-1244

or visit our Web site at:

http://gale.cengage.com/thorndike

OR

Chivers Large Print
published by BBC Audiobooks Ltd
St James House, The Square
Lower Bristol Road
Bath BA2 3SB
England
Tel. +44(0) 800 136919
email: bbcaudiobooks@bbc.co.uk
www.bbcaudiobooks.co.uk

All our Large Print titles are designed for easy reading, and all our books are made to last.